"I like being married to you. It's convenient."

Eva lifted her chin rebelliously.

Raven barked a laugh. "Not as convenient as you might think if we continue to ride the stage. We'd have to sleep together to keep up appearances, *sweetheart*."

Damn, she hadn't thought that far ahead. Eva drew herself up to full stature. She couldn't resist a challenge.

"I can endure sleeping together if you can, *sweetheart*," she countered defiantly. "Turn around, please."

"What for?"

"So I can retrieve the money I stuffed down my dress."

Raven grinned scampishly and shook his head. "Being married and all, there's no reason for me not to watch...."

* * *

The Bounty Hunter and the Heiress
Harlequin® Historical #909—August 2008

Praise for Carol Finch

"Carol Finch is known for her lightning-fast,
roller-coaster-ride adventure romances that are
brimming over with a large cast of characters and
dozens of perilous escapades."
—*Romantic Times BOOKreviews*

McCavett's Bride
"For wild adventures, humor and Western atmosphere,
Finch can't be beat. She fires off her quick-paced novels
with the crack of a rifle and creates the atmosphere of
the Wild West through laugh-out-loud dialogue and
escapades that keep you smiling."
—*Romantic Times BOOKreviews*

The Ranger's Woman
"Finch delivers her signature humor, along with
a big dose of colorful Texas history,
in a love and laughter romp."
—*Romantic Times BOOKreviews*

Lone Wolf's Woman
"As always, Finch provides frying-pan-into-the-fire
action that keeps the pages flying, then spices up her
story with not one, but two romances, sensuality and
strong emotions."
—*Romantic Times BOOKreviews*

The Bounty Hunter and the Heiress

CAROL FINCH

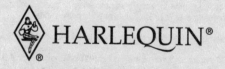

HARLEQUIN®

TORONTO • NEW YORK • LONDON
AMSTERDAM • PARIS • SYDNEY • HAMBURG
STOCKHOLM • ATHENS • TOKYO • MILAN • MADRID
PRAGUE • WARSAW • BUDAPEST • AUCKLAND

ISBN-13: 978-0-373-29509-8
ISBN-10: 0-373-29509-X

THE BOUNTY HUNTER AND THE HEIRESS

This book is dedicated to my husband Ed and our children, Christie, Durk, Jill, Jon, Shawnna and Kurt. And to our grandchildren, Brooklynn, Kennedy, Blake, Livia, Dillon and Harleigh. Hugs and kisses!

DON'T MISS THESE OTHER
NOVELS AVAILABLE NOW:

#907 THE OUTRAGEOUS LADY FELSHAM—Louise Allen
Her unhappy marriage over, Lady Belinda Felsham plans to enjoy
herself. An outrageous affair with breathtakingly handsome
Major Ashe Reynard is exactly what she needs!
*Follow **Those Scandalous Ravenhursts** in the second book of
Louise Allen's sensual miniseries.*

#908 A LOVER'S KISS—Margaret Moore
A Frenchwoman in London, Juliette Bergerine is unexpectedly
thrown together in hiding with Sir Douglas Drury
after they are mysteriously attacked.
*As desire gives way to a deeper emotion, what will become of
Juliette's reputation?*

#910 POSSESSED BY THE HIGHLANDER—Terri Brisbin
Peacemaker for the MacLerie clan, Duncan is manipulated into
marrying the exiled "Robertson Harlot." Despite shadows
lurking over their union, Duncan discovers a love for Marian,
and will stop at nothing to protect her....
*The third in Terri Brisbin's Highlander miniseries. Honor,
promises and dark secrets fuel this medieval tale of clan romance.*

Chapter One

Dressed in her breeches and shirt, Evangeline Hallowell paced back and forth across the Aubusson rug in the spacious study of her home. At irregular intervals, she paused to glance anxiously toward the hallway, then at the window. Muttering a curse, she wheeled around to wear another rut in the imported carpet.

Her younger sister, Lydia, had left earlier that afternoon and she hadn't said where she was going or when she'd be back. Now it was dark and Evangeline was worried. She had the uneasy feeling that something was amiss.

A loud wail erupted near the front door. The sound echoed through the tiled foyer and bounced off the walls. Evangeline whirled around to race to the study door.

She stared incredulously at Lydia's disheveled coiffure, tear-stained eyes and puffy face. "Dear God, what happened to you?"

Dirt soiled Lydia's expensive pink gown. The pristine

lace—that was now a dingy shade of brown—was snagged with leaves and twigs and drooped noticeably over the torn ruffles.

"Oh, Eva, I'm such a fool!" Lydia burst out as she flung herself into Eva's arms.

The sobs and howls commenced in earnest—the outpouring of emotion that had apparently sustained Lydia until she reached the safe haven of their lavish mansion. She clung to Eva as if she was a lifeline and she proceeded to bawl her head off.

Eva let her sister vent her anguish for several minutes before guiding her to the sofa that sat perpendicular to the bookshelves that stretched from floor to ceiling of the north wall. Although Lydia refused to release her hand—and nearly squeezed off the blood flow to her fingers—Eva didn't complain. She had spent years nursing Lydia through one melodramatic, emotional ordeal after another because she had assumed the role of mother, father and older sister.

This high drama, however, seemed to be more serious than usual for Lydia.

"You were right about him," Lydia blubbered, then dragged in a shuddering breath. "I was an imbecile to believe him."

Him, Eva presumed, was the suave, smooth-talking gentleman who had been courting Lydia and escorting her to Denver's elite social functions for the past three months.

Eva tensed as she reassessed her sister's tattered gown. "If Gordon Carter forced himself on you—"

Lydia flung up a trembling hand that sported three broken fingernails. "Worse!"

Eva's dark brows elevated. "Worse than ravishing you?"

Lydia bobbed her head, sending shiny waves of auburn

hair tumbling from her lopsided coiffure to cascade haphazardly over her shoulders. "He broke my heart, stole my buggy and my favorite horse and he swiped my money!" she cried in distress.

Eva went perfectly still, her mind racing back through time to reevaluate Lydia's rather peculiar behavior this past week. She had been in and out of the mansion without bothering to inform Eva or the servants when she planned to return. If Eva hadn't been preoccupied—fending off a particularly persistent suitor—she might have paid more attention.

Should have paid attention, she chastised herself. It was her sworn duty to protect and care for Lydia. She had solemnly promised her father that she would, after he fell ill suddenly then died.

Lydia wiped her eyes with the back of her grimy hand, sniffled loudly then glanced toward the imported grandfather clock that graced the corner. "Gordon and I were going to elope because he said you wouldn't approve and you were jealous because you were interested in him. He said we had to be clever and discreet. He said you would be outraged if you weren't the first to wed."

"What!" Eva scrambled to control her temper then gnashed her teeth, wishing she could take several bites out of Gordon's conniving hide. "I never had any interest in that scoundrel. It was plain to me that he was insincere. He made all the right noises, in his dedicated effort to impress you and others in our social circle, but I didn't trust his intentions. The fact that he tried to pit *you* against *me* is one more reason why I dislike him."

"It worked to some extent," Lydia admitted on a ragged breath. "He suggested that I gather plenty of funds so we could elope—" Her voice broke and she half collapsed on the couch. "Oh, Eva, I'm so humiliated I could die! Gordon insisted that we shouldn't bother with luggage so no one would suspect a thing. With my satchel of money we headed south to Canyon Springs to be married."

Hot fury boiled through Eva's veins as she visualized that silver-tongued, self-serving bastard luring her naive sister beneath his spell. At nineteen, Lydia hadn't learned to be wary and cautious of shysters who sought to separate her from her inheritance. She had fallen for Gordon's flattery and premeditated charm. His scheme had been to divide and conquer the Hallowell sisters so he could manipulate Lydia. Damn that lying, cheating bastard! He would be punished severely for this, she fumed.

Although Eva was silently condemning Gordon Carter to the farthest reaches of hell, she reined in her anger to listen to the rest of the infuriating tale.

"Then what happened?" she questioned intently.

Lydia rerouted the tears on her flushed cheeks, dabbed at her eyes with her dirty sleeve and finally met Eva's unblinking gaze. "Gordon stopped the buggy in the middle of nowhere and shoved me out. He claimed that he was bored with my childish prattle, and I should walk back home because marrying me was the very last thing on his list of what to do with the rest of his life…"

Her voice fizzled out and humiliated wails erupted. Lydia flung herself facedown on the sofa, sprawling in emotional defeat. A few moments later, she raised her tousled head and clutched Eva's hand again, accidentally scratching her with jagged fingernails.

"I'm dreadfully sorry I listened to Gordon's lies. He kept telling me that you were spiteful, stifling and envious because I was happy and you weren't. Since you discouraged me from seeing him I thought it might be true."

Eva shook her head adamantly. "You should have known better, Lydia. I have sworn off men for good reason. I can guarantee that I will never be jealous of my own sister. I want you to be happy, but you need to realize that adventurers will always set their sights on you because you have access to a fortune. That's why we have to be so wary and selective of men."

Lydia nodded and sniffled. "I understand that now, but Gordon kept telling me that he loved me and he'd never met anyone like me. Then his sugary tone changed to disdain once he had my money, my carriage and Hodge. You know how much I adore that horse. He was my last gift from Papa."

Eva promised herself, there and then, that she would hunt down that vermin and see to it that he was poisoned, stabbed, shot and strung up by his heels. Then she would haul his sorry carcass to jail for the duration of his life.

"From now on I'm going to be just like you," Lydia said determinedly. "I'll never again trust a man with my heart or my money."

"I regret that you had to find out the hard way that our family fortune is a burden and a curse. It attracts the wrong kind of men." A faint smile pursed Eva's lips as she brushed the tendrils from Lydia's face and met her watery gaze. "For us, Lydia, all men are the wrong kind of men. They will always want what we *have,* not who we *are* on the inside. They want our prestigious connections, not our companionship. The only way I've found not to be hurt, disappointed or taken advantage of is to guard my heart carefully. You must look beneath the charming smiles and calculated flattery to determine a man's sincerity."

Lydia nodded her head. "I know you speak from experience because you were so sad three years ago and—"

"Past is past and I never look back," she interrupted. "I prefer to profit from my mistakes, not repeat them."

Although Lydia insisted on talking her unpleasant experiences to death, Eva preferred to keep them buried. The man who taught her not to trust, not to expose her heart to pain, was a closed chapter of her life. If she never saw him again, that would be perfectly fine with her. Unfortunately, Felix Winslow owned a successful local jewelry shop—thanks to his new wife's financial backing. He showed up often with his young bride at parties and Eva had taught herself to look through him as if he wasn't there.

When the grandfather clock chimed ten times, Eva glanced up. She tapped Lydia on the shoulder then urged her to her feet. "Why don't you go upstairs and I'll have a warm bath prepared for you. I need to go out for a while, but I'll return shortly."

Lydia levered herself upright and managed the faintest hint of a smile. "If you are off to shoot that lying scoundrel I'll send you out with my blessing, but I know he's headed toward Canyon Springs, and probably to parts unknown. Finding him will be next to impossible."

"You're right. I *would* like to shoot him a couple of times for hurting you," Eva insisted. "It's the only purpose the men in our lives can possibly serve. Target practice."

Lydia snickered but her expression sobered when she surveyed the irreparable damage to her expensive gown. "This was to have been my wedding dress."

"Burn it," Eva recommended. "That's what I did with the one I wore the last time I was with Felix Winslow. I imagined him in it while it burned to ashes."

Lydia shrugged, and when Lydia trudged up the staircase, Eva sailed out the front door. She jogged down the street to the Philbert estate. Roger and Sadie Philbert—

twin brother and sister—were her lifelong playmates and friends. The blond-haired, blue-eyed twosome was returning from a party and they stepped down from their coach just as Eva hurried up the flagstone driveway.

"Rather late to be gadding out in men's breeches, isn't it?" Roger teased as he appraised her unconventional attire.

Eva glanced down, having forgotten that she was still wearing the garments she had donned for horseback riding, while attempting to track down her missing sister.

She shrugged carelessly in response to Roger's playful grin. "You know I've acquired the reputation of an eccentric and free spirit. Why not enjoy it?"

Sadie clasped Eva's hand to lead her to the front steps. "We attended the Jensons' stuffy dinner party. I'm sure you had a more interesting evening than we did."

Eva knew Lydia would be mortified if news of her involvement with Gordon made the gossip grapevine so she waited until she and the Philberts were behind closed doors before she asked, "I want to hire the best bounty hunter in the business, a Mr. J. D. Raven, I believe is his name. How do I go about finding him?"

"Bounty hunter?" Roger and Sadie crowed simultaneously. "Are you mad?"

"No, only vindictive," she said enigmatically.

Roger motioned for her to follow him into the office to ensure complete privacy. Then he gestured for Eva and his sister to take a seat on the brocade sofa. "What the devil is going on?"

Eva shrugged evasively. "The business I want to conduct requires the skills of a particular kind of man like Mr. Raven. He's known to be the best and that's who I want."

"If you need assistance, why not call upon the Rocky

Mountain Detective Agency?" Roger recommended. "You know they are reputable."

Eva had considered it, but since local and state newspaper reporters constantly followed the detectives' cases, she feared Lydia's name might be leaked. The last thing she wanted was a public scandal. Her nineteen-year-old sister was too vulnerable and too sensitive to gossiping peers.

"I came here for information, Roger," she declared, avoiding his direct question. "So how do I contact Mr. Raven?"

"I cannot begin to imagine what you are up to, but it sounds intriguing," said Sadie, her blue eyes glinting with interest.

When Roger crossed his arms over his chest and clamped his lips together, Eva sighed impatiently. "If you won't help me then I'll try another source."

When she bounded to her feet and headed to the door, Roger grumbled under his breath. "All right, Miss Persistence, I'll tell you what you want to know. As luck would have it, J. D. Raven arrived in town earlier today," he reported. "In case you haven't heard, he's half-Cheyenne, half-white. And yes, he's said to be deadly accurate with every weapon imaginable. But he's not the kind of man our friends and colleagues associate with directly."

Eva flicked her wrist dismissively. "You know I refuse to follow the dictates of snobbish society. I associate with whomever I please. I want Mr. Raven because his success rate is legendary when it comes to tracking down men who don't want to be found."

"From what I heard at the party this evening, he showed up at Marshal Doyle's jail with two of the three fugitives he'd been tracking," Sadie declared.

"What happened to the other one?" Eva asked curiously.

"Dead and buried," Roger replied. "According to rumor,

Raven doesn't place a cross on the graves, just an *X* so Indian deities and the Lord Almighty won't have to bother with the sinners. Plus, he plants them in the ground, facing away from the rising sun." He flicked his wrist casually. "I'm told it's some sort of Indian tradition that eternally curses evildoers."

"You are full of all sorts of helpful and interesting information," Eva praised. "Do you also know where I can find this legendary avenger of injustice?"

"You should let me handle this," Roger advised.

Eva shook her head decisively. "This is a private matter and I will take care of it myself."

His shoulders slumped and he shook his sandy blond head in defeat. "Fine, but you should go in disguise so you don't cause a stir. The London House is the place where Raven roosts when he returns from his forays."

"Thank you." Eva grasped the door latch. "I might be out of town for a few days so please check on Lydia for me."

Sadie frowned worriedly, but she said, "Of course, whatever you need. You know you can always count on us."

When she opened the door to leave, Roger burst out indignantly, "You really aren't going to tell us what this is about?"

"No, I'm sorry but I can't right now. I'll explain later," she promised on her way out the door.

J. D. Raven collapsed on his bed, exhausted. He grabbed the bottle of whiskey he'd picked up in a saloon on his way over from Marshal Emmett Doyle's office. He expelled a weary sigh and took a drink. The liquor burned its way down his throat to his belly then he took another sip.

He stared at the saddle and saddlebags he had tossed in

the corner of his hotel room. "Damn sons of bitches," he mumbled before he took another swig.

If life were fair, Buck—the best horse he'd ever had—would be brushed down, eating hay and resting comfortably in the livery stable right this moment. "But life sure as hell isn't fair," he said to the room at large. "I'll drink to that." And he did.

A firm rap on the door forced Raven to roll to his feet. "Who is it?"

"Emmett. I brought your bounty money."

Just to be on the safe side, Raven grabbed his pistol, moved to the left of the door then peeked out to make certain it was the city marshal.

"Besides the bounty, I also have a word of warning for you," Emmett said as he ambled inside. "Buster Flanders's widow just stormed out of my office. She swears revenge after you killed her husband."

"She wouldn't be the first," Raven murmured as he brushed his hand over the three-week growth of beard and mustache he hadn't bothered to shave during the manhunt. "I've had lots of death threats."

Emmett shrugged his thick shoulders. "Well, this woman says she intends to dance on your grave when you end up like her husband. She also wants to know where you planted Buster."

"At the bottom of a deep ravine. Took me an extra two hours to climb down, make sure he had expired, cover him up and climb back to the ledge to retrieve the other two criminals." He glanced at the marshal. "Dance on my grave, huh? That's a new one."

Emmett stared solemnly at Raven. "Buster Flanders has lots of kin and so does his wife. You've been marked for death so you better watch your back, in case she hires

someone to repay you for killing her husband." He dropped
the pouch of money in Raven's hand then gave him three
new bench warrants. "These men are reported to be preying
on miners and prospectors near Purgatory Gulch and the
other camps in Devil's Triangle to the southwest of here."

"These will have to wait until I train a replacement for
Buck." Raven tucked the warrants in his saddlebag. "I'll
get to them when I can."

Emmett nodded. "I'm real sorry you lost your horse.
And remember what I said about the spiteful widow's
threat. She's been passing word around town so be on
guard, Raven."

"Thanks for the warning," Raven said as Emmett exited.

Sighing heavily, Raven plopped on the bed and helped
himself to another drink. Five minutes later a quiet rap on
the door prompted him to reach for his six-shooter. Hell,
now what? he wondered. Considering the possibility of
Buster Flanders's kinfolk gunning for him, plus a few
others along the way who had vowed revenge, Raven
adhered to his motto. Stay alert or die. It was the code of
the Cheyenne and of the wilderness. Carelessness got a
man killed in a hurry.

Raven came silently to his feet. "Who is it?"

No one answered so he eased up beside the door again.
There had been times when outlaws had shot through
doors, hoping he was standing in front of them. Raven
never faced a door directly.

When the quiet rap came again, Raven snapped open the
door, grabbed the unwanted guest by the throat then jerked
him inside. A gurgling yelp erupted from the kid in the
oversize hat and jacket. Snarling, Raven slammed the kid's
thin shoulders against the wall and loomed threateningly
over him. If the widow had hired this brat then Raven

vowed to scare the bejeezus out of him and send him running back to the widow.

"You're messing with the wrong man, brat," Raven growled viciously. "Get the hell out of here and don't come back or I'll gut your carcass and throw it to the wolves."

The kid's chocolate-brown eyes widened then narrowed in annoyance. Raven didn't usually have trouble with his scare tactics, but the kid boldly reached up with a gloved hand to pry his fingers—one at a time—from his neck.

"Back off, you buzzard. I came here to hire you and I can pay good money for your services."

The kid's voice sounded feminine and Raven squinted to appraise the shadowed face beneath the wide-brim hat. When he used the barrel of his pistol to knock off the kid's hat, a cascade of curly auburn hair tumbled free. The woman was young. Twenty-two or twenty-three, he guessed. Despite her smudged cheeks, she was stunningly attractive. Although her thick-lashed eyes were her most striking feature, her Cupid's bow lips drew his rapt fascination.

"Are you the Flanders widow?" he asked, refusing to unhand her until he knew how much of a threat she posed.

"No. I'm the angel of doom who wants a lying, cheating sidewinder of a man hunted down," she replied.

It had been three months since Raven had been anywhere close to a woman. Staring at this woman's lush lips had him wondering what she tasted like. As good as she looked? He was certain of it.

Before he became sidetracked, he shook off the lusty thought. No matter how deprived he had been, his survival instincts always prevailed. *Always.* He trusted only half of what he saw and even less of what he was told. This mysterious female was no different, lovely though she was.

The wary thought provoked him to clamp his hand

around her throat again…in case this was a ruse. The woman coughed then glared at him for cutting off the air in her windpipe. He eased off enough to let her catch her breath.

"Nice to meet you, too, J. D. Raven," she sniped. "Kindly move away. I didn't come here to shoot you. Only to hire you."

"I'm at a disadvantage here. Who the hell are you?"

She looked him up and down and said, "You? At a disadvantage? Rarely, I suspect. I've heard that you're the best in the business. Judging by our unique introduction, you seem to be prepared for anything."

"*Everything*. There's a difference," he corrected. "You didn't answer my question, Miss…? Mrs…?"

He arched a brow when she refused to fill in the blank. Instead, she made herself at home by walking over to plant herself in the middle of his modestly furnished room.

"I'm glad to see the room is tidy and clean. Good. A guest has every right to expect the comforts of home," she commented.

He disregarded her odd remark and studied her closely. She possessed the regal bearing of nobility, but she didn't flash the aloof smiles he usually attributed to the privileged class of white society. Her unconventional style of clothing indicated that she wasn't afraid to be different. Yet, she didn't bear the hard lines of living that he noticed on the faces of women who supported themselves on their backs.

In addition, she possessed exceptional courage or she wouldn't be here alone with him, for fear of damaging her reputation. There wasn't a hint of fear in her dark eyes, only critical assessment and the sparkle of persistence. In addition, she stood up for herself and stood up to him in a way few people dared. He unwillingly admired that about her.

"Who do you want tracked down?" he asked as he set

aside his six-shooter. "An unfaithful husband or fiancé? And what do you want done to him when I find him?"

"Shooting his legs out from under him would be good for starters," she replied. "But he isn't my husband or fiancé. I don't have either one. As I recently reminded my sister, men best serve the purpose of a target for shooting practice."

Raven squelched the makings of a smile when he realized she was perfectly serious. "You're a man-hater, I take it."

She shrugged noncommittally. "What will it cost me to hire you and when can you start this private manhunt?"

"You can't afford me and I'm taking time off." He hitched his thumb toward the door. "Nice meeting you. Close the door on your way out."

She didn't take the hint, just stood there staring at him with the confidence of one seasoned gunfighter bearing down on another.

Who the hell was this woman? he asked himself again. "Bold and determined" only began to describe her. The fact that she had come alone to confront him when most folks in polite society shied away from him was nothing short of astounding. His mixed heritage and his deadly profession usually worked like a repellant.

How desperate was this female? What had the man she wanted apprehended done to provoke her relentless fury?

When he walked over to grab her arm and escort her to the door she set her booted feet and jerked away from him.

"I'm not leaving, J.D. Get used to the idea."

Her challenging stare and the determined tilt of her chin surprised and impressed him. He'd never shared a conversation like this one with a woman. Brief small talk before and after a tumble on the sheets was the extent of his association with women. This female was a novel—but annoying—experience and he wanted her gone. Intimidating her seemed to be the only effective method of shooing her on her way.

He scooped up the whiskey bottle and offered her a drink—which she turned down with a distasteful shake of her auburn head. Then he gestured toward the bed. "If you aren't leaving then disrobe and climb in. We'll negotiate the terms of our agreement later." He waggled his eyebrows suggestively.

He could tell right away that he'd offended her. Hell, he could practically see steam rolling from her ears.

"That's what you want for your fee?" she snapped, disgusted. "All dealings between a man and woman are to be resolved in bed? You are an ass, J.D."

"I've been called much worse. And it's just Raven," he replied, undaunted.

In his effort to route her from his room he removed his shirt and tossed it toward the towel rack on the washstand. When he reached for the clasp to the double holsters that held his ivory-handled Colts, she didn't blink, just held her ground as the weapons clanked on the floor. Raven unfastened the top two buttons on the placket of his breeches and smiled wickedly.

She stared at his bare chest then at his gaping trousers, before raising her gaze to meet his challenging grin.

"You wouldn't dare," she muttered.

"I've dared plenty in my life. More than you have, I suspect. So how far do you plan to go with this game of chicken?" He shoved his breeches a little farther down his hips. "All the way…?"

Chapter Two

Eva silently fumed at the ornery rascal known as Raven. It was bad enough that this man, who was six foot three inches of brawn and muscle, appealed to her in ways that baffled logical thinking. The hard, defined muscles of his chest, shoulders and belly drew her admiring gaze and held it fast.

His Indian heritage was evident in his bronzed, angular face. With the growth of the dark beard, mustache and shaggy hair—not to mention his black shirt, buckskin breeches and moccasins that made him appear as wild and untamed as the rugged Rocky Mountains—he looked formidable.

Yet none of that seemed to bother her because he was such a magnificent study of masculinity. His powerful physique suggested he had tested himself to the very limits of endurance time and again and that unwillingly impressed her.

He possessed none of the sophisticated gestures or polished manners of the affluent. Come to think of it, that was a point in his favor. He was not particularly handsome, though who could tell with that wooly facial hair that concealed the sides of his face and his jaw. *Striking* was a better word to describe him, she decided.

His large, almond-shaped eyes were the intense combination of green and gold. They were translucent, intelligent, alert and alive. Similar to the cougar she and her father had happened upon during one of their mountain excursions a dozen years earlier. The beast had watched them from an overhanging ledge, its gaze missing nothing in its surroundings. The great cat had intrigued Eva then, just as this man intrigued her now.

"Well? What's it gonna be?" he said, jostling her from her pensive thoughts. "In my bed or out the door?"

"Neither," she replied. "My sister fell for the wiles of a conniving swindler who professed his undying love and devotion. They were supposedly on their way to elope when he took a share of her inheritance and left her afoot. I want the bastard tracked down. I want the money returned to my sister and I want retribution for her humiliation and heartbreak."

Raven stood there, his hands on his lean hips, shaking his coal-black head. "No, I just returned from three hard weeks of tracking thieves. They shot my horse out from under me and I need time to train a dependable mount. Get someone else to help you."

"Then name someone reliable and trustworthy," she demanded. "And he better be as good as you're reported to be."

"There's…" He paused, frowned then flicked his wrist dismissively. "No, he's too trigger-happy. But you might try…" He shook his head again. "Never mind him. He's a drunk."

Eva elevated her brow and stared pointedly at the whiskey bottle on the nightstand. "Seems to me that the pot is calling the kettle black."

"I'm lamenting the loss of a good horse and celebrating the end of three weeks of exhausting hell," he defended righteously. "That's different from a man who has whiskey for breakfast, lunch, supper and a bedtime snack."

Eva crossed her arms over her chest and tapped her foot impatiently. "Who then, if not you?"

Raven raked his hand through his long hair then shrugged impossibly broad shoulders. "Try the Rocky Mountain Detective Agency."

"That is not an option," she said in no uncertain terms.

He studied her curiously. "Why not?"

She refused to meet his green-gold eyes and stared over his wide shoulders. "I have my reasons. I want you and apparently you can't think of anyone good enough, either, so it's settled. We will leave in the morning and I'll pay you half your fee then. You'll receive the second half when the fugitive is brought to justice."

"We?" He barked a laugh. "That wouldn't happen. If by some remote chance it did, it would cost you double because I'd have to babysit a tenderfoot sissy like you. No thanks. I've got better things to do with my time."

Frustrated, Eva stamped her foot. "You are exasperating and infuriating!" she muttered.

He flashed a mischievous grin. "Part of my charm."

"Charm?" She scoffed as she raked him up and down, trying exceptionally hard not to become sidetracked by his rippling muscles and bronzed flesh. Not to mention those fascinating eyes and the seductive gap at the waistband of his breeches. Try as she may, she couldn't keep her gaze from straying to the dark furring of hair that disappeared into his buckskin breeches.

He unstrapped the dagger tied to his thigh and tossed it on the nightstand. She watched him cautiously, wondering if he was going to drop his breeches in front of her, wondering how she was going to react to seeing her first naked man.

Despite her bravado, the only person she had seen naked was herself and she didn't think it was going to be at all the same.

"I'm not taking your case," he declared as he heeled off his moccasins. "I'm going to bed because I'm about as worn out as a man can get. So take a hike." He bent at the waist to untie his leather leggings. "I'm through talking to you."

Eva noticed the scars on his muscled back. Two long, deep strips of discolored skin resembled claw marks. The other scars must have come from a whip, she speculated. It left her to wonder at the torture he'd endured as he passed back and forth between Cheyenne and white culture.

Her thoughts scattered like buckshot when he did the unthinkable and shoved his breeches down his lean hips. Her face went up in flames and she whirled away before he disrobed completely and she received an education she hadn't anticipated.

She heard the low rumble of his chuckle as she faced the wall. The bedsprings squeaked, assuring her that he had sprawled out. She hoped he had covered the lower half of his torso with the sheet and bedspread. But no matter what, she wasn't going to allow this contrary rascal to get the best of her. She had made a pact with herself three years ago that no man would ever put her at a disadvantage again.

Drawing herself up to full stature, she gathered her courage and spun around. She was greatly relieved that he had covered his torso with the sheet. Even as he reached for the whiskey bottle, she noticed the look of surprise on his rugged face. Clearly, he thought she'd bolt and run.

"You can try to dismiss me, but you haven't seen the last of me, J. D. Raven," she assured him.

He settled back against his pillow and cushioned his head on his linked hands. Muscles rippled over his arms and down his washboard belly. "Thanks for the warning, sugar." He took a swig of whiskey. "This is your last chance to climb in bed with me."

"Thank you but no. I also sleep naked and I'd likely be cold because you probably pull covers," she countered sassily before she turned to leave.

"We won't need covers for what I have in mind," he drawled suggestively. "And I have every intention of warming you up, sweetheart."

Eva flashed him a go-to-hell glare as she swooped down to retrieve her discarded hat. She wrapped her hand around the doorknob—and wished it was his throat. He tossed her another scampish grin and waggled his eyebrows.

J. D. Raven might have won this skirmish but she wasn't one to give up easily. This bounty hunter and legendary gunfighter was exactly the kind of man she wanted to track down Gordon Carter. She wasn't taking no for an answer and that was that. All she had to do was sit herself down and figure out how to convince Raven to take this assignment, for which she would pay him a premium.

Eva pulled her hat down to shield her face then descended the steps. She detoured over to pay the hotel clerk for Raven's rented room before she exited. Raven didn't know it yet but he was on her payroll—starting now.

"Where have you been?" Lydia questioned the moment Eva strode past the bedroom suite.

"I'm in the process of making arrangements to hire a highly trained bounty hunter to track down Gordon," she reported as she came to stand beside Lydia's canopy bed.

Lydia blinked her dark eyes. "My goodness. Already?"

"Well, we are still negotiating terms," Eva hedged. "But I will be monitoring his activities to ensure I get my money's worth. I'll be gone a few days."

"You're leaving me here by myself?" Lydia wailed. "You know I can't go out in public ever again after the embarrassment I've suffered."

"First off, no one but the two of us knows what happened and we'll keep it confidential. But the next few days will determine what you're made of," she told her sister. "You will appear in public and answer questions about where Gordon got off to by saying you decided to go your separate ways."

Lydia shuddered and clutched the sheet to her chest. "I'm not sure I can do that. I'm too ashamed."

"If you say that you are no longer interested in sharing his company that won't be a lie," Eva pointed out.

For Eva, she hadn't had the luxury of voicing a pat comment because Felix had used her to introduce him to another wealthy heiress. He had turned his attention to a younger and less independent-minded woman. Then he had paraded her around in public and married her five months later, leaving Eva feeling like a cast-off bride candidate.

"I told Roger and Sadie that I was going to be out of town and I asked them to stop by here to check on you. You can always count on our friends."

"Thank you," Lydia murmured. "I'm sorry that I've been such a burden to you the past six years since Papa died."

"You are not a burden," Eva contradicted. "You are my sister and sisters stick together. Also, they stick up for each other." Eva patted her arm affectionately. "Now get some rest so you can walk out to face the world and convince the high society of Denver that you couldn't care less about Gordon."

Eva turned toward her room. For all her words of encouragement, she had yet to figure out how to convince Raven to take this assignment. He didn't back down easily, but then neither did she.

A warm flood of pleasure washed over her as she discarded her clothes and lay down on her bed. Raven's teasing words rolled over her and she wondered what it would be like to join such an incredibly masculine man in bed, to feel his muscled contours gliding alongside her—

"Stop it this instant!" Eva scolded herself. Damn his scampish hide for planting the erotic thoughts in her head.

She owed him for that and she'd make him pay.

Eva stretched leisurely then stared at the twinkling stars framed by her spacious bay window. If someone in her social class discovered her alone in the hotel room with Raven, there would have been a scandal of gigantic proportions. For years, the Hallowell name had been widely known throughout the area and gossip would be flying.

Thanks to her father, who had made his fortune prospecting for gold and had invested wisely, the Hallowells were always newsworthy. Her father had built businesses to outfit other prospectors. Also, he had established hotels and restaurants to house and feed his fellow prospectors. In addition, he had organized two local banks to grubstake miners who needed a helping hand.

Although her family name was familiar, Eva was rarely recognized on the street. She went to great effort to maintain a low profile. She spent most of her time at the expansive estate, overseeing various family businesses and contributing to worthwhile causes. Raven, on the other hand, was easily identified. His unique manner of dress signified that he had a foot firmly planted in two contrasting civilizations.

If their names were linked together, especially while he

was half-dressed in her presence at his hotel room, she might have been forced to marry him, just to salvage her family's good name and her reputation....

She jerked up her head when creative inspiration struck. A mischievous smile worked its way across her lips and she snickered. "I told you, J. D. Raven, you haven't seen the last of me," she said to the vision floating above her. "And indeed you haven't. Just wait until tomorrow."

"The kid did *what?*" Raven crowed in astonishment the next morning when the hotel clerk informed him that his bill had been paid in full.

The balding manager stepped back apace, his gaze darting apprehensively left and right. "Yes, sir, Mr. Raven. The boy said to thank you kindly for your time and any inconvenience. He also said to have a good day."

Raven ground his teeth as he lurched around to see that his raised voice had sent three men darting to the door. He could clear a room in two shakes. Not that he cared most of the time because it was a powerful tool of intimidation, which was vital in his line of work.

If he looked and sounded like hell's avenging angel then that was half the battle against defiant outlaws. As for men who turned tail and ran from him, they were usually guilty of something and that made them easy to flush out.

When involved in a showdown, Raven had learned not to display the slightest fear or hesitation. And when he barked an order, he had to make it stick. Otherwise, his intimidating reputation was useless. Raven knew how to make orders and ultimatums stick and he had the souvenirs of battle scars to prove it.

Just ask the man frying in hell after he put the whip

marks on Raven's back for no other reason except that he was half-native.

Cold fury trickled down his spine at the thought, but he quickly shifted his attention to the cowering clerk. The man assumed he'd somehow offended him by permitting that female masquerading as a young boy to pay for the room.

Raven fished a silver dollar from his pocket then tossed it to the clerk. "Thanks for the good night's sleep. It was a long time in coming after sprawling on the ground while chasing down thieves for three weeks."

The balding clerk relaxed and smiled slightly. "My pleasure, Mr. Raven. I'll pass along your kind words to the hotel owner."

"Yeah, be sure to tell the Hallowells I enjoyed my stay," he said and silently smirked as he envisioned the highfalutin family members who reportedly owned half of the damn town.

"It's always good to have you stay here," the clerk added. "Come back again."

Raven nodded before he walked outside. He was no fool. He knew exactly why the clerk at London House was eager to have him stay here. He had quelled three disturbances with drunken patrons during the past four months. Now there were no disruptions when word spread that he was renting a room here.

A cynical smile quirked his lips when two prissy females reversed direction the instant they spotted him standing on the boardwalk. The fashionably dressed pair scurried off. Apparently, they had heard circulating legends. He had overheard the rumor that he was half-human and half-Cheyenne ghost spirit. Damn, where did whites come up with that superstitious nonsense?

His smile faded as he carried his saddle with him to the

restaurant to have breakfast. He noticed the manager opened his mouth to object, recognized him then turned away to speak confidentially with the waitress, who scurried over to take his order immediately.

Raven ignored the stilted silence that descended on the café. He wondered if the mysterious woman, who had barged into his room the previous night, would be as well-received in *her* unaccepted attire as *he* was. He stuck out like a sore thumb—and on purpose. She would, too, if she removed her oversize hat and allowed those silky auburn curls to tumble around her alluring face.

A knot of unwanted attraction tightened in his belly when the image of the fascinating woman who dared to visit his room sprang to mind. Hell, half the reason he had refused her request was that he felt an admiration and sexual interest that could have spelled trouble.

J. D. Raven had one hard-and-fast rule. He never, ever became emotionally involved in a case. It was strictly business because anything less might make him hesitate, make him think with his heart, not his head. Like carelessness, distraction could get him killed before his time.

After eating the hastily delivered breakfast Raven exited the restaurant, much to the relief of the proprietor and customers, he noticed. He halted on the boardwalk to survey Denver's hustling, bustling citizens, who cast him cautious glances then hurried on their way.

Above the clatter of wagons and carriages in the street, a train whistle pierced the morning air. Glancing absently toward the depot, Raven strode off to deposit his bounty money in the bank. Fifteen minutes later, he entered the dry goods store to replace the shirts damaged during his recent foray. In addition to ground-in dirt and mud stains—the result of wrestling Buster Flanders on the edge of a cliff—

smears of blood and ripped fabric made the garment better
suited as a rag.

Raven plucked up two black shirts then set them on the
counter. As an afterthought, he picked up a plaid shirt and
brown breeches for Hoodoo Lemoyne, the older man who
kept the home fires burning in Raven's mountain cabin.
The clerk hastily tallied the expenses so he could get Raven
out of his store as quickly as possible.

Ah, how he longed to be working around the mining
camps tucked in the mountain valleys. At least there, where
the lines of civilization weren't so strictly defined, he
wasn't treated as such an outcast. Then again, he reminded
himself, he wasn't accepted readily much of anywhere and
he'd become accustomed to his solitary existence.

Tucking his purchases in his saddlebag, Raven scooped
up his saddle, rifle and gear then spent a long moment lamenting his fallen horse. That buckskin called Buck had
listened patiently while Raven rambled. He knew what
Raven expected of him during a frantic chase and he trotted
loyally to him when he whistled. Losing Buck was like
losing a trusted friend.

Raven strode deliberately down the boardwalk,
sending citizens veering off like the Red Sea parting for
Moses. Once inside the stagecoach depot, Raven purchased his ticket to travel south. He sprawled negligently
in a chair—away from the three men and the woman
who would soon be wedged in the coach with him during
the journey.

Hat pulled low on his forehead, Raven crossed his arms
over his chest. Stretching out his long legs then crossing
them at the ankles, Raven settled in to get some more shut-
eye before the stage departed.

The whiskey he'd consumed the previous night left him

with a dull headache. Missing several nights of sleep to remain on constant alert was catching up with him.

From beneath the shadowed brim of his hat, he could see the men and woman fidgeting nervously at the prospect of sharing confining space in the coach. If he cared in the least—which of course, he didn't—their distaste of what he represented would dent his pride. But, like a cougar in the wilds, he had come to terms with his isolated lifestyle and didn't brood about it.

Tracking criminals for bounty was what he was good at. He supposed he could sign on as a deputy marshal or city marshal in some nameless little town. As long as he clipped his hair, dressed strictly in white's man's clothing and made a conscious effort to look civilized. Yet, the very idea…

His rambling thoughts scattered like a covey of quail when the door creaked open and a woman entered. Raven had learned to school his facial expressions and give none of his thoughts away years ago. But he was stunned to the bone when he recognized the woman whose curly auburn hair danced like flames in the sunlight. She was the very same female who had dared to approach his room and make demands the previous night. She was even more fetching in daylight, especially when she discarded shape-less masculine clothing in favor of feminine apparel.

This morning she had dressed in a modest but flatter-ing calico gown that accentuated every voluptuous feminine curve and swell. And she had plenty of them in all the right places, he noted. She carried a matching parasol and wore a hat that boasted a couple of feathers and ribbons. War bonnet, most likely in her case, he mused as a wry grin crossed his lips. Indian custom had nothing on white civilization, he decided. Undoubtedly, the woman had girded herself up for another confrontation to urge him to take her assignment. Waste of time though it was.

Without acknowledging her arrival, he surveyed Miss Calico. She stood about five foot six inches and weighed about one hundred and ten pounds—give or take. She passed a polite smile around the depot then focused her full attention on him. Still he didn't move or alert her that he recognized her from the previous confrontation.

If she planned to open another lively debate with an attentive audience on hand then he would refuse her not only in private, but also in public. No matter what, Raven wasn't taking the assignment. He needed time to rest, relax and to train Buck's replacement. Period. End of story. No exceptions.

He shouldn't have been surprised when the gutsy female walked straight up to him—but damn if he wasn't. Then she shocked him speechless when she said, "Did you purchase my ticket, J.D.?"

Calling him *J.D.* suggested they were on intimate terms. He sat there, too stunned to react, while the three men and woman glanced back and forth between him and the daring female. Even the agent at the ticket window perked up at the unexpected scene unfolding in the depot.

She sighed dramatically, shook her curly auburn head then smiled at him in tolerant amusement. Miss Calico, with her matching parasol, set her two carpetbags on the empty chair beside him.

To his further astonishment, she doubled at the waist, pushed his hat back to stare him squarely in the eye and said, "Honestly, love, I know we were married recently but you'll have to remember you have a wife to consider now."

You could have heard a pin drop on the planked floor of the depot. Everyone's jaws sagged with incredulous disbelief. If Raven hadn't trained himself not to show the slightest reaction, his mouth would have dropped open and his teeth would have clattered to the floor.

Married? What the hell was she talking about? Sure, he'd been drinking last night but he certainly would have remembered something like *that!*

Seemingly unaware or unconcerned with the rapt attention she'd attracted, Miss Calico kissed his bearded cheek then sashayed over to purchase her ticket. She returned to take her place beside him. By that time, Raven had managed to sit up a little straighter in his chair and shake off the alluring scent of her perfume that had clogged his senses.

When Miss Calico brushed her shoulder affectionately against his and smiled at him as if he were the sun in her universe, something very strange and unfamiliar unfolded in the region of his chest. It was probably indigestion, he decided. He'd wolfed down his breakfast in a rush so he'd have time to swing by the bank and dry goods store before catching the southbound stagecoach.

When she glided her hand over his, giving it a seemingly affectionate squeeze, his tongue stuck to the roof of his mouth. He wasn't sure he could have formulated a sentence at the moment if his life depended on it.

"I'm very much looking forward to the rest of our honeymoon, J.D.," she said in a stage whisper.

Beneath lowered lashes, Raven observed the expressions plastered on the faces of the other passengers. Something in the way they stared at him had altered drastically since his supposed bride arrived to make over him as if he were special to her. He seemed to have acquired instant respectability because everyone thought he was married to the stunning female—whose name he still didn't know, damn it.

"The stage has arrived," the ticket agent announced.

Miss Calico was the first one on her feet. She grabbed her satchels then tugged him from his chair. "Don't forget your saddle, sweetheart. And I'm so sorry about the loss of your favorite horse. I know how much he meant to you."

The comment confirmed to the other passengers that she knew specific details about him. She sealed their connection by adding, "I'm anxious to watch you train the replacement. In time, I'm sure the new saddle horse will be as invaluable as the last one."

Then, to his absolute amazement, and that of the onlookers, she pushed up on tiptoe to press another kiss to his bearded jaw. Again, the tantalizing fragrance of her perfume infiltrated his senses and fogged his brain. He couldn't recall, but he presumed she had led him outside like a stupid lamb to slaughter. Then she directed the other passengers where to sit so the newlyweds could cozy up side by side in the coach.

It was only while Raven was tossing his saddle and the satchels into the luggage compartment on the back of the coach that his head cleared long enough for him to realize that he hadn't shut down the woman's charade and sent her packing. Worse, several passersby heard her call out to him. When she referred to him as *sweetheart,* she stopped traffic on the boardwalks and attracted owlish stares.

While she stood there, all smiles and cheery disposition, he stepped up beside her and bent his head to ask confidentially, "Who in the hell are you?"

"Evangeline Raven, of course. Really, J.D., you've been calling me Eva for weeks. Last night you swore I was the love of your life."

"Ha, curse of my life is more like it," he said and grunted. "Last night you interrupted a perfectly good drunk. And here you are this morning to ruin a perfectly good hangover. Be warned that you're going to regret this little charade of yours, I guaran-damn-tee it, *Eva*."

He wheeled around to tuck his Winchester rifle beside his saddle and she followed after him. Flashing an impudent grin, she said, "I told you that you hadn't seen the last of me. You were warned, darling."

"I thought you were a man-hater."

"Can you think of a better way to get even with a man than to pretend to marry one of the worst offenders?" she countered in a syrupy tone.

"What the hell—?" came a startled voice from overhead.

Raven looked over the top of Eva's auburn head when the stage driver's gravelly voice boomed above him. From his elevated perch, the grizzled driver, whose bushy hair, long beard and mustache concealed most of his wrinkled features, stared at him in bewilderment.

"You're married?" the driver croaked like a bullfrog. "To her? You must have more charm than I thought."

Raven inclined his head to take a better look at the driver. He recognized George Knott, the man he had interviewed after a stagecoach holdup the previous year.

"He has oodles of charm," Eva defended as she laid her hand on Raven's forearm. "I'm honored to be his wife."

Raven noticed the speculative glances coming his way again. This new respectability in white society beat anything he'd ever seen. One attractive female in calico, who testified to his charm and claimed to be his new bride, and wham! Suddenly he wasn't the dangerous bastard everyone thought he was. He was considered almost human.

Eva tapped his hand, then lifted her full skirts so he could assist her into the coach. He took his cue. However, he gave her a bit more of a boost than she needed. She yelped when she nearly sprawled facedown on the other passengers' feet. He noted that she reacted quickly and that she was agile enough to catch her balance. She eased a hip onto the seat and settled in for the ride. Raven expected her to glare daggers at him for the spiteful stunt but she grinned sportingly.

"How clumsy of me." She tucked her skirts beneath her legs then scooted sideways to pat the empty space beside her.

Raven wedged into the space between Eva and the window. In the close quarters, it was impossible to rail at her without being overheard by the other four passengers. Presently, he was too irritated to keep his voice to a whisper so he held his tongue. He did what he always did during the rare occasion when he was forced to travel by stagecoach. He pulled his hat low on his head, crossed his arms and caught a catnap.

Unfortunately, visions of his impish bride kept intruding into his dreams and jolting him awake. And sure enough, she was still cuddled up beside him, smiling triumphantly at him.

He sighed inwardly, aware that he had lost control of the situation the instant she appeared in the stage depot to shock him speechless. He decided to give her high marks for ingenuity and let her enjoy her crazed charade for the first leg of the journey. But that was as far as this pretend marriage went.

Biding his time, he closed his eyes to nurse his headache and vowed to get even with Eva Whoever-she-was for trying to outsmart him.

Chapter Three

An hour into the overland journey Eva was still feeling exceptionally pleased with her ingenious scheme to attach herself to the stubborn bounty hunter. Of course, she wasn't so smug to think that just because she had stunned and out-maneuvered Raven that he would take the assignment to avenge Lydia's humiliation. She figured she had some fast talking to do before that happened.

However, he hadn't shouted her from the depot, de-nouncing her claim. It was a start. Either she had caught him completely off guard while he was hung over or he hadn't wanted to make a scene in public. Maybe it was a little of both. Whatever the case, he had kept his trap shut and they were sharing the same stagecoach that was headed south.

Eva glanced discreetly at Raven. She knew he wasn't sleeping at the moment. He was like a lounging panther, intently aware of his surroundings, ready to pounce at the first sign of danger. Beneath those long thick black lashes, she could see a slash of golden green.

Although she knew he wasn't going to let her com-pletely off the hook for duping him, she enjoyed her reprieve and played her new role to the hilt. She even spun the simple gold band on her finger—the one that had belonged to her departed mother—calling the other passengers' attention to the ring that implied marriage.

She smiled cordially at the woman across from her, who looked to be a few years older. The thin brunette with the sad smile also wore a wedding band.

"Are you meeting your husband, ma'am?" Eva asked.

The brunette nodded. "He's an officer at the army post near Canyon Springs. I'm returning from a visit with my family in St. Louis."

Within five minutes, Eva knew her fellow travelers by name. Clara Morton had left her seven-year-old son with his maternal grandparents for a month. Delbert Barnes, the effeminate little bookkeeper, wore thick, wire-rimmed spectacles. He had a bald spot on the crown of his head and a cleft in his chin. He was on his way to Pueblo to begin his new job as an accountant with a coal smeltering company.

The other two men looked like gamblers, judging by their frock coats, brocade vests, snappy black hats and expensive pocket watches that dangled from gold fobs. Eva reminded herself that gamblers were a nickel a dozen in the area. They frequented saloons that catered to miners. One look at the rings on Frank Albers's and Irving Jarmon's fingers suggested their hapless opponents at gaming tables had lost their bets and paid their debts by surrendering their jewelry.

Irving Jarmon had a long, horselike face and large horselike front teeth. His tuft of hair reminded Eva of a horse's mane. Frank Albers was average height and slim build. His blond head seemed too large for his thin-bladed shoulders.

Frank Albers and Irving Jarmon—if those were their real names—claimed they were headed to Mineral Wells, before venturing to the mining towns in Devil's Triangle. According to reports, visitations to the numerous bawdy houses, gaming halls and saloons were the order of the day in Mineral Wells.

She wondered if that's where she'd find Gordon Carter—con man, shyster and God knew what else. She suspected he planned to lay low in the isolated mining camps before reappearing in society to fleece another young, unsuspecting heiress.

"Stage stop ahead. We'll exchange horses," George Knott called down from his perch.

Eva stirred on the bench seat, eager for a reprieve from the jostling ride that left her posterior numb and cut off the circulation in her arms, which were jammed between Raven's broad shoulders and Frank's narrow ones.

The instant the coach rolled to a stop, a plume of dust rose around it. Like a great cat surging to its feet, Raven exited then pivoted to clamp his hands around Eva's waist. The instant he touched her, strange fissions of heat rippled through her body. Stunned, she glanced into his hypnotic eyes as he slowly, deliberately lowered her to the ground.

Eva cleared her throat. "Thank you, dear."

"Anything for you, my sweet," he purred. "We'll partake of a cool refreshing drink and enjoy a private moment alone."

Eva wasn't sure she wanted to be alone with him just yet. He might strangle her and toss her behind a tree as a snack for wolves, mountain lions and such. Nevertheless, he clamped hold of her hand and strode off swiftly, forcing her to scurry to keep up with his long-legged strides.

The reckoning, she predicted as he led her out of earshot. She expected him to chew her up one side and down the other—and he was entitled because she felt a little guilty about the deception. But she wasn't one to give up easily. Especially when it came to an important cause like avenging Lydia's shame and recovering Hodge and the money Gordon had extorted.

Her thoughts trailed off when she noticed the unhitched buggy sitting behind the stage station. Eva thrust out her free hand excitedly. "That's it!" She set her feet, only to be uprooted by Raven's superior strength. "That's my sister's carriage. Gordon has been here."

"Good for Gordon and good for you for finding the first piece of the puzzle," Raven muttered caustically. "But that doesn't change the fact that I have a few choice comments to make to you. And be warned, none of them are very nice."

When he halted by the creek, she was surprised that he allowed her time to cup her hands and sip the refreshing drink of cool water from the stream before he launched into his scathing lecture. Apparently, he wanted to wet his whistle, too, before he laid into her.

Rising, he fisted his hands on his hips and widened his stance. His thick brows swooped into a sharp *V* and he glowered ominously at her. "You think you pulled a fast one on me because I didn't call your bluff, don't you, Eva? If that truly is your name."

"It is," she confirmed. "What does J.D. stand for?"

"Jordan Daniel."

"Your white father's name," she presumed.

"Yes, not that it's your concern," he snapped curtly.

"Jo-Dan," she mused aloud. "That's the pet name I'll use for you."

His bearded face puckered in a scowl. "No, you won't. I hate it. Furthermore, I'm not taking this case, even if you did spring for my hotel room. I pay my own way. Always have. I'll not be kept by a female."

"It was the least I could do since I interrupted your evening." She smirked. "After all, I did interrupt your designs on your whiskey bottle. Any of it left, by the way?"

"Yes." He waved her into silence. "Now listen, lady, this marriage you concocted is a bad idea. In order to remedy that problem, we are about to stage a big argument and you aren't going to speak to me again.

"I'm going my way to my mountain cabin to train a new horse and you're going to Canyon Springs…or wherever," he instructed. "Our disagreement should gain you sympathy from the driver, guard and passengers. Especially if you work up a few crocodile tears. After I abandon you, you can annul this pretended marriage by waving your magic wand of a parasol."

She lifted her chin rebelliously and said, "No, I like being married to you. It's convenient."

He barked a laugh. "Not as convenient as you might think if I continue to ride the stage line until we have to bed down for the night. We'd have to sleep together to keep up appearances, *sweetheart*."

Damn, she hadn't thought that far ahead. When she winced, he noticed. Those green-gold cat eyes missed nothing.

"What? This isn't the grand love affair you've made it out to be for the benefit of the passengers?" he taunted.

Eva drew herself up to full stature. He wasn't going to intimidate her with that snarly scowl and threats of intimacy. She was sorry to say that she couldn't resist a challenge. It was one of her many faults.

"I can endure sleeping together if you can, *sweetheart*," she countered defiantly.

He gave a sarcastic snort. "I'd hang around until tonight to find out just how far you'd take this charade, but I've had enough companionship for one day. I'm heading west after we stop for lunch."

"Fine, but do me one favor," she negotiated. "Check the barn to see if a chestnut gelding is stabled there. Maybe Gordon traded the thoroughbred for a mountain pony to make the next leg of his journey. Meanwhile I'll question the stationmaster about the buggy…. Turn around please."

He frowned, bemused. "What for?"

"So I can retrieve the money I stuffed down my dress. I want to buy back the carriage," she explained. "The horse, too, if Hodge is here."

He grinned scampishly and shook his head. "Being married and all, there's no reason for me not to watch."

She rolled her eyes in annoyance then reached into the bodice of her gown to fish out the money she'd brought with her. Despite the blush that splashed across her cheeks, while she watched him stare deliberately at her bosom, she didn't turn away, either.

He was still staring at her gaping gown when he said, "Checking on the horse is all the effort I'm putting into this case. I'm still taking time off to train a new horse. Maybe you can hitch a ride with your two new friends, Irving and Frank, to check the mining towns for your sister's missing boyfriend. *If* you really have a sister and you aren't making up this tale the same way you made up the story about our marriage."

It was plain to see that Raven didn't trust easily. Besides, she hadn't offered conclusive evidence. But still…

He wagged a lean finger in her face. "No matter what, sugar, I'll be gone this afternoon. No more of your clever charades. I'm fresh out of patience and this headache and hangover are hard on my good disposition."

"Didn't know you had one," she couldn't help but sass.

When he pulled a face and muttered something under his breath that she didn't ask him to repeat, she frowned curiously. "For the life of me I don't know why this bothers me, but why don't you like me? Is it because you don't find me particularly attractive? Because I talk too much to suit your tastes? Because I'm headstrong and pushy?"

"All of that, plus you're a royal pain in the ass," he told her bluntly.

"Maybe I am, but I can't let a thing like that get in my way while I'm serving a noble purpose and I need your help."

"I'm not helping and the very last thing I need is a wife, pretend or otherwise. Especially one like you."

Even though his comment stung her pride a bit, she angled her head to peer up at him. "How do you know you don't need a wife? Have you had one before?"

"No, but I travel light. A wife is extra baggage that might get in the way or become another hazard in my profession. As it is, your charade will cause complications. When I return to Denver, everyone will have heard the news. It's your job to quell the rumors when you get home."

"I intend to pretend to be married for a good long while so get used to the idea," she said stubbornly.

Considering her place in high society, having a pretend husband, especially one with J. D. Raven's legendary reputation, would discourage insincere proposals from fortune hunters. She should have hired a husband impersonator earlier, she mused. It would have solved dozens of problems.

"Lady, you are loco," Raven said with a marveling shake of his shaggy black head.

She tossed him a teasing smile as she handed back the comment he'd made to her. "Part of my charm." She lurched toward the station to inquire after the stolen buggy. "And don't forget about looking for the horse."

"Nag, nag."

"No, Hodge is a gelding," she insisted, grinning.

He frowned darkly. "I wasn't talking about the horse."

Raven stared after the bundle of irrepressible spirit wrapped in calico. He didn't recall having this much trouble winning arguments until he clashed with a woman who possessed an incredible amount of fortitude and determination.

Muttering under his breath, Raven raked his hands through his untrimmed hair then hunkered down to drink his fill from the clear stream. Despite his irritation with the madwoman, he was unwillingly impressed by her uncanny ability to draw information from the passengers without seeming nosey.

She had even mentioned Gordon Carter offhandedly then inquired if anyone knew him. She had discovered quickly that the passengers didn't reside in Denver. They were passing through and no one had heard of the con man.

Glancing this way and that, Raven decided to take advantage of the privacy and sink into the cool water. If nothing else, the quick bath eased his hangover and helped to curtail the inappropriate thoughts that hounded him after being nestled beside Eva in the coach.

Watching her dip her hand into her bodice to retrieve her money intensified his unwanted awareness of her. Hell, even their lively debates stimulated his interest. She intrigued and aroused him all too easily. He didn't want to like her or give her a second thought.

This was going to be a very brief acquaintance, he promised himself. Wife indeed! That had bad idea written all over it. If his longtime associate, Hoodoo Lemoyne, and his only surviving cousin, Blackowl, got wind of this, they would laugh themselves into comas.

The thought of Hoodoo Lemoyne, the crippled man who lived at Raven's mountain cabin, while he tracked notorious criminals, made him grin. Raven hadn't been able to get rid of that chattering Cajun any easier than he'd gotten rid of Eva.

Raven just sort of inherited the gabby older man who had been his father's acquaintance. In addition, Raven thought, now he had a pretend wife and she had more grit and gumption than most men he knew.

Raven blew out his breath, shook off the cold water and dressed hurriedly. He hiked to the barn to watch the stage attendants trot out fresh horses. He glanced around the stalls but there wasn't a chestnut gelding in sight.

"Did you happen to see the man who left the carriage behind the station?" he inquired.

"No," the first worker replied. "I showed up for work this morning at seven and the buggy was already here."

"Same for me," the second man chimed in. "You might ask the station owner. He's around all the time."

The first worker surveyed Raven's attire. "You're Raven the bounty hunter, aren't you?"

He nodded.

"Heard of you," the man murmured. "Congratulations on your marriage. Your wife is one of the prettiest females I've ever laid eyes on. You must be proud."

Raven was no such thing. He was baffled by the newfound respect he'd acquired because of his association with Eva. The uncharacteristic chattiness from men who usually ignored him was difficult to grow accustomed to. Raven glanced toward the doorway of the station house where Eva was deep in conversation with the potbellied owner, who was only a few inches taller than she was.

"She's the prettiest female I ever laid eyes on, too," he admitted.

"How'd you meet her, if you don't mind my asking?" the second attendant said interestedly.

Raven smiled in wry amusement. "A young kid, a mutual friend, introduced us."

He pivoted around to amble toward Eva. He was ten feet away from her when the report of a rifle echoed around the rugged canyon walls overlooking the stage station. Raven reacted instantly. He lunged forward to hook his arm around Eva, forcing her to roll across the ground with him. The stage station owner yelped and leaped backward when the bullet whistled over their heads and thudded into the water barrel outside the door. Water dribbled into the dirt, leaving a puddle that could easily have been Eva's blood.

While Raven lay atop Eva, her lush body melded familiarly to his, she gaped at him in astonishment. He was surprised to note that curiosity, not fear, flickered in her chocolate-brown eyes.

"Here's another reason why being married to me is unwise. It puts you in harm's way," he murmured against her ear. "Criminals dislike me and so do their vindictive kinfolk. I might as well have a bull's-eye painted on my back."

"How do you know that someone is shooting at you and not at me?" she retorted. "It could be Gordon. The stationmaster informed me that late last night he bought the buggy from a man who matches Gordon's description. He bought a saddle and rode off on Lydia's horse. Gordon would recognize me easily and I predict he would be anxious to have me off his trail."

Raven rolled sideways then pulled Eva up beside him. He kept her protectively behind him while he scanned the towering peaks that were rife with hiding places behind rocks and trees. Wherever the sniper was lurking, Raven couldn't locate him. What's more, it disturbed him to no end that he'd been so distracted and preoccupied with Eva that he wasn't as attuned to his surroundings as he usually was.

She was a liability he could ill afford. The sooner they parted company the better for both of them, he told himself.

"You okay, ma'am?" the driver questioned—and Raven was quick to note the smell of whiskey on George's breath.

Eva adjusted her cockeyed hat and smiled reassuringly at George. "I'm fine," she insisted as she dusted herself off.

"This is one of the drawbacks of marrying a man who has a target on his back," the driver slurred. "Somebody's always gunning for him, I reckon."

"Then I'll have to take extra good care of J.D., won't I?" she murmured as she stared adoringly at him.

Raven studied her blankly. He couldn't recall anyone offering to take care of him. A moment later, he remembered that her comment was part of her act and he shrugged off the pleased sensation that had no business taking root.

"Are we going to be ambushed again?" Delbert Barnes asked warily as he readjusted his drooping spectacles. "I haven't begun my new job and I could be dead before I start."

"Relax, Delbert," Raven said he as brushed off his buckskin breeches and black shirt. "Stay inside each station along the way or in the coach and you'll be just fine."

Flustered, the little man fidgeted from one foot to the other, glanced apprehensively toward the stony peaks of the mountains then dashed headlong toward the coach.

Raven had expected a reaction like that from Eva. She, however, was amazingly unruffled by her near brush with disaster. Another blossom of admiration unfurled inside him as he watched his pretend wife walk purposely toward the stagecoach. She halted halfway then turned to wait for him to catch up.

"Surely you aren't going to pick a fight with me so soon

after I was nearly gunned down, are you?" she murmured as he strode up beside her.

"No, but I'm leaving eventually so don't think I've changed my mind," he said gruffly.

An impish grin spread across her bewitching face. "Of course not. I'm your proverbial pain in the ass."

"Exactly right and don't you forget it."

And he better not, either.

His tone wasn't as sharp as it should have been, not if he hoped to convince her that he considered her a nuisance. To his dismay, she noticed the lack of intensity in his voice and looked excessively pleased with herself.

"Help me into the coach, will you, darling? Being knocked off my feet during the ambush affected me more than I first thought. I feel a bit shaky."

Shaky? This ironclad daisy? Ha! Nothing shook her up that he could tell. Not his terse rejection, his intimidating threats or flying bullets. Raven gave his head a marveling shake as he assisted his wife into the coach.

Wife? The word rang through his mind like a clanging gong. She was not his wife and she never would be, he reminded himself realistically. Let her have her fun while it lasted. By nightfall, he'd be long gone and she could track Gordon by whatever means available—as long as it didn't include him.

Raven continued to chant that mantra, even when she held his hand and smiled up at him so sweetly during the next leg of the journey. Eva? Sweet? He chastised himself for getting soft when she poured on the feminine charm. He didn't want to warm up to her. But when he stared at her enchanting face and gazed into those twinkling brown eyes he knew she was getting to him. He'd better put a stop to it quickly if he knew what was good for him.

* * *

"Damn, I knew she'd come after me." Gordon Carter spewed a string of foul expletives as he watched Evangeline and her brawny bodyguard pile into the stagecoach.

He'd botched the perfect opportunity to remove that female thorn in his side…permanently. But his aim had been slightly off the mark. Now, instead of disappearing for a few months to live on the money he'd swiped from Lydia, he had to deal with Eva breathing down his neck.

Gordon had expected as much from that willful woman, which is why he went to roost in the rocky terrain near the line of stage stations that flanked the mountains. He hadn't considered that she would hire that half-breed bounty hunter called Raven to help track him down. Gordon knew he had to strike suddenly and quickly because getting hold of Eva and making it look as if she had an untimely accident had just become more difficult than he originally planned.

Scowling, he tugged on the reins and led his confiscated horse along the mountain trail. Too bad he hadn't been able to resolve his problem with one well-aimed shot, he mused sourly. Next time, however, he'd take his time and make the bullets count. On that cheering thought, he mounted the chestnut gelding and trotted off.

"In all the excitement of the ambush I forgot to ask if you gathered any information about the man who stole your sister's carriage," Raven whispered in Eva's ear five miles down the road. "And no, the attendants haven't seen the horse named Hodge that you described to me."

"That's because Gordon rode off on Hodge last night, after selling the buggy to the stationmaster and buying a saddle," she murmured against his bearded jaw. "I bought back the buggy, of course."

"If you leave it sitting where it is for too long the owner might sell it twice," he warned.

"That's why I left a message to be delivered home so my friend can pick it up." She squirmed to find a more comfortable position in the cramped space. There wasn't one.

Raven smirked. "What if the agent isn't honest enough to forward the message? Let me tell you something, sugar. You won't get far in this world if you're too trusting. Cheaters, backstabbers and liars are as thick as mosquitoes."

Eva stared pensively at him. Cynical and wary though she had become—after dealing with a long line of gold diggers who tried to smooth-talk her out of her inheritance—she couldn't hold a candle to this bounty hunter. No doubt, chasing bloodthirsty renegades distorted his perception of everyone.

Taking into account Raven's mixed heritage, she suspected he had encountered racism, bigotry, brutality and who knew what else. The scars on his back indicated that he'd endured difficult times and he'd lost his faith in humanity. Raven had become isolated because of his Native background and insulated by his indifference to other people's opinion of him.

As much as she wanted to probe into Raven's past to understand what made him the hard-edged, mistrusting man he was, this wasn't the time or place. In the coach, whispering in his ear was the extent of the privacy between them. And so, she scrunched down the way Raven had and closed her eyes to catch up on the sleep she'd lost while making last-minute arrangements for this trip.

Chapter Four

$\mathcal{A}$n hour later, someone poked Eva on the shoulder. Groggily she opened her eyes, shocked to find her head on Raven's chest and her hand flung across his abdomen. She nearly recoiled to sit upright but she remembered she was playing a charade. Cuddling up to her supposed husband wouldn't be considered improper.

A shiver of unexpected pleasure riveted her when Raven's warm breath caressed her neck. "Better move your hand off my lap before you embarrass both of us. I'm going to need a cold bath if you plan to sprawl all over me until lunch. Good thing the relay station is up ahead."

Heat suffused her face. She shifted her hand and arm then levered herself upright as casually as she knew how. The fact that she felt innately secure and comfortable with Raven disturbed her. She supposed that since he was straightforward and assured her that he considered her a nuisance she wasn't as leery of his intentions. She couldn't say the same for the men who moved in her social circle, however. They told her what they presumed she wanted to hear to draw her interest. They relied on effusive flattery to win her affection.

That wasn't a problem with Raven.

How refreshing to encounter a man who wanted her out of his hair rather than schemed to part her from her fortune, she mused as she silently appraised him.

"Why are you looking at me like that?" he asked warily.

She cast him a drowsy smile. "Because I'm only half-awake. I'll be my old self in a few minutes."

"Sorry to hear that," he murmured against her ear, causing a stream of unwanted tingles to trickle through her.

She ignored the taunt and the arousing sensation by focusing on the landscape outside the window. The stage route skirted the fissured mountain range, providing a scenic view of craggy precipices bracketed by rugged ridges and mesas. Some of the towering summits were snow-capped while others were a tumbling cascade of boulders. There were also peaks that stood like green-clad soldiers barricading the entrance to the wilderness. Colorful wildflowers between crests waved in the breeze, making Eva wish she had time for exploring.

She had made an excursion into the mountains two years earlier with Roger and Sadie Philbert. The invigorating climb and panoramic views had captivated her. Although the Philberts decided one strenuous adventure into the wilderness was enough for them, Eva had enjoyed the rugged beauty and the challenge.

The trip reminded her of the hikes she'd made with her father when she was a child. Hoping her sister would delight in the experience, Eva had hired a guide to take her and Lydia on a short jaunt the previous year. Lydia also decided that city life appealed to her more than roughing it in the mountains. She had announced that Eva would have to make her next excursion alone. And here Eva was, striking off to overtake that slimy weasel Gordon.

Her thoughts trailed off when George Knott shouted out that they were near the rest stop at the base of the looming cliff. She noticed Raven had come to alert attention and he was the first to step down from the coach. Like a great cat scanning the terrain, he searched for signs of trouble before pivoting to help her down.

Eva tried to control the baffling tingles she experienced when his hands encircled her waist. Erotic speculations ricocheted around her mind as her body brushed suggestively against his masculine contours.

"We'll be here 'bout fifteen minutes to check the undercarriage. A brisk walk is usually a good idea to get circulation goin' again," George suggested in a slurred voice.

While two scraggly-looking attendants hunkered down to check the wheels, hubs and carriage sling, Raven grasped her hand and veered away from the other passengers, who stretched this way and that to work kinks from their necks and backs.

"You're being extremely careful, I see," she said as he zigzagged in and out of the pines and cottonwoods that lined the narrow creek.

"I don't want you hurt because of me," he insisted. "Besides, it makes me look bad if I can't protect my own wife." He halted abruptly then spun to face her. "I've been thinking it over for an hour and I've decided you should go home on the next stage that comes through here."

She stared disparagingly at him. "Just because I'm pretending to be your wife, don't think you can tell me what to do, Jo-Dan."

"Don't call me that," he said and scowled.

"Don't tell me to go home," she countered. "I'm going to find that lowdown, good-for-nothing swindler and recover the horse and every red cent he stole from Lydia."

"How many red cents are we talking about?"

"Doesn't matter." She flicked her wrist dismissively. "It's the principle of the matter."

Raven barked a laugh. "You're in the wrong neck of the woods to avenge your strong sense of fair play to your personal satisfaction. I can tell you from experience that life isn't a damn bit fair. If you don't believe it, ask the Cheyenne people whom Colonel Chivington massacred at Sand Creek in Colorado, and then suffered through George Custer's ambush on the Washita River in Indian Territory."

Eva grimaced at the thought of Raven's family encountering such a disastrous fate. She remembered reading about the Sand Creek Massacre investigation. Her private tutor had described it as one of the most brutal and insensitive crimes in the country.

"Were you there?" she asked gently.

He nodded abruptly. "I was twelve years old when Chivington and his soldiers killed my mother, uncle and all of my cousins except one," he said in a grim voice. "Blackowl and I survived by pretending to have drowned. We floated facedown in the stream until the soldiers passed. Then we came ashore to confiscate a horse. We headed for cover in the mountains and then took refuge with a band of Utes."

"I lost my mother to illness when I was five and my father died when I was sixteen," she confided. "But I cannot fathom how awful it would be to endure a cruel massacre that senselessly took your family from you."

"It was hell," Raven muttered as he stared at the towering precipices. "Two years later I located my father at the trading rendezvous near Pine Crest. He thought I had perished, too. In the meantime, he'd married a white women and settled into town life. Although I wasn't accepted into polite society more readily than I am now, my father was determined to indoctrinate me into white culture." He pulled a face. "It didn't help that I inherited a racist stepbrother who made my life miserable. When my father died, I cleared out. At eighteen I hired on to ride shotgun for coaches and express trains before venturing out on my own."

"But you never used your impressive skills to scout for renegades for the army," she presumed.

"Hell no," he grumbled. "Soldiers in uniforms bring back too many bitter memories. I'll be damned if I'll help them track runaway warriors from other tribes so they can herd them like cattle to those hated reservations."

To say that Raven harbored hard feelings was an understatement. Not that she blamed him. She was still bitter about being used by Felix Winslow, who professed to love her until his dying day…and discarded her for another woman so fast it made her head spin. So who was she to pass judgment?

"Stay here." Raven drew a peacemaker from his holster then pressed it into her hand. "Do you know how to use this?"

"Sort of," she hedged.

"You can always use it as a club if you're desperate," he suggested before he slinked away.

"Where—?"

She compressed her lips when Raven disappeared into the bushes. She glanced around, wondering what his trained senses had seen or heard that she had missed. Then, in the near distance, she heard the thud of retreating hoofbeats. A moment later Raven appeared, swearing in what she presumed to be the Cheyenne language.

"Did you see who it was?" she asked as he approached.

"No. Which is all the more reason for you to wait at this station to catch the returning stage."

"I made it perfectly clear that I'm not abandoning my mission," she retorted sternly.

"How many more times do I have to win this argument?" he shot back. "Any association with me puts you in danger. How do you think you're going to avenge your kid sister if you're dead or worse?"

"What's worse than dead?" she said, smirking.

"Don't ask." He clutched her hand to lead her down to the creek for another refreshing drink from a spring-fed stream.

Eva had the unmistakable feeling that Raven had seen the worst humankind could do to one another. In comparison to his exploits, she was hopelessly sheltered and naive. Nevertheless, her fierce sense of justice and her devotion to her sister refused to let her give up when the going got a mite tough. She would see this through, whether Raven approved or not—which he obviously didn't.

"All right, how about a compromise," Raven suggested as he reclaimed the pistol so she could sip water with her cupped hands. "You go home and I'll track this Carter character after I've trained a dependable saddle horse. Give me two weeks to work with a green-broke mount then I'll search for Carter."

"In two weeks Gordon could be anywhere," she argued. "Even out of the state if he's so inclined. I don't have to tell you that cold trails are difficult to follow. Gordon is obviously in the area because he sold the carriage just last night. If he heads for the hills there are but three mining camps in the area called Devil's Triangle for me to search. I intend to visit Purgatory Gulch, Satan's Bluff and Hell's Corner before I give up and go home."

"If you think that claiming to be my wife, while you tramp around in those rowdy camps, is going to keep you safe then you're sadly mistaken," Raven said harshly.

"Some of those men working claims haven't seen a woman in months. Years maybe. Don't expect the polite consideration you're accustomed to in civilization. There are no laws and no rules, except survival of the strongest and you'd be an easy mark."

She knew he was trying his damnedest to impress upon her the danger she might face, but she wanted to apprehend Gordon so badly that it was an obsession.

Besides, she had vowed to her father on his deathbed that she'd protect Lydia. She had failed miserably. And because she hadn't sought revenge on Felix Winslow for hurting her, she wanted to make an example of Gordon to compensate for her ill feelings toward the conniving con men of the world.

"I can take care of myself," she assured Raven.

His reply was a contradicting snort.

"I can hold my own with you, can't I? I'm not afraid of you, Raven. Fear is not the feeling tormenting me."

Compelled by some emotion she refused to name or delve into too deeply, she framed his bearded face with her hands. His catlike eyes glowed as she drew his head to hers. When her lips touched his mouth experimentally, she realized she'd wanted to taste him since… Well, she couldn't remember precisely when the forbidden craving began, but the casual pecks she'd planted on his cheek and chin earlier today had only whetted her appetite.

Despite his stubborn refusal to assist her, in spite of their ongoing conflict and her solemn vow never to let a man matter to her again, she wanted something from this man that she craved from no one else.

Raven's kiss was surprisingly gentle and the taste of him urged her closer—as close as she'd been when she'd used his muscular body as a cushion during her nap on the stagecoach. As close as they had been when he sprawled on top of her to shield her from the flying bullet.

In this fanciful moment outside the realm of time and reality, in this secluded cove by the creek, Eva cast off her wary inhibitions and looped her arms around Raven's neck. She leaned into him, enjoying the feel of her body meshed against his masculine contours, marveling at the fact that she'd taken the initiative with a man for the first time in her life.

"You aren't playing fair and this is no way to win an argument," Raven rasped after he broke the kiss. "Next thing I know you'll be offering me this lush body of yours if I'll take this assignment."

She grinned at him, feeling oddly confident and comfortable in the circle of his brawny arms. "Would you take it? In addition to a premium rate for bounty?"

He smiled down at her, his fascinating eyes flickering with playful mischief. Eva felt her heart thud against her ribs and stick there momentarily, even when he said, "No, hellion, I told you that you are a pain in the ass."

He angled his dark head and his gaze locked with hers as he took her mouth beneath his. His words were in direct contrast to the smoldering heat and hunger in his kiss.

Eva felt herself being swept up in the reckless moment. His arms contracted, lifting her off the ground. He pressed her against his hips as his tongue plunged between her lips. She felt his aroused flesh between her thighs and her body responded instantaneously. She couldn't get close enough to satisfy the burgeoning craving, couldn't kiss him hard enough or deeply enough to appease the white-hot need that suddenly burned her alive.

Sweet mercy! Where had all these wild, desperate feelings and sizzling sensations come from? Had she suppressed physical desire for too many years, in her effort to avoid the wiles and entrapments of cunning adventurers? And why did this man, who didn't particularly like her, have to be the one who inflamed her with incredible hunger?

Eva's head was still spinning like a windmill when Raven suddenly set her to her feet and stepped away. He stared at her as if she were insane. Or he was. Then his thick brows bunched over his green-gold eyes and he scowled at her.

"You *are* trying to seduce me into taking this assignment, aren't you? Damn it, Eva!"

She puffed up with offended dignity. "I did no such thing! You're the one who tried to lure me into your bed last night." Shame and anger flooded her cheeks. "I can't begin to explain why I thought it was a good idea to kiss you. It was foolish and reckless and I don't care if you strike off to train a blasted horse while I track Gordon myself. No matter what, I will get the job done!"

Furious with herself for her lapse of good judgment—and feeling incredibly self-conscious to boot—she lurched around to hike back to the relay station. She must be out of her mind to be so attracted to a man who had no use for her whatsoever.

"Don't kiss me like that again," he called after her.

"Don't worry, I won't," she said over her shoulder.

Besides, she'd liked kissing him way too much and she would cut out her tongue before she admitted it to that infuriating man.

"Don't go haring off by yourself without paying attention to your surroundings," Raven warned as she stamped off without so much as a backward glance.

Raven blew out his breath. He hadn't meant to pick a fight with Eva right now. Apparently, it came naturally for him. She made him feel reckless and vulnerable. Plus, she was as headstrong as he was, no doubt about that.

The more conflict between them, the better off he'd be. He wished he'd remembered that *before* he kissed her and discovered that she tasted like honey, smelled as fresh and wholesome as the whole outdoors…and felt like heaven in his arms.

Holy hell! Dealing with the scalding sensations she set off inside him was the last thing he needed to distract him while an unknown sniper lurked around. Already Eva had come dangerously close to being shot by a bullet meant for him.

He cringed at the thought of her being hurt or killed because of her association with him.

Marshal Doyle in Denver had warned him the Widow Flanders and Buster's family were hell-bent on revenge. Since that clan of ruffians was as thick as thieves, whomever she'd hired to gun him down must be taking the job seriously.

The fact that someone wanted him dead was nothing new. Besides, he faced danger on a daily basis. He had made peace with the prospect of his own demise after watching the massacre that had destroyed most of his Cheyenne family. But he was not prepared to claim responsibility for Eva's death.

He barely knew that firebrand but that didn't seem to matter. She provoked all sorts of intense sentiments and sensations that he usually had no difficulty controlling. But here she was, the picture of beauty and spirit, right in his face, right in his arms…and now she was the lingering taste on his lips.

The disturbing thought prompted him to take another sip of water, hoping to wash away her taste. It was a waste of time. And he had no idea how to erase the memory of her shapely body imprinted on his.

"Hell and damnation." Raven expelled an exasperated breath then inhaled fresh air, hoping to clear his head and get his unruly male body under control.

He stood in the exact spot where he'd kissed Eva with wild desperation—and she had kissed him back the same way. When the memory and sensations tried to overpower him again, he focused his concentration on scanning the hillsides. He'd encountered enough precarious situations the past decade to sense trouble. And he definitely sensed trouble now. Hell, he could practically hear death rattles.

The hair on the back of his neck stood at attention, prompting him to retreat into the pockets of shadows in the trees. He knew there was a narrow trail leading to the ridge to the west because he'd followed it as a child and had used it three years ago while searching for the drunken murderer wanted in Leadville.

Raven stared up the rocky slopes and noticed a flash of color among the trees. Someone was lying in wait. Thankfully, he hadn't become an easy target for another ambush attempt.

A horse nickered in the distance, confirming his suspicion. Raven jogged off when he heard the driver announce it was time to board the coach. He circled to step into the opposite side of the coach, convinced that he was being stalked and that he had been marked for death.

No one in the coach uttered a word when Eva piled onto the seat. She sat catty-corner to him and never once glanced in his direction. It was clear to everyone that she wasn't speaking to him.

"Lover's spat?" Frank Albers questioned as he rolled a silver dollar deftly over his fingers.

Apparently, Eva overheard because she looked over at

Raven and held his gaze while he replied, "Just a difference of opinion. Now that I think about it, I was probably wrong."

Frank snickered when he noticed the smile on Eva's lips. "A wise man once told me that if husbands knew how to say they were sorry and they were wrong, marriages would run smoother." He winked at Raven. "You're halfway there."

For the life of him, he didn't know why he'd bypassed the chance to fuel the anger that had sent Eva stamping off earlier. The only explanation was that he was turning into mush—all because of a beautiful but feisty female who couldn't possibly be more than a footnote in the chronicles of his hardscrabble life. Why should he care if Eva Whoever-she-was was annoyed with him? He shouldn't...

Then she smiled and those luminous brown eyes twinkled with inner spirit. He turned into a mindless sap and smiled back at her.

Raven was reasonably sure that goofy smile was still plastered on his face when a loud clap of thunder shook loose his stalled thoughts. He glanced through the window to see a thunderstorm skirting the mountains. The bank of gray clouds that had scraped the summits left a curtain of rain sweeping over the stagecoach. The driver cracked his whip over the team of horses, hoping to outrun the cloudburst.

Rather than huddling against the seat, Eva outstretched her hand to catch the oversize raindrops then she inhaled a deep breath of rain-scented air. Spellbound, Raven watched her tilt her face to the mist swirling around the window. A woman who embraced storms? What else did she like? he wondered.

Was she really the sister of the woman Gordon had betrayed? Or was *she* the woman scorned? There was also the possibility that she had been Gordon's accomplice and he had double-crossed her by riding off with the extorted money. Perhaps she wanted her cut and wasn't giving up until she found him.

Why wouldn't she divulge her last name? he wondered. That made him highly suspicious. He knew she wasn't telling him the whole story. He could sense it.

You're thinking too damn hard, Raven. Before long, you'll be gone and Eva will continue her crusade with or without you.

Raven glanced away, watching the curtain of rain sweep past the stagecoach then fizzle out as if it hadn't been there at all. If nothing else, the shower settled the dust. At best, the midday storm might have waylaid the unidentified bushwhacker. Better yet, he might slip and fall on the treacherous mountain trails. If he ended up at the bottom of a canyon, it would be one less thing for Raven to fret about.

Of course, that would be too easy. When had life been easy? Never that Raven could recall.

"Lunch will be served at the upcoming station!" George called down to the passengers. "Eat heartily, friends, because it will be a long ride before we stop for supper."

Raven noted the slur in George's voice. Stage drivers were known to be heavy drinkers, he recalled. George had been tipping his stashed bottle all morning. That explained the bushy-haired man's daring when he'd asked how Raven possibly could have married a woman like Eva. He hadn't taken offense to the tactless question. It was obvious to everyone with eyes in his head that he and Eva didn't belong together.

When the coach clattered to a halt then lurched unexpectedly, Eva was catapulted into Delbert Barnes's lap. The bookkeeper grunted uncomfortably then hoisted her upright. Her stylish hat snagged on Delbert's jeweled stickpin and stuck there. Her coiffure came untangled and tumbled over the side of her face when Delbert tried to settle her back in the seat across from him.

"Goodness." She leaned forward to retrieve her hat from Delbert's jacket and surveyed the two broken feathers that hung like limp antennas. "I should have worn a helmet."

When she flung open the door, preparing to climb down without assistance, an eerie sensation—like another death rattle—overcame Raven. "No!" he yelled when she surged forward to place her foot on the step.

Eva's startled yelp was followed by the unmistakable sound of a whizzing bullet that thudded into the wall of the coach. The shot missed her head—and Delbert's shoulder—by a scant few inches.

"Get down and stay down!" Raven roared as he lunged over the passengers to grab the nape of Eva's dress and jerk her back inside.

Another gunshot whistled over Eva's head as Raven sent her sprawling on Delbert's lap again. Crawling over bodies, Raven somersaulted from the coach and came to his knees, firing both pistols in the direction of the shot.

"Run for it," he barked at the startled passengers. "Use the coach and horses for cover and take Eva with you!"

Raven fired repeatedly while the passengers piled from the opposite side of the coach then scurried into the stage station. He cursed foully when he heard the clatter of hooves beating a hasty retreat on the rocky trail above the station.

Then and there, he decided that the sniper was ex-army or part Indian because of his guerilla fighting skills. He attacked and retreated before Raven could pinpoint his exact location and the sniper was on the move constantly. Which is exactly what Raven would have done if he were in the bushwhacking business. The only good news was that the sniper didn't have the unerring accuracy of a sharpshooter.

Scowling at the new complication he'd encountered, Raven stuffed his pistols into his holsters and strode inside. "This day just keeps getting worse," he muttered to the world at large.

Chapter Five

James Archer jerked his horse to a halt and swore sourly. "Damn J. D. Raven to hell and back," he sneered as he reloaded his Winchester.

He'd had several confrontations with Raven in the past and his hatred had festered as Widow Flanders's had. The opportunity to dispose of Raven was too good to pass up. He could have put an end to that half-breed bastard and his lady friend if he hadn't gotten trigger-happy and overanxious.

James had expected Raven to be the first one to climb down from the coach, not that auburn-haired chit in calico.

The horse James was riding whinnied—just as it had at the previous stage stop, alerting Raven to his presence on the hill. James glared mutinously at the horse then walloped it upside the head for spoiling the ambush attempt earlier. The horse danced skittishly and James yanked hard on the reins, causing the bit to dig deeply into the animal's tender mouth.

"I'll break you, you contrary beast," he muttered then gouged his heels painfully into the horse's flanks.

The horse nickered again as it pranced on the stone path.

James sneered impatiently then used the barrel of his rifle as a club on the horse's neck. Before the animal reared up and unseated him, he dug in his heels again—hard. He rode away, mentally planning his next attempt to bring down the legendary J. D. Raven and leave him for buzzard bait.

Eva appraised the damaged hat she had clamped in her hand and silently fumed while she sat at the table in the stage station. It seemed she had encountered one disaster after another since Gordon had deceived Lydia then stolen her carriage, her horse and her money. Now the scoundrel was trying to blast Eva off the face of the earth.

She would dearly love to return the favor.

Clara Morton, the other female passenger, halted to pat Eva's hand consolingly. "Are you all right? You were jostled all over the place, even before the shooting started."

Eva rotated her tender arm—the one Raven landed on accidentally after he shoved her facedown. She had slammed her forehead into Irving Jarmon's boney knee as Raven somersaulted from the coach to return gunfire. She had to admit it had been a rough morning—and she hadn't even had lunch yet.

"I'm a little shaken up but otherwise fine," Eva admitted. "Thank you for asking."

Clara smiled down at her. "It must be comforting to have such a capable husband who will risk life and limb to protect you. I wish my husband was that attentive and—" She closed her mouth then patted Eva's hand again. "I'm glad you're okay."

Eva got the impression that all wasn't well in Clara's marriage to the army officer. Which made her wonder if Clara had taken her son to St. Louis so she could return to pack up and leave her inattentive husband at the fort.

Delbert Barnes plopped down across the table from Eva and mopped his brow with his handkerchief. "Are you all right?" When she nodded he said, "I don't mind telling you that the ambush scared ten years off my life. Mercy, that was too close for comfort. Honestly, I couldn't believe you poked your head out the door after the first shot was fired."

"I was hoping to get a good look at the sniper."

"One of your new husband's sworn enemies, no doubt," he remarked before he sipped the whiskey the waiter set in front of him. "It's not my place to say, of course, but I fear you'll be hounded constantly by Raven's past—unless you pack up and move out of state. Of course, that's no guarantee."

"And miss all the excitement that makes life interesting? Where is the fun in that?" she replied flippantly.

Delbert couldn't decide if she was kidding or crazy so she snickered lightheartedly and he smiled tentatively at her. When he noticed that Raven had entered the station house he got up, grabbed his glass of whiskey and walked over to join the other passengers, who had gathered around the larger table.

It only took one glance into those intense green-gold eyes to realize Raven was displeased with her. *So what else was new?* she mused as she absently massaged her left wrist, which had been hyperextended during the shooting incident.

Considering Raven's sour expression—which she'd noted several times during the course of the day—she wondered if she brought out the worst in him. Or maybe bad moods were the order of all his days. She hadn't known him long enough to say for certain.

She would have thought he'd be looking exceedingly pleased. After all, he was leaving the stagecoach after lunch. He was hiking off to his secluded mountain cabin, never to see her again.

He loomed over her in that formidable way he had about him. His thick black brows flattened over his slitted eyes. His lips were stretched thin and his jaw, covered with the thick black beard and mustache, was clenched tightly. His chest swelled up like a striking cobra. Eva could understand how he was able to intimidate outlaws. He could look absolutely ominous when he felt like it.

However, she had discovered how tender and gentle he could be when he'd held her in his arms and kissed her until nothing else in the world mattered except the sizzling sensations he set off inside her. Whatever he said to the contrary—and dangerous though he looked, and he definitely did—she knew he had a gentler side. That knowledge prevented her from being frightened of him.

He doubled at the waist to slap his hands on the table so he could get right in her face. "Do not ever do that again," he said with a snarl. "You nearly got yourself killed. When I tell you to get down then you get down right then and right there. Do you understand, Eva?"

"No," she sassed him. "Maybe you could be a bit more specific about what you want me to do and when you want me to do it."

Her smart remark obviously took him by surprise because he stared at her as if she were a curious creature he'd never seen before. Apparently, he wasn't accustomed to a woman talking back to him. Good, she didn't mind being the first at *something* for him.

Raven expelled his breath, shot her another annoyed look then plunked down across from her at the table. "You're driving me crazy."

"Only for another half hour," she reminded him. "You'll

be gone after you have lunch. If I get my head blown off this afternoon it won't besmirch your reputation or encroach on your time because I won't be your concern."

"Look, Eva, the—"

Raven swallowed whatever he intended to say when the waiter set down two plates of beans floating in the grease dripping off two slices of bacon. The corn bread was nearly burned beyond recognition.

Eva stared at the unappetizing food. "I've heard that meals on the stage line leave a lot to be desired, but I've never eaten one. The train serves better food. Too bad you didn't choose to ride the rails. You could have saved both of us from bushwhacking attempts." She directed his attention to the knot on her forehead then gestured to her injured arm. "Not to mention bypassing a few bumps, sprains and bruises."

"I don't recall inviting you to come along, *dear,*" he retorted as he picked up his fork.

Eva grimaced as she watched him scoop up a bite of bacon and beans then munch on them. Well, she thought, if he could choke down the unappealing food so could she. Unfortunately, she couldn't hide her distaste when the foul-tasting beans landed on her tongue and tasted like poison. Because he was watching closely, waiting for her gag and make a run for the door, she swallowed with defiance and quickly chased the food with a half a glass of water.

"Best food I ever had," he declared.

He took another bite, but she couldn't match him forkful for forkful. Defeated, she rose to her feet and walked out.

"Don't become a live target again, sugarplum," he called after her. "The third time might be the charm."

She wished she spoke the Cheyenne language so she could tell him where to go and what to do with himself when he got there—without the passengers overhearing her.

* * *

Raven sat there for a half hour during the lunch break, debating with himself about what to do next while Eva did whatever the hell she was doing outside. Since no one was shooting at her presently, he presumed he was the primary target and the sniper had gotten in too much of a hurry.

He intended to leave the stagecoach and head up the mountain trail. But what to do about Eva…? She could concoct an explanation to feed to the curious passengers about where he'd gone. Or maybe she'd give up and go home where she should've stayed in the first place…*if* the story she had fed him was really the truth. He couldn't swear it was.

Then again, as daring as she was, she might arrive in Canyon Springs, outfit herself with a horse and supplies and travel alone to the mining camps in Devil's Triangle to search out Gordon. Bold and determined as she was, that wouldn't surprise him one damn bit.

"All aboard!" George slurred out as he propped himself negligently in the doorway.

The driver looked two sheets to the wind with his glassy eyes and slouched stance. It was no small wonder that stagecoaches occasionally overturned during trips. A besotted driver made matters worse while negotiating rough roads. Six months earlier, he'd heard that the stagecoach from El Paso to Santa Fe had overturned three times. He wondered if George Knott had been driving it.

Raven recalled the injuries Eva had sustained thus far then he muttered under his breath, "Hell and damnation."

He surged to his feet and made a beeline toward George. "If this stagecoach lands upside down during the next leg of the journey I'm coming after you, Knott," Raven growled as he halted in front of the inebriated driver. George's eyes widened as Raven bore down on him. "I don't make idle threats. That's a promise, guaran-damn-teed."

George straightened to let Raven pass through the door.

"I'm grabbing my saddle and luggage and I'm leaving," Raven called over his shoulder.

"Good. Maybe that bushwhacker will leave us be if you aren't on the stagecoach," George mumbled when Raven was a safe distance away.

Glancing around, Raven tried to locate Eva. Using the horses and coach as a shield—just in case—he stepped up to grab his belongings from the cargo compartment. Reluctantly he dug around until he found Eva's two bulging satchels.

"I must be out of my mind," he muttered as he carried the luggage to a nearby tree then dropped them at his feet.

"Board the stage!" George shouted as he wobbled outside.

Raven saw Eva emerge from the underbrush. Apparently, she had hiked down to the stream because her face looked freshly scrubbed and her glorious mane of auburn hair tumbled loosely over her shoulders and down her back. When she heard George's slurred summons, she broke into a run, her flaming hair flying out behind her. She squawked when Raven stepped from the shadows to snag her arm unexpectedly.

"You're coming with me," he said, silently castigating himself for being a hypocrite.

Her long lashes swept up and she focused those luminous brown eyes on him. "I am? I thought—"

"Changed my mind."

"Why?"

"Because I'm crazy about you, of course. One day with you and I want you for life," he said caustically.

She scoffed at his insincere tone. "Sure you do, Jo-Dan."

He bared his teeth. "I told you not to call me that."

"You coming or not, Mrs. Raven?" George called to her.

"She's with me," Raven answered for her as he crammed her damaged hat in her satchel. "We're married, aren't we?"

As the coach clattered away Eva flashed him a radiant smile. "Thank you, Raven. You really are a sweetheart. You won't regret taking this assignment."

"Whoa, honey," he said quickly. "I didn't say anything about taking the case. You can spend a few days at my cabin then I'll bring you down the mountain to catch the stage."

"Now wait just a blessed minute!" she protested hotly. "If you aren't going to help me then I need to be on that stage!" She waved her arms wildly, trying to gain the driver's attention but George had picked up speed and didn't look back. Furious, she wheeled on Raven. "Damn you! You purposely misled me. That was a cheap trick!"

"Sort of like pretending we're married?" he mocked.

If looks could kill Raven was sure he would have been pushing up daisies. Having survived the murderous glare—just barely—he scooped up his saddle and rifle and walked off.

"Gordon Carter has nothing on you. You're a conniving rascal, Jo-Dan," she spluttered at him.

"I prefer to think of myself as crafty." He stared pointedly at her satchels. "Make yourself useful. Carry your gear. Either that or leave it behind. I don't care which."

"Just when I think I'm beginning to like you a little…you do something to annoy me to the extreme," she muttered as she followed him through the cover of the trees. "I'm curious. Is there anyone on the face of this planet that you like or respect enough to treat with kindness and consideration?"

"Yes, my cousin, Blackowl, and Hoodoo."

"Who's Hoodoo?"

"The man who keeps the home fires burning at my cabin while I'm on forays," Raven explained as he ducked beneath a low-hanging tree limb.

"You have two friends in the world? That's two more than I expected," she taunted. "They must overlook your sour disposition because they're desperate for companionship."

Raven halted so abruptly that Eva slammed into him. He pivoted to face her wicked smile.

"You should be a helluva lot nicer to me," he told her. "I'm the only thing standing between you and *lost*."

"Has it occurred to you that this might be as nice as I ever get?" she countered, undaunted.

He nodded pensively. "Yeah, that's right. A man-hater. I almost forgot after you put on that sugarcoated act to fool the stagecoach passengers."

When he spun around to walk away she said, "I'll pay you an extra five-hundred-dollar bonus to take this case."

"Are you made of money?" he asked as he sidestepped up the rocky slope then tossed his saddle onto the ledge.

"I have a modest inheritance," she replied. "I'll gladly share it with you if you'll help me put Gordon behind bars so he can't swindle another unsuspecting woman out of money."

"The Rocky Mountain Detective Agency is still your best bet. General David Cook is as a good man and so are most of his assistants," Raven recommended.

"Still not an option," she mumbled.

He pulled himself upon the ledge then stretched out his hand to hoist her up. "I don't get it. *Why me?*"

"Because you're the best and that's exactly what I want."

The comment inordinately pleased him. Damn if he knew

why. After all, he was making a colossal effort to find fault with Eva at every turn so he wouldn't like her too much.

"Let me know if the pace is too rigorous. Nothing worse than dragging along a sissy girl," he baited purposely.

She slung her leg over the ledge and flopped beside him. "I love you, too, J.D.," she cooed in a sticky sweet tone.

He surged to his feet and turned away before she noticed his grin. "Let's move, wife. We're wasting daylight."

Eva huffed and puffed her way up the winding footpath. They had been climbing toward the sawtooth peaks with their eroded cliffs and weather-beaten bluffs for what seemed like hours, but she vowed she would give out long before she gave up. Sissy indeed! Raven was testing her, pushing her to pinpoint her limitations, forcing her to admit she was out of her element and inferior to his strength and survival skills. She knew she was, but she wouldn't give the infuriating man the satisfaction of hearing her admit it.

Despite her willful determination, her feet were killing her and her arms ached from lugging the heavy satchels. She could see why traveling light in the mountains was important. Any extra baggage weighed you down and zapped your strength and stamina prematurely.

Eva managed to keep walking for another half hour before her knees gave way and dumped her unceremoniously on the rocky path. She was on the brink of tears, knowing she'd have to beg for a short break. To her surprise, Raven halted. He dropped his saddle, grabbed her arm and boosted her onto a boulder.

"Ouch," she mumbled, massaging her tender shoulder.

"Sorry, I forgot about your previous injury." He glanced overhead and frowned. "I wonder what's drawing buzzards."

Eva shaded her eyes with her hand and glanced at the

four vultures circling in the cloudy sky. Then they swooped down and disappeared on the upper ledge. That didn't bode well. Someone or something was about to become an afternoon meal.

"Here, take this," Raven ordered as he handed her one of his Colt .45s.

"I still don't know how to shoot it," she reminded him.

"Cock the hammer, aim at anything that doesn't announce itself and squeeze the trigger. I'll give a shout when I return, so don't accidentally blow my head off."

She flashed him a mischievous grin. "At last, an excuse I can work with."

"Two hours ago you said you loved me," he recalled.

"I've decided I'd love to *shoot* you instead."

"Fickle woman. You change with the wind." His smile faded and his expression sobered. "Seriously, minx, pay attention to your surroundings. This could be a setup by my sniper. He might have killed a rabbit and left it to the buzzards to provide a distraction for me while he moves in for the kill."

"*My* sniper," she corrected. "I told you Gordon despises me because I never trusted his premeditated flattery. I was rude to him every change I got."

"Gee, can't imagine that," he said flippantly as he clutched her hand to lead her beneath the overhanging stone ledge. "Rule number one in the wilderness—*pay attention.*"

"I'd rather come with you," she requested.

"This is not negotiable." He wagged his finger in her flushed face. "You better be exactly where I leave you…or else."

"Or else what?" she asked with a challenging smile.

"I'll dream up a suitable torture while I'm gone."

After he disappeared around the bend on the path, Eva

removed her shoes and sighed in relief. She had blisters on her feet and she'd give anything for a pair of those thick-soled moccasins Raven wore. She leaned back to wiggle her bare toes, closed her eyes and begged for a quick nap. Amazingly, she dozed off but she was startled awake by the sound of a gunshot reverberating around the canyon walls.

Afraid Raven had become a target because of his association with her, she padded barefoot along the path, ignoring the pain of sharp pebbles digging into her feet. When the trail became even more rugged, she paused to fashion her hindering skirts into a pair of breeches by tucking the hem into her belt. Then she took off again with pistol in hand.

She stumbled to a halt when she saw Raven hunkered down on one knee on the path. "Oh, God, no!" she railed in horror.

"Damn it, Eva, I told you to stay put," Raven all but yelled at her.

He watched her hand fly to her mouth as she staggered back three paces. The pistol he'd given her hung loosely in her fingertips. She stared at him in anguish.

"Sweet Jesus…"

Her knees folded up again and dumped her on the pebbled path. Raven swore foully as tears welled up in her dark eyes then dribbled down her cheeks. This courageous woman, who defied flying bullets to search out a sniper and who stood up to him when no one else dared, was brought down by the sight of her sister's horse dangling half-on, half-off the ledge of the narrow trail. Or was it really *her* horse, he wondered.

The fact that Raven had to fire a shot to put the animal out of its misery, because of its broken leg, didn't make him feel any better about the situation. It was the second time in ten days that he'd had to dispose of a downed horse.

"Oh, Hodge, I'm so sorry I didn't catch up to you in time," she whispered as she crawled over to stroke the chestnut's muscular neck. Dark eyes spilling shiny tears, she looked up at Raven. "Papa bought this horse for Lydia's thirteenth birthday. When Papa died six months later, Lydia was so grief-stricken that she rode off on Hodge and it took me two days to find her. Hodge took care of her, but I wasn't here when he needed me most—"

Her voice broke when she noticed the telltale signs the horse had been abused by its rider. Someone had fastened leather straps around the gelding's jaw and muzzle to keep him silent. The rider had whipped him recently, leaving fresh welts on his hindquarters and shoulders. Raw strips of skin on his hocks indicated that he'd been tethered tightly to restrain him.

She stared stonily at Raven as she draped herself across the lifeless horse, as if to give it one last affectionate hug. "For this alone I swear I will kill Gordon myself."

"You don't know for certain that Gordon used the horse," Raven pointed out as she continued to stroke Hodge's neck. He gestured toward the wild tumble of rock and trees that filled the ravine below. "For all we know the horse might have tripped and catapulted the rider off the cliff. Finding dead bodies in these mountains isn't easy, especially if you don't know precisely where to look. It took me a long time to find Buster Flanders and I knew approximately where he landed."

"I'm not banking on the fact that Gordon is at the bottom of the ravine," she said between sniffles. "He exposed his vicious streak to me only once, when he didn't know I was there to watch him take a makeshift club to a drunken partygoer who did nothing more than poke fun at him."

"Nonetheless, your smooth-talking gold digger might have been overtaken and killed for possession of this well-bred horse and the stolen money," Raven contended. "I've seen it happen countless times before. Gordon might have been knocked off the side of the mountain or dragged into a cave or into an abandoned mineshaft and left to rot. My best guess is that my sniper confiscated this horse from Gordon. He is still gunning for *me,* not *you.*"

He set Eva to her feet then retrieved his six-shooter, which she'd dropped on the ground. "We need to keep moving."

"We can't just leave Hodge here for the buzzards."

"Let it go, Eva," he said quietly. "There's nothing we can do for him now."

"Did you bury your horse?" she wanted to know as she swiped at the tears rolling down her grimy cheeks.

"No. I was in the middle of a firefight with three desperados. There was no time for sentiment. And I didn't have time afterward, either. But that doesn't mean I didn't say a heartfelt farewell to Buck in my own way. Same goes for you and Hodge. That's the code of survival, Eva, like it or not."

She was silent as Raven escorted her downhill to retrieve their gear. He pulled her to a halt before they rounded the corner—just in case an unwanted visitor lay in wait. When he was sure the coast was clear he led the way to their discarded belongings.

Raven noticed the blisters on her feet and made a stabbing gesture toward the oversize boulder. "Sit."

Learning the fate of the horse had taken the wind from Eva's sails. She sat down dutifully. Raven rubbed the healing poultice that he carried in his saddlebags over her blisters.

"What is that stuff? It feels wonderful," she sighed.

"Cheyenne potion. A little of this and that."

He twisted on his haunches to fish out gauze to bind her

feet then paused to scan the jagged slopes for any sign of trouble. He wondered if the bushwhacker was out there somewhere, watching them constantly, trying to deceive them into thinking he was dead so they'd let their guard down. Had the mysterious sniper stolen this horse from Carter? And what had happened to Carter?

"Jordan, I'm sorry I fell apart earlier," Eva said quietly. "I don't do it often. Not since—" She dodged his direct stare. "Not for a long time. I'm sure you don't approve of any sort of sentimental weakness. Neither do I. I'm not a bleeding heart ordinarily. I'm a realist."

He could see that pride refused to let her decompose again. She strived to be strong-willed and rational. He admired her for that. Hell, he felt the same way himself. He couldn't name one time in his life when bawling his head off had resolved a crisis or eased emotional pain. All it did was waste valuable time and slow him down.

Eva was a woman after his own heart—if he had one left after all his ordeals. Life hadn't been kind and he held very low expectations. Mostly Raven just did his job and survived the only way he knew how. Then Eva came along to complicate an existence that was difficult—even on a good day.

"Let's get moving. Since we aren't on horseback, we won't use the wagon trail. We'll take a shortcut that we can only access on foot," he said as he hoisted her back to her feet. "I'll carry your lug—"

She jerked the satchels from his fingertips and tilted a determined chin. "I'll carry them myself. I have no intention of weighing you down like a pack horse."

And off she went. She didn't look down as she sidestepped around the downed horse he'd had to put out of its misery.

"The footing will become precarious during this next stretch," Raven warned as they hiked uphill. "There is a detour on this trail that leads to the Cheyenne tribe's sacred site. It's worth the extra time to see it."

"Not a problem," Eva insisted. "I can go anywhere you can. I'm not going to let a piddly mountain slow me down."

Raven smiled in amusement as he surveyed Eva's proud stance and determined expression. She had no idea what she was in for, but she was about to find out….

Chapter Six

Thirty minutes later Eva wanted to retract her cocky comment about keeping up with Raven on this difficult mountain trail. When he'd mentioned the footing would become a mite precarious at times she hadn't expected to be inching along the side of a stone peak like a mountain goat. He'd secured their belongings to a rope so they could concentrate on getting themselves across the narrow trail then drag the saddle and satchels to them later.

The path had become a wedge of rock that was eighteen inches wide—and dropped into a chasm filled with jutting boulders. One false step and she would swan dive to her death.

"Sweet merciful heavens! Where do you live? In an eagle's nest atop some craggy summit?" she asked, out of breath.

When she halted to flatten her back against the vertical rock wall, Raven glanced at her in concern. "You okay?"

"Not very okay," she said shakily. "I've just discovered that I have a slight aversion to perching on narrow ledges. The whistling wind isn't helping, either."

"Look at me," he demanded sternly.

Eva dug her nails into the rock behind her and slowly turned her head to stare into those cougarlike eyes that glittered a deep shade of gold in the sunlight. She didn't notice a speck of fear in Raven—probably because she was afraid enough for both of them. In his eyes, she saw only that unblinking, uncanny alertness she envied.

"Slide your feet sideways without picking them up," he instructed. "In those shoes you might step down on loose pebbles and that will toss you off balance."

"Was this tight-wire ledge part of your Cheyenne training?" she asked, trying to keep her mind off the forty-foot drop into nothingness that yawned before her.

"Yes. Blackowl and I were training to become members of the elite society of Dog Soldiers. We tested ourselves to our limits so we would know how far we could go and how much improvement we needed to make. Then we pushed ourselves further to see what we were made of…. No, don't look down," he commanded sharply. "Keep looking at me."

Eva swallowed hard and dug in her nails, certain the gust of wind that swirled around her was going to blow her off the narrow ledge. She dragged in a ragged breath then met Raven's unblinking gaze.

"What are you really made of Eva? Grit or putty?"

He was challenging her and she silently thanked him for it. Trying to conquer her weakness, she continued to stare into those captivating eyes as she glided sideways on the ledge.

A sense of pride and accomplishment consumed her when she completed the feat and noticed a wider path a few feet ahead of her. She half turned a moment too soon and yelped when her left foot skidded on pebbles then dropped off the ledge. When she felt herself tilt toward the abyss, she reared backward. But that didn't help because she threw herself off balance and couldn't get a handhold on the rock wall.

Raven's guttural growl erupted as he clamped his hand around her elbow to jerk her sideways in the nick of time.

One second later and she would have pitched off the ledge into nothingness.

Eva gasped in pain when Raven inadvertently yanked on her tender arm. She told herself that it was the burning ache in her shoulder that prompted her to throw herself against his broad chest and hold on to him for dear life.

She was rattled, was all, she tried to convince herself. She'd nearly taken the short way down the mountain and it had frightened her senseless.

Even after several heart-pounding seconds passed, she still had her head buried against his shoulder. Her good arm was clenched around his waist like a vise grip. Try as she might she couldn't breathe normally. Thin air, she told herself. She was at all sorts of disadvantages in this unforgiving terrain. This misadventure exposed each and every one of her vulnerabilities and rattled her composure—to the extreme. Which made her look like… What had he called her? Ah, yes, a sissy.

"I'll let go of you in a minute," she mumbled against the fabric of his shirt.

"Take your time. It isn't every day that you nearly cartwheel off a cliff and get shot at a few times," he said as he rested his chin on the crown of her head.

There was no censure or ridicule in his deep baritone voice and his strong arms felt wonderfully protective. This was the second time today that she'd snuggled up against Raven. She had better not get used to it, she cautioned herself. Raven had assured her that he wouldn't be around for long, so depending on him would become a habit she'd have to break.

Eva inhaled a bolstering breath, and then another. Careful where she stepped, she backed from Raven's arms.

"Thank you. It seems I have a lot to learn about trekking through the wilderness."

"If you want to survive you do." He pivoted to reclaim the rope he'd used to anchor their belongings while crossing the narrow stretch of the trail. Hand over hand, he dragged his saddle, rifle and their bags up to the ledge. "I told you this country is no place for the faint of heart."

An hour later, Eva paused to survey the incredible scenery that spread out before her like a secluded fairyland. "What is this place?"

"Garden of the Gods," he said. "This is sacred ground to my mother's people. The place I mentioned earlier."

Eva dropped her satchels and studied the gigantic rock formations that rose from the earth at horizontal and vertical angles. The unusual blades of stone caught and reflected the hues of afternoon light. The site was positively magnificent and she had never seen anything like it!

"My people gathered here in the old days to worship the gods, before the whites routed them from their land," he murmured as he stared into the distance, as if glancing through the window of the past. "The elders, who knew it was their time to travel the stairway into the sky, scratched and clawed their way to the top of the stone slabs. Exhausted, they waited to draw their last breath as the first rays of sunlight shined on their aged faces and led their way to the happy hunting ground."

"It's spectacular," she whispered reverently. "In case I don't survive the journey to your cabin, leave me out here with the spirits of your people. Perhaps I'll fit in better with them than I do with my own kind."

He chuckled at that. "I do believe you would, Eva. Women command a great deal of respect and authority in the Cheyenne culture."

"Show me where to join up," she insisted. "What initiation rites must I undergo?"

Raven waved his arms and called to the gods, using his native language. A moment later, he said, "There. It is done. After a ceremonial baptism in the nearby warm springs and the presentation of a headband and eagle feather you'll be one of us."

"How far to the springs?" she asked eagerly. "I'm dead on my feet and I'd love a good soaking."

"We'll be at the springs in a quarter of an hour," he reported.

"Lead the way, oh great chief," she said with a sweeping bow. "I'll be right behind you."

"This surely must be paradise," Eva proclaimed as they stood side by side, overlooking the warm springs that trickled from cracks in a vertical stone wall to collect in a hollowed-out basin of rock.

Raven couldn't suppress a smile when Eva's face lit up with undeniable pleasure. He'd like to be the one who put that smile on her bewitching face….

He jerked upright when that dangerous thought rattled through his brain. He must be tired, he decided. He usually had more mind control. Nevertheless, he'd let his guard down with this spirited female because she had endured considerable emotional upheaval recently. Yet, he couldn't let her get to him. Already he'd gone back on his word by bringing her with him to his mountain retreat.

She's here with you because she was the target of gunfire meant for you, the sensible side of his brain argued. *Yes, but still…*

His thoughts flitted away when Eva dropped her satchels and began unfastening the buttons on the front of her calico gown while she sidestepped downhill. Raven caught a glimpse of her lacy chemise and the enticing swells of her breasts while he stood above her on the ledge. He held his breath, his body stirring with erotic anticipation as she shoved down the sleeves, exposing the creamy flesh on her chest and shoulders.

If she'd been trying to seduce him, she couldn't have aroused him more. However, he realized that she was so completely focused on the inviting spring that she had almost forgotten about him.

Raven wondered what it would be like to be the absolute focus of Eva's attention while they were swimming naked in the spring.

"Hell!" he burst out, aggravated with his betraying thoughts.

His voice carried downhill, causing Eva to stumble to a halt and glance up at him. He knew the exact moment when she became aware that she had partially undressed in front of him. She caught him staring directly at her bosom.

"Are you going to watch?" she challenged.

He grinned wickedly. "Do you want me to?"

She cocked her head to regard him speculatively as she stepped out of her gown, revealing the short chemise that extended to midthigh. Desire hit him like a rockslide and he had to brace his feet to prevent swaying when the appealing sight made him light-headed.

"Well, we are married, aren't we?" she teased. "And you did partially disrobe in front of me last night, so I suppose turnabout is fair play."

"I was trying to shock you into leaving last night," he retorted in a strained voice as his gaze roved helplessly over the ripe swells of her breasts, the tempting curve of her hips and the tantalizing sight of her long shapely legs.

"The tactic worked for you," she recalled. "Is it working for me?"

He chuckled wryly. "No, it's having the reverse effect. You don't see me running away, do you?"

The admission seemed to please her enormously and he regretted making it when she said, "So you are saying that you find me attractive, J.D.?"

He wasn't giving her another inch, even if she was the most alluring female he'd ever seen. He tried to concentrate on the fact that her stubborn, headstrong persistence drove him crazy, not the fact that he craved the chance to get his hands all over her luscious body.

"Don't flatter yourself, sugar. I find a lot of women attractive. Most of them in fact. I'm a man, after all." He shooed her on her way, as if he'd lost interest in staring at her—which he doubted he ever would. "Go soak your head while I scare up supper. Oh, and keep this handy…"

When he tossed her a six-shooter, she caught it in midair, causing her high-riding chemise to expose a few more inches of silky flesh on her upper thighs. Raven forgot to breathe. He battled the enticing image that suddenly became branded on his brain. Not to mention the flare-up of lust that urged him to bound downhill to join Eva in the spring.

Cursing his faltering willpower, he spun on his heels. "Watch out for snakes and such," he said in a strangled voice before he strode off.

Eva sank into the warm pool and sighed tiredly. The swirling water eased her aches and pains and she swore she could soak until she shriveled up like a prune. But she knew Raven wanted to reach his cabin by nightfall and she had slowed him down too much already.

A mischievous smile pursed her lips before she sank beneath the surface to douse her hair. Seeing Raven towering above her on the hill a few minutes earlier, staring at her with those uniquely colored eyes, had stirred something dangerously intriguing inside her. True, she hadn't intended to undress in front of him. Yet, when she had, she hadn't minded having his gaze fixed on her.

What did that mean? she wondered. Had she wanted to test him? Was he right? Was she trying to seduce him, if only to see if she could? Or because she wanted him in ways she'd never wanted another man?

"What the blazes is the matter with you?" Eva admonished herself as she burst to the surface.

She had spent the past three years protecting her heart from deceptive men and their wily schemes. Then along came J. D. Raven, a man who insisted she was no more than an inconvenience, a nuisance. He didn't ply her with flattery or cater to her whims. Just the opposite, in fact. He pushed her to her limits, challenged her and didn't treat her as if she were special.

Maybe that's why she wanted to impress him and gain his respect. Because he was the kind of man who was hard to impress, hard to rattle, hard to catch.

"You are going to give yourself a headache by doing too much thinking," she scolded herself.

However, she did admit that of all the men who had tried to charm her, J. D. Raven was the man she wanted to want her for who and what she was on the inside. However, she wasn't about to tell him who she really was. Neither did she want to disclose that she had inherited a fortune and the Hallowell family owned several successful businesses in Denver. That would change everything. It always had before. Eva delighted in her unique association with Raven and she was reluctant to change it. Even ruffling Raven's feathers gave her pleasure.

A movement on the rocks beside the pool caught Eva's attention. She swallowed a gasp when she saw a snake curling up beside her shoes. Damn it, Raven had warned her to remain alert but she'd been lollygagging. When the serpent raised its head, as if preparing to strike, Eva yelped impulsively. She lunged for the pistol three feet away from where she sat. She heard a warning hiss as she grabbed the pistol and whirled around to take aim.

She'd never shot a weapon before but beginner's luck prevailed. She hit the snake halfway between its head and tail and it dropped into the pool. Eva squealed like a sissy and thanked her lucky stars that Raven wasn't around to mock her. If the snake was still alive—and there was a strong possibility that it was since she hadn't hit it in the head—it still had plenty of bite left. Frantic, Eva scrambled from the pool and stood naked as she took better aim and fired again.

The snake sank. Whether it was dead or alive, she couldn't say. But the incident ruined her bath and she wasn't climbing back in.

"Eva!" Raven's voice boomed around her. He appeared on the ledge above her and she squawked in embarrassment as she shielded herself as best she could and scurried to gather her clothing.

"What the hell happened?"

"Snake," she bleated.

"Did you kill it?"

"I'm not sure. It fell in the pool. I'm not fishing it out."

She noticed he was staring politely over her head, trying to ignore the fact that she was dripping wet and naked behind the calico gown she clutched to her chest.

"Would you mind tossing down my satchels," she requested. "I'd like to put on clean clothes."

"Fetch them yourself while I deal with the snake."

Eva gnashed her teeth and slipped on her shoes. She sidestepped uphill to retrieve her carpetbags while Raven jogged over to break off a tree branch. Like a bounding mountain lion, he descended the boulders on the opposite side of the springs.

Meanwhile, Eva pulled on her breeches and shirt. No need dressing like a proper lady if she had to trek along death-defying ledges and battle snakes, and bears and only God knew what else she'd encounter during this misadventure.

Once dressed, Eva scurried downhill to watch Raven use the long branch to scoop the snake from the bottom of the pool. He uplifted the motionless creature to survey the two gunshot wounds.

"Not bad," he praised as he set aside the snake.

"Thank you. It was my first time. It's perfect practice for the sidewinder named Gordon Carter."

"I told you not to get your hopes up about blasting him to kingdom come because he might be dead already."

She shrugged. "Perhaps, but I want to check the obscure mining camps. That's where I'd go if I wanted to hide out."

He stared somberly at her. "You really aren't going to give up on this crusade, are you?"

"Whatever made you think I would? A misstep on a narrow ledge? A few flying bullets that came out of nowhere? A snake in my makeshift bathtub?" She shook her wet head. "No, J.D., This manhunt is for all the misfortunate women who have been conned by silver-tongued shysters who got away scot-free."

"You included? Is this about the one you didn't avenge because you were embarrassed and ashamed? Or is Gordon really your runaway fiancé who took your money and your horse and now you're out for your own revenge?"

Leave it to Raven to ask the straightforward questions. Well, considering the ordeals they had endured together today it made him her most trusted companion to date. She had spent more quality time with him—learning his moods and seeing his depth of character—than she had with her dandified suitors. She'd cursed him, cried on his shoulder and kissed him until she was dizzy and light-headed. She'd run the gamut of emotions and he'd been there through thick and thicker to watch her. She owed him the truth, mortifying though it was.

"I made the same foolish mistake Lydia did when I was nineteen," she confided. "I believed the charming phrases, the flattery and the gushing words of affection. The lying cheat named Felix Winslow used me to make the acquaintance of a friend, then he married her because he claimed she was younger and more easily controlled. He needed her backing to expand his floundering jewelry shop.

"The embarrassing ordeal wasn't as financially costly for me as it was for Lydia. I didn't have to risk public humiliation by consulting the local detective agency to reclaim stolen money. That's why I came to you for this."

"So this man betrayed you and you swore not to trust another one as long as you lived," he guessed accurately.

When she nodded her head, he shrugged his massive shoulders. "Can't say that I blame you. I swore to hate all whites forever after the two bloody massacres that claimed my family. But being half white, I realized I had to be more specific with my distaste because I had white man's blood flowing through my veins, too."

"So you're saying I should be selective in which men I hate," she said, paraphrasing.

He smiled. "I suppose there are good men in the world, just as there are a few good whites."

"But too few and too far between," she contended as she strode to the edge of the pool.

"My sentiments exactly." Raven unbuttoned his shirt and dropped his holster. "My turn at the spring. Your choice. You can watch or gather wood for a campfire. The matches are in my saddlebag."

She watched him discard his shirt. Her curious gaze flooded over his bare chest. For certain, he and Eva were becoming entirely too familiar with each other, Raven mused. He'd seen too much of her enticing body this afternoon and the tantalizing memory played hell with his self-control. He also knew how it felt to hold her in his arms and how she tasted on his lips.

His thoughts evaporated when she reached out to trail her forefinger from one male nipple to the other, then traced the wedge of hair that dipped into the waistband of his breeches. Raven tried to swallow but his throat closed up. He tried to drag in a breath of air but his lungs refused to function.

Only his heart worked; it pounded like a herd of stampeding buffalo.

Then she lifted her gaze to his face and focused on his mouth. *Hell! Say something before things get too far out of hand—or in hand, as the case might be*—he ordered himself.

"You aren't going to kiss me again, are you?" he asked, his voice nowhere near as steady as he'd hoped.

Damn it, need was hammering at him and he had to force himself not to reach for her, for fear that he couldn't stop touching her until he was buried deep inside her. Which was precisely what he wanted, even though he had enough sense to know that would be a disastrous mistake for both of them—for at least a dozen sensible reasons.

She might be curious about the possibility of passion between them right now, but she would never forgive him if he took advantage of the emotional whirlwind she'd endured the past twenty-four hours.

"I already told you that trying to seduce me isn't going to convince me to take your case," he reminded her bluntly.

The comment served its purpose. She jerked her hand from his chest and stopped staring at him with curious speculation. Her dark eyes flashed in annoyance as she lifted her chin.

"Sometimes, when I think I'm beginning to like you, you ruin it by aggravating the hell out of me, *Jo-Dan!*"

He knew why she was calling him Jo-Dan. And sure enough, it aggravated the hell out of him.

"Are dignified ladies allowed to curse?" he taunted as he unstrapped the sheathed dagger wrapped around his thigh, then dropped it beside his discarded holster.

"I never professed to being proper or dignified," she growled before she lurched around. "I live by my own rules and I thumb my nose at the restrictions men place on women. Never doubt that."

"Really? Glad you brought that to my attention. I never would have noticed…. Hey!"

He ducked when she hurled a rock at him. It missed his head with only an inch to spare.

"Keep your eyes peeled," she warned, glaring at him. "Someone around here might be tempted to sneak up and drown you. Want to guess who?"

He chuckled after she stalked off then he dropped his breeches. Eva was feisty, daring, gorgeous—and he cursed himself up one side and down the other for liking her, faults and all.

To cool the lust that was becoming ever present when

he was with her, he dropped into the spring. He didn't realize he was so tense until he began to relax. Being on guard to protect himself from an unidentified assassin and from his growing attachment to Eva was wearing him out.

Raven decided he was in desperate need of a buffer. When they reached his cabin, Hoodoo would be there to talk Eva's leg off and to distract him. Thank the powers that be for Hoodoo Lemoyne, Raven mused as he sank into the pool and told himself to forget how temping Eva looked naked.

Nothing was going to happen between them, he promised himself resolutely. But that didn't prevent the lusty side of his brain from conjuring up a fantasy that left him hard and aching. Raven sighed in exasperation as he came up for air. He wondered if anything short of dying was going to erase the thought of Eva's sassy temperament and her luscious body from his mind.

He seriously doubted it.

Chapter Seven

After Eva gathered firewood, she dug into Raven's saddlebag to locate the matches. Her hand folded around a necklace and she pulled it out to have a closer look. The Cheyenne side of Raven's persona, she mused as she surveyed the intricate jewelry. She could easily picture him wearing the bead-and-bone necklace…and nothing else.

She glanced over her shoulder to make certain he hadn't arrived to see her snooping in his saddlebags. She found three bench warrants for men who had robbed miners in Purgatory Gulch—one of the isolated camps in an area to the west known as Devil's Triangle. A place where she suspected Gordon might be lying low—if he wasn't dead already.

There were also two new black shirts, like the ones Raven favored, and a brown plaid one that didn't suit Raven. There was a pair of breeches, a breechcloth…Eva studied it curiously, wondering how Raven would look wearing it with his bead-and-bone necklace.

"Looking for something in particular?"

Eva practically leaped out of her skin when Raven's voice tumbled over her. She hadn't heard him coming.

However, in her defense, who did? The man moved with the silent grace of a panther.

Despite the profuse blush pulsating on her cheeks, she painstakingly replaced the items in his saddlebag. "I didn't have the opportunity to study the contents of the other bag. Is there anything in there I *shouldn't* see? If so, I want to see it."

He spread his arms wide. "I have nothing to hide. Can you say the same, Evangeline Whoever-you-are?"

The comment struck her conscience like a barb. She hadn't been honest about who she was. But she didn't want his attitude toward her to change because she *liked* the teasing camaraderie between them. Matching wits and challenging J. D. Raven was more fun than she'd had with a man in a very long time. If ever.

"Eva?" he prodded, scrutinizing her all too closely.

She held up his breechcloth and grinned. "I'd pay good money to see you wear this."

"In your dreams," he said and chuckled.

"Probably," she said under her breath.

"Come again?"

"Nothing." She surged to her feet with matches in hand. "I'll start the fire."

"You already did," he murmured as she walked away.

Coming from J. D. Raven that was most likely the closest thing to a compliment that a woman would ever get, so Eva took it as one.

"What is that?" Eva questioned, pointing at the grilled meat on a stick.

"A delicacy. Taste it," he encouraged, handing it to her.

"Not until you tell me what I'm eating."

He sank down cross-legged to munch on the meat.

"Seems fitting to me that you should take a bite out of the snake that nearly bit you."

Her eyes widened and she wrinkled her nose distastefully. "You must be kidding."

He shrugged nonchalantly. "The other meat is rabbit if you're too squeamish to try snake."

To his surprise, she rose to the taunt and took a bite of snake. She chewed, swallowed and said, "Not bad, but I think I'd prefer fried Raven."

"Cute," he said between bites.

"How far to your cabin?"

"A good hour if we set a swift pace."

"Any more towering ledges to tackle before we get there?"

"No, a few steep, rock-strewn cliffs to scale, but nothing an experienced climber like you can't handle while wearing your breeches." He was silent for a moment then he added, "About Hoodoo Lemoyne…"

"What about him?"

"He was maimed by a grizzly bear five years ago and I let him stay with me until he recuperated. He never left. Sort of stuck around, like you today."

She smiled at his teasing remark and munched on her meal.

"William Lemoyne came west from Louisiana after fighting for the South in the war," Raven explained. "He lost his family's land to carpetbaggers and his fair-weather fiancée to a man who acquired wealth and property by preying on misfortunate Southerners. He came here to hunt and trap. In the early years my father took him under his wing to teach him the trade, then Hoodoo struck off on his own."

"How bad were his injuries?" she asked attentively.

"Bad enough to alter his lifestyle," Raven replied. "I was gathering wild horses in the mountain meadows to add to my herd when I heard his call for help. William managed to get off a shot but that only enraged the bear that attacked him. By the time I got to William, he'd lost part of his left ear and the skin on the side of his face. He mangled his knee badly enough that he still walks with a limp."

Eva looked around uneasily. She had encountered a snake and a two-legged predator who tried to separate her from her head already. She definitely needed to brush up on her survival skills if there were bears in her future.

"While I was helping Will get away, the bear shredded my shirt and left the claw marks on my back," Raven continued. "Now, Will has a gimpy leg and disfigured facial features that make him self-conscious. I can't get him to venture to trading posts or to town these days. So, if you're going to stare at him in fanatical fascination do it when he isn't looking."

"You bought him the breeches and a shirt," she commented. "That's very sweet of you, Raven."

Raven snorted. "I've been called many things. Sweet isn't even on the list. But yeah, I thought a store-bought shirt and breeches might be a treat since he makes his own clothes. Plus, he makes my moccasins and deerskin garments."

She smiled playfully. "Now I understand why you said you don't need a wife. You have a valet who tends to your needs."

"Not all of them," he said pointedly.

She remembered his earlier comment about how she was trying to seduce him to gain his cooperation. "Right," she said, smirking. "But you prefer a woman who wants no strings and no favors. Not someone manipulative and deceptive like me."

He shrugged noncommittally and kept eating.

Eva had hoped he would retract that hurtful remark he'd made after she'd kissed him. But not J. D. Raven. He didn't give an inch. Which was probably why she liked and admired him so much—in an exasperating and infuriating kind of way.

Raven rose agilely to his feet then kicked dirt on the fire. "We should get moving."

Eva stared longingly toward the spring, wishing for another relaxing bath to ease her strained muscles.

"Sorry," he said, accurately reading her expression. "There is another spring near my cabin that will serve you just as well."

"I prefer that the next spring is on the path to the mining camps I plan to search."

"Wild-goose chase," he declared as he gathered his gear. "Do yourself a favor and go home. I think that Gordon character is at the bottom of a ravine and you're tramping around here for nothing."

"Then why didn't we find any of his belongings with Lydia's horse?" she questioned.

"They were likely stolen," Raven speculated. "For all we know he was robbed and shoved off the cliff by the man who is gunning for me. Men disappear mysteriously and all too often in this lawless part of the state. I'm as close to a peace officer as most folks get in the areas around mining camps. Men literally get away with murder in that neck of the woods. I don't want you to be the next victim."

Doubt and uncertainty began to intrude in her mind but she refused to abort her mission just because she faced difficulty. She wanted Gordon to become an example to other calculating men who preyed on naive women. If he were still alive and kicking, she would track him down and see justice served.

Raven halted in the trees lining the mountain meadow to survey the herd of a dozen sturdy mountain horses he'd rounded up the past few years. He'd worked with them to ensure they were green-broken but they were a far cry from a seasoned mount like Buck that he'd lost during his last assignment.

"They are beautiful," Eva murmured as she came to stand beside him.

He looked down to see the pastel shades of sunset framing the exquisite features of her face and dancing like colorful flames in her silky hair. *She* was beautiful, he mused, admiring her while she was unaware. She was much too refined-looking and too civilized to associate with a social outcast like him, but no one said he couldn't appreciate her until they parted company.

"Which one do you plan to train for yourself?" she asked interestedly.

He pointed out the skewbald pony with patches of brown and white and a brown mane and tail. "The horse reminds me of the one I had when I was a child. The soldiers slaughtered the paint pony, along with a hundred others during the Sand Creek Massacre."

"I'm sorry," she commiserated. "Losing a horse like Buck or Hodge isn't easy." She glanced sideways at him. "Which one will you allow me to purchase? Since I'm headed to the mining camps I prefer not to walk."

Raven studied the determined glint in her dark eyes and noted the unyielding tilt of her chin. She had that come-hell-or-high-water-or-both look that he admired and disliked at once. She aggravated him. She aroused him. She impressed him.

Hell, no wonder he had trouble dealing with Eva. She touched off so many conflicting emotions he didn't know which one to battle first.

When he didn't respond immediately she gestured to the

herd grazing in the meadow. "I'd like to ride that blood-red bay with the black mane and tail."

Raven shook his head. "No, that horse is the very devil."

"According you, so am I," she reminded him. "We should get along grandly."

"That red devil gelding is too much horse for a woman," Raven insisted.

"We shall see about that later. Right now I want to meet Hoodoo Lemoyne."

Shoulders thrust back, a satchel in each hand, she strode toward the cabin. Raven smiled begrudgingly. Eva Whoever-she-was was a strong-willed, independent-minded, persistent woman. His smile faded when his thoughts stalled on the fact that she still refused to divulge her last name.

That bothered the hell out of him.

Was she really Mrs. Gordon Carter, who was out for blood and revenge? Or was she the woman scorned who lost her pride, her money and her horse?

The galling truth was that Eva could be feeding him one tall tale after another and he wouldn't know it because he was too far from Denver to verify what she told him. If he knew what was good for him he wouldn't put stock in anything she said. But when he looked into that exquisite face, surrounded by a curly mass of auburn hair, and recalled how she looked naked he lost the good sense he'd spent thirty-three years cultivating.

Mustering his resolve, Raven hiked off to view Hoodoo's reaction to their unexpected houseguest. He mimicked the sound of a hoot owl to forewarn Hoodoo that he had arrived.

The door opened wide enough to accommodate the double barrels of a shotgun.

"It's me!" Raven called out.

"'Bout time you got here. I expected you a week—" Hoodoo's voice stopped when he saw Eva walking directly toward him.

"Hello, Hoodoo," she greeted cheerfully. "Raven has said many nice things about you. It's a pleasure to make your acquaintance."

As she marched up the steps Hoodoo's bumfuzzled gaze leaped back and forth between her and Raven.

He had to give the woman credit, Raven thought. Nothing shy or hesitant about her. She didn't blink or stare at Hoodoo's scars, just met his gaze head-on and flashed a dazzling smile.

"I'm J.D.'s wife," she announced as she halted on the porch beside Hoodoo.

"The ornery hellion," Raven muttered under his breath. Why did she have to blurt that out?

"Wife?" Hoodoo hooted incredulously. His blue eyes were as round as goose eggs. "You married him of your own free will?"

"That's right." She leaned forward to plant a kiss right smack-dab on his scarred cheek. "Mind if I go inside and make myself at home? It's been a long, exhausting trip."

Hoodoo watched her walk inside then pivoted toward Raven. His gaze narrowed as he snapped his shotgun into firing position. "Damn it, boy, there better not be a baby Raven on the way because if you forced yourself—"

Raven dropped his saddle and flung up a hand to silence the wild conjecture. *And thank you so much, Eva,* he thought irritably. "There is no baby Raven and she's not exactly my wife," he told Hoodoo.

"What's that mean?" Hoodoo demanded impatiently.

"That means she's so determined to get me to track

down an outlaw who wronged her family that she pretended to be my wife so she could hitch a ride on the stagecoach with me from Denver."

"No kidding?" Hoodoo used his shotgun as a crutch then half turned to stare into the open doorway. "Must be a very determined she-male to make such a daring claim."

"And then some." Raven leaned his rifle against the outer wall and dug into his saddlebags to retrieve the new clothes.

"For me?" Hoodoo smiled appreciatively as he appraised the new garments. "Thank you, Raven. That was thoughtful."

Raven chuckled. "Eva said I was sweet to do it."

Hoodoo glanced through the doorway. "That's interesting."

Raven quickly changed the subject before Hoodoo started prying into his dealings with Miss Hell-on-wheels. "I lost Buck during a firefight with three fugitives last week so I'm afoot."

"Aw, damn, I'm sorry. I know how partial you were to Buck. That big buckskin gelding was a remarkable horse."

Raven stared into the distance and nodded mutely. Then he said, "Have you seen Blackowl recently?"

"Not in six weeks. You know how he is. He shows up when the mood strikes."

Raven wished his cousin would stop in for a visit. He could use the assistance. "I want to begin training a new horse immediately. I was wondering if you could entertain Eva for me."

A lopsided grin spread across his scarred face. "Sure. I'll dance a jig and pick out a few tunes on my banjo."

Raven was grateful for the reprieve. He'd never spent so many consecutive hours with a woman, and never with one who challenged, irritated and aroused him—simultaneously—as much as Eva.

If that was her real name, he thought skeptically. He couldn't rule out the fact that she might be the *Lydia* she kept mentioning. He supposed he should torture the truth out of her, but he was afraid if he touched her, he would have entirely different designs on her tantalizing body.

Raven walked back to the herd, forcing himself to concentrate on the task at hand, not the woman who had disrupted his life like a churning tornado.

Eva stood in the middle of the rustic log cabin, admiring the bear rugs, the buckskin coats hanging on hooks beside the door and the boots and moccasins that Hoodoo had made meticulously by hand.

Pine railings and steps led to the spacious loft that was divided by two buffalo hides strung up to provide privacy. A small stone fireplace served a dual purpose—for cooking and for warmth. Everything inside the cabin was hand-constructed—a testimonial to living modestly and in harmony with the wilderness.

"Raven already had the cabin built before I came here." Hoodoo limped across the planked floor to set aside his new clothes. "I added a few things to make it feel like home."

Eva surveyed the wiry, five-foot-ten-inch man who looked to be in his mid-fifties. Then she pointed to the item on a shelf behind his rocking chair. "A few things like voodoo dolls?" she teased as she walked over to pick up the small effigy that had pins sticking clear through it. "I presume there's a story behind this."

Hoodoo grinned broadly and Eva realized it wasn't difficult to overlook the disfigured side of his face because he had a lively sparkle in his sky-blue eyes. When his full lips curved up at the corners, she felt instantly at ease with the man who spoke with an unmistakable Louisiana accent.

"That's to remind me of the woman I was supposed to marry when I returned from the war and of the swindler she cozied up with," he explained. "Call me spiteful, but to this day I still bear ill feelings toward both of them."

"I don't blame you." Eva sank down in the oversize rocking chair that she assumed belonged to Raven. "I'm harboring a few vicious sentiments myself. I'll get around to forgiving those who trespassed against me eventually, I hope. Just not yet."

Hoodoo plopped into his chair. "Who might that be? The man that Raven says you're chasing after right now?"

Eva nodded. "He and a few others I know who deserve a good shooting."

"Would you care for tea?" he asked, suddenly remembering his manners. "It's one of Raven's medicinal teas made from plants, roots and bark. With a spoonful of honey added, it's mighty tasty. It also helps a person relax and rest."

"Sounds heavenly. If it's not too much trouble, I'll take a cup of tea."

"Trouble? Hell…er, heck, little gal, we almost never have guests. Except for Raven's cousin. Mostly we have unwelcome intruders who try to steal what we have. You just can't trust some folks, ya know?"

"Amen to that," she murmured as she slumped tiredly in the comfy chair.

Five minutes later Hoodoo handed her a cup of tea. "Here ya go. This will make you feel better, guaranteed."

Eva awoke the next morning, startled to find herself sprawled in Raven's bed. The last thing she remembered was sipping the brewed tea. The rest of the night was a blur.

Pushing herself upright, she glanced over the railing to see that she was alone in the cabin. Since she was still dressed in her shirt and breeches she got up and went down-stairs. When she stepped onto the covered porch, she blinked in amazement. The two horses that she and Raven had singled out for new mounts lay on their sides in the distance. Their legs were bound up with rope and blindfolds covered their eyes. Raven was bare-chested, down on his knees between them. Speaking softly, he brushed his shirt over their nostrils then stroked his hands over their bodies.

"What is he doing?" Eva asked when Hoodoo appeared from the side of the cabin, followed by a flock of chickens that eagerly pecked the grain he tossed on the ground.

"Training horses," Hoodoo replied.

"I've never seen horses trained this way."

"Probably because the Cheyenne and the other Plains Indians have more effective methods than whites. Last night Raven roped them and left them sprawled on the ground. He slept between them so they would grow accustomed to his scent very quickly since he's short on time."

She wondered if that meant Raven had decided to escort her to the camps or if he was simply doing a hurry-up job to get her on her way.

"Raven said the horses needed a quick lesson in training because you're headed to the mining camps soon." He squinted at her. "Those are dangerous places, little gal, es-pecially for unchaperoned females."

"So I've been told."

"But you didn't listen," he guessed.

"No, because I'm on a crusade," she insisted, as if that made everything all right. In her book it did.

Hoodoo chuckled and shook his frizzy brown head. "Raven was right. You are a headstrong woman. Just don't get yourself killed because of it," he warned.

When Raven noticed she was standing on the stoop

he waved to her. "Glad you're awake. Come here," he called softly.

She approached, careful not to startle the downed horses. "How can I help?"

"I want you to sprawl all over this red devil," he instructed. "Talk to him so that he recognizes your voice and your scent. Since I've had both horses down on their sides all night they are going to require a little time to get their circulation going when I let them up. That's when we'll saddle them and climb on their backs. Until then, we'll get to know them and they will become familiar with us."

"I get to break my own horse?" she asked.

"Unless you're afraid to," he teased.

"You know perfectly well that I'm not afraid to try anything at least once," she sniffed, affronted.

"Then have right at it." He gestured for her to get down on her knees beside the blood-red bay.

She watched and listened attentively while Raven told her to half-straddle the horse, while he draped his arm and leg over the spotted skewbald pony. He whispered constantly while he stroked the horse's rigid neck and head and she emulated his every technique to ensure the powerful bay gelding recognized her scent.

"Let this red devil become very comfortable with your touch so that he realizes he has nothing to fear from you. Touch him everywhere until he doesn't flinch."

Eva felt a wave of forbidden warmth flood over her as she watched Raven's hands stroke gently, continuously, over the pinto. She wondered how it would feel to have his fingertips gliding expertly over her body in a languid caress….

Guiltily, she glanced over to see Raven's gaze fixed on her. Embarrassment stained her cheeks. She swore the ornery rascal could read her mind because he smiled rakishly. Eva looked away quickly and continued to stroke her horse so he'd become unafraid of her.

"What was in that tea Hoodoo gave me last night?" she asked in a singsong voice—for her horse's benefit.

"Lots of Indian remedies, plus peyote," he murmured as he lay completely atop the paint pony.

"It worked so effectively that you had to carry me upstairs to your bed," she observed.

"That's an interesting way to phrase it…. Does it have anything to do with the way you were looking at me a moment ago?"

He was purposely trying to annoy her…and it was working. However, Eva refused to be baited this morning. Two could play his mischievous game, she decided.

"I was disappointed when I woke up alone in your bed," she said as she rubbed sensually against the big bay gelding. "I've been wondering what it would be like to be with you. It's obvious that you have a way with horses. How are you with women?"

She looked up then grinned when he choked on his breath. Never in her life had she felt so delighted about getting a man's goat. Catching J. D. Raven off guard and leaving him speechless was gratifying and empowering.

"I'll get the saddles," he croaked as he surged to his feet. "You can seduce both horses while you're at it. You're a natural siren."

Raven walked off, his body throbbing with every step. Damn it, he had teased Eva and the taunt had blown up in his face. Her comments left desire pulsating through him while the image of Eva—naked—gliding provocatively over him very nearly burned him into a pile of frustrated ashes.

"Are you all right, Raven?"

He flinched when he realized Hoodoo had walked up beside him while he was completely distracted. "No, that woman makes me loco."

"I'm impressed with her," Hoodoo commented. "Don't know many gals who are willing to get down and wallow with the horses like she's doing. She's as bold as she is beautiful." He stared up at Raven. "Thanks for bringing her here. After my fiancée betrayed me, I swore off all women everywhere for the rest of my life. But a man can't help but like a spirited woman like Eva."

Don't I know it, thought Raven.

"I got some stitching to do while you're training the horses. After lunch, you should show Eva Cheyenne Canyon and Phantom Springs. I suspect a free-spirited adventuress like Eva would enjoy both sites immensely."

After Hoodoo limped off, Raven grabbed two saddles from the shed. He wasn't sure he wanted Eva's memory attached to all the scenic locations near his cabin. Hell, he could easily visualize her in his bed, because he'd placed her there last night—and had to summon every ounce of willpower he possessed not to join her.

This mountain cabin was his haven from the harsh, demanding world where he worked. He lived near the sacred Cheyenne haunts but he didn't want the place disturbed by memories of a woman who wouldn't be a part of his life. He would still be tracking criminals—they were never in short supply. She would return to Denver after she discovered the whereabouts of Gordon Carter.

If the rigorous manhunt didn't get the better of her first— and there was a very real possibility that it would, he mused.

"Okay, Eva, let's move to phase two," Raven said in a hushed voice so he wouldn't alarm the horses. "Untie the red devil's hind legs first. Then the front ones. Your horse will have trouble gaining his balance since he's been down overnight. Back off so he doesn't stumble over you."

She did as instructed, speaking softly to the gelding all the while. Raven decided that if she used that husky whisper on him very often he would become her willing slave. Already, her voice was working its magic on his mind and body and he had to fight the erotic sensations spilling through him.

He cautioned himself against putting absolute faith and trust in her, tempting though it was. However, it was better than being disappointed if she betrayed him eventually, he reminded himself.

Forcing himself to concentrate on the upcoming task, Raven eased a saddle over the bay's back. The horse quivered momentarily, but didn't object. Couldn't. He was still trying to orient himself, which was difficult since Raven hadn't removed the blindfold.

"Now for the bridle," Raven murmured, handing it to her. "Lead your horse around, force him to depend on you for direction and keep talking to him to reassure him."

Eva slid the bridle in place and cooed at the horse continuously. "This is amazing," she said as she led the bay around the meadow. "I'm definitely using this training method on Lydia's new mount."

Raven kept a watchful eye on her while he practiced the same technique on the skewbald pony.

Thirty minutes later Raven boosted Eva atop the muscular bay gelding that remained blindfolded. Raven led him around while she stroked his black mane and praised him constantly.

"He hasn't bucked or reared up once," she murmured. "This gelding should be ready for a jaunt into the mountains by tomorrow."

"You're getting entirely too far ahead of yourself," Raven countered as he halted the horse. "Gunfire might send him into a headlong dash down the mountain. We don't know how easily he spooks because he hasn't been tested. That's critical information."

"How long will that take?" she asked impatiently.

"Depends on the temperament of the horse."

She frowned at his evasiveness. "Generally speaking."

He shrugged a broad shoulder. "At least two days of intense training. I'd prefer a week, but you're as impetuous as they come."

He handed her the reins then stepped back. "Now pay attention, Eva. I'm going to remove the blindfold. Either this red devil has accepted you and doesn't object to a rider or he'll try to unseat you. If you hit the ground, tuck and roll." He stared somberly at her. "I'd rather you hang on for dear life so he understands that you'll stick to him like glue, no matter what he does. This is one exceptionally spirited horse. I shouldn't have given into you when you singled him out, but I did. Now he needs to know you're his boss…. Ready?"

"As I'll ever be," she said determinedly.

Chapter Eight

Raven tensed, prepared to leap into action in case Eva's horse ducked his head and kicked his heels for all he was worth. But when Raven removed the blindfold, the blood-red bay snorted, stamped a hind hoof then turned his broad head to sniff Eva's leg. She curled over his back to brush her hand over his muzzle, whispering softly to him. He walked dutifully toward the cabin when Eva clucked her tongue at him.

"That ornery horse is a sucker for a female," Hoodoo called from the front porch. "I wouldn't have thought that big brute had a gentler side."

Raven mounted the paint pony. The horse stepped sideways when he removed the blindfold. At first, he walked tentatively with the extra weight on his back, but he didn't object to carrying a rider.

When Raven glanced over at Eva, watching her touch her knee to the bay's ribs to rein him to the right, he decided she possessed several equestrian skills. That was good. She'd need them where she was going.

Since she seemed to have control of the horse—for now,

at least—he motioned for her to join him. "Follow me. There's a place I want you to see."

Five minutes later, he drew the pinto to a halt on top of the hill. "Keep talking to the red devil while we negotiate this narrow path. If he bumps the rock wall beside him he might spook so be prepared."

Eva blinked in amazement when they descended to level ground and she noticed the bubbling spring. "This is another paradise," she breathed appreciatively.

"It was before the whites trespassed all over the place," he grumbled as he dismounted to tether the skewbald pony. "This is the place the Cheyenne call Phantom Springs."

"I never want to leave this place," she declared as she slid to the ground.

Eva led her horse to the inviting spring to survey the small waterfall that gurgled from the stone wall. Trees surrounded three sides of the spring and she swore the sketches she had seen of Greek and Roman bathhouses were less spectacular than the sunlight dancing on the rippling pool below the trickling falls.

When her horse dropped its head to drink, she went down on one knee beside him to sip the cool water. Raven and the pinto drank from the opposite side. She glanced up warily when she heard what sounded like a whispering voice echoing around the rock walls above her. No doubt, Phantom Springs was appropriately named. Either that or the pesky sniper was cursing them for still being alive.

"Another sacred site," she presumed.

"Bathhouse for the Cheyenne gods," Raven replied. "Drinking and bathing here is said to restore the body and spirit. Hoodoo swears by it. He couldn't walk at all until he soaked here daily for weeks on end. But then Hoodoo is superstitious by nature and by habit. Hence his voodoo doll and its curse."

Raven came to his feet. "I have one more place to show you before we *un*spook the horses."

He held the reins while Eva mounted the powerful bay. Then he swung into the saddle to lead the way across another panoramic mountain meadow. A quarter of an hour later, Eva heard the sound of rushing water. As they came around the bend of the trail, the hillside opened into a plunging, one-hundred-eighty-foot-deep canyon where seven distinct waterfalls tumbled from one outcropping of rock to another then splattered into the stone-rimmed pool below.

"Incredible," she murmured, awestruck. "You live in the most spectacular region this side of heaven."

"All of my people were free to roam our homeland in days gone by." Raven's solemn gaze swept over the scenic canyon and frothy falls. "Only a few of us can visit our ancestral haunts these days. The others are confined to reservations like criminals housed in penitentiaries."

Eva knew Raven's freedom had come at great expense and she predicted it must be bittersweet for him to visit the sites. He had become the guardian of these sacred haunts because his white heritage allowed him to purchase land. Ironically, his father's people had taken the land from his mother's tribe. The conflicting emotion left Raven caught in a vise because of the circumstances of his birth.

On the way down the steep trail, Eva savored the majestic beauty of the canyon and the magnificent falls. She would love to revisit this site in the future, to spend more time…

Her thoughts scattered when a rumbling sound overhead jerked her from her musings. The earth shook and pebbles pelted her head. Her horse pranced backward and flung its head nervously.

"Get off of him," Raven ordered. "Rockslide!"

Eva slid from her mount and plastered herself against the jagged rock wall. Her horse was wild-eyed and jittery, and he tried to bolt away. Despite the potential disaster, Eva whispered reassuringly to the horse, hoping he wouldn't stumble over the narrow ledge and end up like Lydia's horse.

She grabbed a quick breath and held it while dust and boulders tumbled downhill. She glanced anxiously at Raven, who was also plastered against the stone wall, a death grip on the pinto pony's reins.

A long moment later, the fog of dust drifted over the canyon. Eva coughed and blinked to clear her vision, then took a quick inspection to ensure she and Raven were still in one piece. A film of dirt covered his coal-black hair, beard and mustache. He was swearing colorfully, switching back and forth between English and Cheyenne, as he stared up at the stone wall.

The sound of a discharging rifle erupted in the silence that followed the earth-shaking rockslide. Then the call of an owl drifted across the canyon.

Raven scanned the area while Eva wiped her eyes and squinted into the sunlight to see a brawny man, dressed in buckskins and wearing a wide-brimmed sombrero, waving at them from the opposite side of the canyon.

"That was no accident," the man bellowed as he gestured to the hillside above them. "You must have a bitter enemy who strikes quickly then retreats like a shadow."

Raven craned his neck to look above him again. "Did you get a good look at the man who set off the landslide?"

"Not much of one," the new arrival called back.

"Who is that?" Eva asked as she dusted herself off.

"My cousin, Blackowl."

"The cousin who took refuge with you in the Ute camp after the massacre," she recalled. "I'm anxious to meet him."

"He's less fond of whites than I am." Raven gestured to the blood-red bay gelding whose shiny black mane and tail had taken on a dull brown hue. "Mount up before that devil horse decides to take off on his own."

"Apparently *my* would-be assassin is still alive and kicking," Eva remarked as she followed Raven uphill.

"I think *my* sniper disposed of yours," he speculated. "He isn't giving up, which suggests that he was paid a lot of money to dispose of me. Either that or he's nursing a vicious grudge of his own because of a past confrontation."

James Archer swore ripely as he rode away from the canyon. "Another near miss," he grumbled then glanced back at the unexpected arrival who had taken a shot at him.

Muttering at his rotten luck, James headed for the protection of the trees on the rugged mountain trail. When he spotted an unsuspecting rider ahead of him, he smiled fiendishly. His attempt to rid the world of that pesky half-breed gunslinger would have to wait until later. For now, he had encountered another pigeon ripe for plucking.

Raven drew the pinto to a halt when Blackowl appeared on the outcropping of rock. His cousin's thick brows flattened over his dark eyes as he critically appraised Eva.

"What is this, Raven?"

"It's a woman," he replied wryly. "Surely you've seen one before."

Blackowl looked Eva up and down. "Not in breeches, I haven't. Why is this paleface tagging along with you?"

"I'm pleased to meet you, Blackowl." Eva rode over to extend her hand cordially to the tall, powerfully built

Cheyenne warrior, who looked to be only an inch shorter, a few pounds lighter and a few years younger than Raven.

Blackowl stared at her hand as if her fingers dripped poison and he refused to touch them.

"I'm training for a trek into the nearby mining camps," she explained as she withdrew her hand.

Blackowl snorted in disapproval. "Even a woman in breeches will face danger if she goes into Devil's Triangle."

"That's what *I* said," Raven chimed in. "Head-Like-A-Rock refuses to heed my warnings."

"That's her name?" he asked, staring owlishly at Eva.

"No, but it could be," Raven insisted, grinning. "Maybe that will be my pet name for her."

"I'm his wife," she declared for shock value.

Blackowl's onyx eyes nearly popped out of his head. His mouth opened and closed like a fish but no words came out.

"She's kidding," Raven said quickly.

"I should hope so," Blackowl grumbled when he found his voice. "You must marry one of our kind. It is your destiny, Raven."

Raven didn't know what his destiny was. Didn't care at the moment. He simply wanted to hunt down the annoying assassin who kept trying to catch them off guard and finish them off.

"Can you describe the man who set off the rockslide?"

Blackowl nodded sharply. "Broad-brimmed hat like mine. Flannel shirt, suspenders and high boots. He wasn't too thin or too heavyset. Average height."

Raven rolled his eyes. "Hell, that describes ninety percent of the male population of prospectors in Colorado."

"If you wanted to kill someone, wouldn't you prefer to blend in?" Blackowl questioned reasonably. "Even the man's horse was nondescript brown with no identifying markings. I took a shot at him but he was already scampering away and he was beyond rifle range."

Raven blew out a frustrated breath. "This is the third attempt on my life."

"On *my* life," Eva corrected. "He's after me, not Raven."

Blackowl's gaze bounced back and forth between them then he said, "Why is she here?"

"Because I'm crazy about J.D. and I swore I'd follow him to the ends of the earth," she said smartly. "Are you always as blunt as J.D.?"

Raven watched Blackowl smile reluctantly. Her feisty temperament was getting to his cousin and it was beginning to show. Eva was simply irresistible.

"You have a sassy mouth, Paleface," Blackowl said to her then glanced at Raven. "Did you not know this when you let her tag along?"

"Yes, but I can't get rid of her."

Blackowl inclined his dark head toward the trail. "The sniper nearly got rid of both of you in one fell swoop."

Raven didn't need to be reminded of how close Eva had come to being struck by a falling boulder and knocked over the edge of the cliff. Remaining in his presence, when he was most likely the target of an assassin, was the equivalent of signing her own death certificate. He needed an extra pair of eyes until he overtook the assassin. Blackowl was his first choice.

"What are you doing for the next few days?" he asked.

"I was going to take the furs I hunted and trapped to the rendezvous site at Pine Crest to exchange for white men's money." He hitched his thumb toward the stack of hides tied behind his saddle. "Business has been brisk."

"Eva will pay you well to accompany her to the mining camps," Raven informed him.

"Travel with a paleface and then brush shoulders with the gold diggers?" Blackowl scoffed caustically. "I do not look that stupid, do I?"

"I'll buy your furs and save you the trouble of riding to the rendezvous site," she offered.

Blackowl glanced questioningly at Raven, who shrugged. It occurred to him that Eva seemed to have plenty of money. Perhaps she was relying on the funds Gordon had stolen in Denver. Hell, she might even be his partner. If Gordon had double-crossed her, it made sense that she wanted to recover her share of the loot—the whole kit and caboodle would be even better for her.

Stop it, Raven scolded himself. Eva deserved the benefit of the doubt. Just because he'd become cynical and mistrusting, didn't mean he had to pick apart every comment she made. Then again...

He sighed in annoyance. Unwanted feelings for Eva interfered with logical thought and made it difficult to remain objective.

"You have a deal, Paleface," Blackowl declared. He extended his hand, palm up. "Pay now."

"I don't have the money with me," she explained.

Raven felt the shadow of doubt creeping up again. Until Eva said, "It's in my satchel in the cabin."

Maybe she was telling him the truth after all.

"Maybe I will help my cousin instead," Blackowl remarked. "You should stay here while Raven and I search the mining camps to locate the fugitive."

Her chin came up. Her back went ramrod stiff as she squared her shoulders. "This is not negotiable, Blackowl. I'm going after Gordon Carter myself and that is that."

As Raven rode toward the cabin, he muttered under his breath. There was no talking Eva out of her one-

woman campaign to track down Gordon Carter. Her unfaltering determination kept her on course, no matter
who discouraged her.

Raven frowned, realizing the more adversity Eva faced
the more hell-bent she became. The obstacles she encountered during her mission challenged and motivated her. He
sat up a little straighter in the saddle and blinked when he
realized that he possessed the same exasperating trait that
refused to let him be bested by wily outlaws. Hell, he was
as headstrong and competitive as she was.

"Something wrong?" Eva asked, scrutinizing him carefully.

"Yes, but I'll deal with it." He urged the skewbald
gelding into a trot then into a swift gallop to see how well
he responded.

Eva decided Raven was right. He didn't need a wife. He
had Hoodoo Lemoyne, who cooked like a skilled chef,
trained horses, made clothing and provided all the conversation anyone could possibly hope to have. The food he
prepared was so scrumptious that Eva ate like a field hand,
while the three men chatted nonstop. It reminded her of her
close connection to her sister and the Philbert twins. But
here *she* was the outsider, the unwanted female the men
merely tolerated and sometimes overlooked.

It was a rude awakening for a woman who was a valued
guest at parties hosted by the socially elite in Denver. Now
that she was partially ignored, she gained insight into how
Hoodoo, Raven and Blackowl felt when they were
excluded and rejected by polite society.

"I'm going to see if I can pick up the sniper's trail,"
Raven announced as he carried his empty plate and tin cup
to the wooden counter.

"I'll go with you," Blackowl volunteered.

"No, I'd rather you stay here while I borrow your horse," Raven requested. "You and Eva can put the two new mounts through the next phase of training. Eva can learn a lot from you."

"Work with the paleface?" Blackowl smirked, disgruntled. "I'd rather track your assassin."

"It's my assassin so I'll track him," Raven insisted.

"It's *mine*," Eva spoke up. "I'm not convinced that Gordon is lying at the bottom of a ravine. It's more likely the sneaky scoundrel disposed of the prized horse to fake his own death or that he traded horses with someone else."

"Where's the money for my furs?" Blackowl questioned abruptly. "I'll teach you to take the spook out of that red devil but you have to pay me first. I don't work for palefaces for nothing, you know."

Eva rose from the planked table then carried her dishes to the pan of water. She smiled at Hoodoo on her way past. "The meal was wonderful. I can name several restaurant owners in Denver who would stampede over each other to hire you."

"There, ya see? Somebody appreciates me," said Hoodoo, grinning smugly.

"We do appreciate you, but if we start dishing out praise all the time there'd be no living with you," Raven teased as he loaded his six-shooters then grabbed his rifle. He turned back to Blackowl. "Don't leave yourself or Eva vulnerable to become an open target."

Blackowl bobbed his coal-black head. "Don't fall into a trap, cousin. We are the last of the Bird Clan. Besides, that would leave me to take Paleface on her mission alone."

Eva glanced into Blackowl's ebony eyes. She didn't know him well enough to know if he was teasing or dead serious. Then she noticed the hint of a smile on his clean-shaven face. She was relieved that he didn't dislike her completely.

"Behave or I won't pay you for the furs," she threatened.

"No one expects Indians to behave," Blackowl countered, unabashed. "Ask Raven."

"So that's the standard excuse, is it?" she replied. "Raven insists that I don't behave, either. He says I'm a pain in the posterior."

"She's a bona fide lady and you should both be nice to her," Hoodoo lectured as he hobbled over to scrape the plates. "Now go on about your business, all of you. I'll clean up the dishes then start my stitching."

Eva was sorry to say she was disappointed when Raven walked away without a backward glance. His cousin and friend were taking her off his hands for a few hours and he was glad to be rid of her. That stung her pride... because she seemed more attracted and aware of him than he was of her.

Men! Here was another shining example of why she should avoid them all. The ones who catered and fawned over her made her suspicious and didn't interest her in the least. The one who cautiously kept his distance intrigued her. It was enough to drive a sane woman crazy.

Lost in thought, Eva rummaged through her satchel to retrieve the roll of banknotes. "How much are your furs worth?" she called down to Blackowl.

"One thousand," he called back.

"No, they aren't," she contradicted. "I'm not completely ignorant of the market value so don't try to swindle me. I'd say more like five hundred dollars."

"The other five hundred is for teaching you to be Cheyenne and for guiding you through the mountains. I told you, I don't work cheap, Paleface."

Eva smiled in amusement. In some ways, Blackowl reminded her of Raven. The Bird Clan of the Cheyenne tribe was obviously a straightforward, plainspoken, dry-humored bunch.

Tucking the remainder of her money in a new place, she descended the steps to see Blackowl staring attentively at her. She arched a curious brow but he didn't say a word, just extended his arm.

She slapped the money into his hand then said, "I'm paying you a premium to teach me to be a survivalist and a horse trainer so let's get at it."

With a wave to Hoodoo, Eva followed Blackowl outside.

"First things first," he declared as he rounded on her. "Do not hurt my cousin. He's all the family I have."

"Hurt him?" she echoed incredulously. "Impossible."

"Not as impossible as you seem to think, Paleface," he said somberly. "He let you come here, didn't he?"

"He only feels sorry for me because I narrowly escaped being shot twice with bullets he's convinced were meant for him, not me," she explained. "Besides, I nagged him incessantly to help me and he finally threw up his hands and gave in."

Blackowl frowned pensively as he hiked off to select a protected location to work with the two horses. Eva followed him, feeling more than a little guilty about with-holding information about herself from Raven, Hoodoo and Blackowl. And yet, she didn't want any of the three to change their attitude toward her because of who she was. She enjoyed her association with them and she wanted to keep things the way they were.

She knew it wasn't fair to attach herself to Raven the way she had. She had needed expert assistance, but that was no excuse for practically forcing her presence on

Raven and putting his life in danger. Now she had involved his cousin and his friend in her crusade.

Curse it, her conflicting feelings of revenge and guilt were tormenting her to the extreme. Maybe she should strike out on her own after her horse was adequately trained. Then she wouldn't have to worry about the men being injured because of her.

"Pay attention, Paleface," Blackowl said sharply. "Slap this gunnysack all over the red devil until he no longer shies away or tries to bolt and run."

Eva did as instructed but the blood-red bay strained against the lead rope she'd secured to a tree for five consecutive minutes while she flung the gunnysack at him. "How long—?"

"As long as it takes and a moment longer," he interrupted.

Eva noted the brown-and-white pinto stood still while Blackowl swatted him from head to rump. She reached out to reassure her horse and he quieted instantly.

"I'll be damned," Blackowl mumbled while she kept her hand on the horse's black mane and flung the gunnysack over his withers and back.

"Now shake this tree branch with its rattling leaves over him," Blackowl directed, handing the limb to her.

Again, the blood-red bay tolerated being whacked lightly with the branch as long as Eva's hand remained on his neck.

"That explains it," Blackowl said insightfully.

"That explains what?"

Blackowl grinned and gave an evasive shrug. "Keep working with the horse by walking all the way around him. Remain as close to him as you can get. He can't kick if you're practically sharing the same skin."

"Where did you learn such perfect English?" she asked as she did precisely as he instructed.

"From Raven. His father taught him as a child and he taught me. It has helped me to communicate with the whites at the trading posts and at rendezvous."

"How long did you remain with the Ute tribe after the massacre?" she questioned interestedly.

Blackowl's thick brows shot up his forehead. "He told you about that?"

"I tortured it out of him," she teased.

"I'm beginning to believe it." He walked the skewbald in ever-widening circles while slapping its shoulder with the branch. "We spent about two years with them, biding our time, before Raven went looking for his father. Jordan thought we were dead and he settled in white society to remarry. I hunted and trapped with the Utes while Raven was indoctrinated into his father's world."

"Raven mentioned a stepbrother," Eva prompted while she leaned against the bay's ribs and draped her hand over his back. "Where is he now?"

"I don't know and I don't care," he said flatly. "Neither does Raven. The brat was rude, disrespectful to Jordan, insulting and belittling to Raven. After Jordan died, all Raven's belongings disappeared from the house and his stepmother told him he was never welcome there again."

"And what about you, Blackowl? What have you been doing for the past dozen years? Dodging white society every chance you get to avoid being labeled a renegade and marched to the reservation in Indian Territory?"

He shot her a narrowed glance. "You are too smart for your breeches, Paleface. But yes, I skirt the towns heavily populated with whites. The Mexican settlements are more tolerant of an Indian who partially dresses like a white, a Mexican and a Cheyenne, all rolled into one."

Suddenly Blackowl drew his pistol and fired off two

shots, causing the horses to bolt sideways. Eva latched onto her mount, whispering reassuringly until he calmed down.

Then out of the blue Blackowl pounced on her. He shoved her roughly to the ground and plunked down on her belly, forcing the breath from her lungs in a whoosh. She stared up at him, realizing there were two different person-alities housed inside those doeskin clothes. The man sneering at her now was definitely a threat.

Eva tried to knock him backward but he grabbed her hands and held them beside her shoulders. She yelped in outrage and writhed wildly beneath him, but the muscular Cheyenne warrior snarled viciously and refused to release her. The biting pressure on her manacled wrists prompted her to yelp in pain and struggle for all she was worth to escape this surprise assault.

Chapter Nine

"What the blazes are you doing?" Eva demanded angrily as Blackowl bore down on her.

"Attacking you. What are you going to do about it?"

"Curse you, for starters," she muttered.

"That won't keep you alive," he said gruffly. "Throw an elbow and kick at me. You fight or you die, Paleface. It is the code of the wilderness. No one is going to go easy on you because you're a woman."

Eva tried to jab him in the chest and lash out with her boot heel but he was too shifty and agile. Then he jerked her hands over her head and held them there as he settled exactly upon her. She upraised her knee, but it didn't deter him.

"What the hell is going on here?" Raven's voice boomed from the underbrush like a discharging cannon.

His ominous tone didn't faze Blackowl, who grinned wickedly at her. "Survival training."

Eva arched her neck to look behind her. She saw Raven striding toward her, rifle in hand. The look on his face would have been frightening if she didn't know he wouldn't lay a hurtful hand on her. But he directed his icy glare on his cousin, who hadn't moved and was still smiling in scampish glee.

"Get off of her," Raven snapped brusquely.

"She hasn't learned to unseat me yet," Blackowl replied. "She's untrained and helpless. Is that what you want?"

"What I want is for you to back off, damn it!" he exclaimed, voice rising to a roar.

Blackowl pushed onto his knees then climbed to his feet. His shoulder brushed Raven's as he walked past and said, "Just as I thought."

"What did you think?" Eva questioned irritably, rubbing her wrists as she sat up. "That I can't take care of myself and you wanted to make that point *in spades?*"

"That, too," Blackowl said enigmatically as he grabbed the reins to his own horse—the one Raven left nearby— then ambled away.

Eva frowned, bemused. She was still staring after Blackowl when Raven reached down to draw her to her feet.

"Did he hurt you?" Raven asked in concern.

"Only my pride. I thought I could protect myself better than that."

"Obviously you can't, which is why Blackowl and I need to track Carter while you keep Hoodoo company at the cabin."

Eva glared at him then at Blackowl's departing back. Then it dawned on her that she had been set up. "So that's what that little demonstration was all about."

He frowned. "What are you talking about?"

"You told Blackowl to make me look foolish and ill-prepared then you *conveniently* showed up, seemingly offended by his harsh methods so I wouldn't blame you. But you put him up to roughhousing, didn't you?"

"Of course not," he said, and snorted.

"Couldn't prove it by me," she muttered as she brushed the grass and leaves from her clothing. "You want to get rid of me and you've made it plain as day to me and your friends."

"And you've been leading me along with claims of theft against your sister, but how do I know you and Carter aren't in cahoots?" He stared pointedly at her wedding band. "Are you married to him? Is that why you refuse to tell me your last name? Are you after him because he didn't give you a cut of the loot? Don't lie to me this time, damn it."

Eva staggered back as if he'd slapped her. The harsh questions cut to the quick—and even deeper. In most circles, her word was honored and respected, but she was beyond upset that Raven didn't trust her, even after he'd gotten to know her. Yet, fool that she was, she was hopelessly attracted to the big cynical brute.

Honestly, she didn't know if she was angrier with him for distrusting her so completely or at herself for allowing him and his opinions to matter so much to her.

She hated getting emotional, especially in front of other people. And most especially in front of someone as invincible as Raven. Refusing to cry in front of him, Eva lurched around and dashed off before she decomposed. "I'm going to the springs and don't try to talk me out of it."

"Not without a chaperone," he called after her.

"Go to hell!" she shouted as she broke into a run.

"Damn it, Eva, I lost the sniper's tracks on the rocky hillside. He could be anywhere."

"I'll deal with him myself if he shows up."

And off she went, without looking back.

Raven blew out his breath, slapped his hat against his thigh and cursed his runaway tongue.

"You do have a way with women," Blackowl taunted as he circled back to where Raven stood.

Raven rounded on his cousin. "You caused that."

"I was testing you. And her. You both failed."

"How did you know I was nearby?"

Blackowl scoffed sarcastically. "I'm Cheyenne. I know these things. I also know you have feelings for the woman."

"You're right. I do. She drives me crazy and I'd like to strangle her," Raven grumbled resentfully.

Blackowl shook his dark head. "No, cousin, she is taking the mean off your rough edges. Her magic is powerful and you should be wary. She is not right for you."

"Tell me something I don't know," he said dryly.

"Very well then, I will. You became possessive and jealous when you thought I was a threat to her. You disapproved of my methods of assuring Eva that she is not prepared for unexpected attacks. I had to make it *feel* real if she was to take me seriously and fight back. She needs to learn skills to protect herself. Will you teach her or shall I? If I do it then do not criticize my techniques."

"I'll do it," Raven insisted.

"But don't enjoy it too much, cousin." Blackowl smiled wryly. "It's hard not to, I can tell you from experience."

Raven scowled as his cousin took the reins to lead all three horses away so he could continue the training. Eva's blood-red bay gelding pranced away from him, drawing his annoyed snort.

"You have several strong, sturdy horses in your herd," Blackowl pointed out. "Why did you pick this contrary beast for Eva?"

"She picked out the red devil herself."

"That explains it," Blackowl said as he watched the horse sidestep then lay back his ears. "If he bites me I'm going to bite him back."

As Blackowl walked off, Raven glanced toward the

copse of trees where Eva had disappeared, then he sighed in frustration. Hell! He should have kept his trap shut about his ongoing suspicions of her ulterior motive. But he'd been insulted when she accused him of siccing Blackowl on her to make a point.

In addition, the woman was complicating his life until hell wouldn't have it. Now his cousin was rubbing his conflicting feelings for Eva in his face.

With one last glance toward the springs, Raven strode back to the cabin. He decided to give Eva—and himself—a few minutes to cool off before he stood guard over her. Otherwise, it might become a contest over who killed whom first.

Gordon Carter smiled devilishly as he stared through the spyglass, watching Eva storm off alone. "Perfect timing," he snickered. He'd like nothing better than to take Eva hostage to lure in her protectors and dispose of them one by one.

He changed his clothes hastily then grabbed another hat. Leaving his horse tethered in the rocky hills, so that pesky half-breed couldn't find it, he transferred his gear to the sturdy mule he'd acquired from its recently deceased owner.

Like a mountain lion on the prowl, he went in search of the woman who had made the crucial mistake of venturing off alone. He grinned, calculating how much money he could make when he ransomed Eva to her naive little sister, who had played right into his hands and provided him with plenty of money already. Gordon never bypassed golden opportunity.

And there was a lot more money where that came from, Gordon reminded himself. It was his for the taking.

* * *

Roger Philbert trotted his horse toward the stage station that Evangeline Hallowell had specified in her note. He still had no idea why his longtime friend and neighbor had left the carriage there and why she wanted him to fetch it. This entire affair was puzzling to him, but he did as she asked of him.

Dismounting, Roger dusted off his stylish jacket and breeches then entered the crude building to locate the off-duty agent. The barrel-shaped proprietor was sweeping crumbs from the floor and tossing them to the furry dog waiting outside the window.

"I've come to retrieve the buggy for my friend," Roger announced.

"Who might you be?" The owner leaned heavily on his broom handle then huffed and puffed for breath.

"Roger Philbert. Did Eva tell you to expect me?"

The man nodded then wiped the sweat from his brow. "She also said you'd pay me for keeping a close eye on the carriage until you showed up."

Roger snorted caustically. "I know Eva exceptionally well and I'm absolutely certain she paid you generously for your services. Now, where is the horse?"

"Didn't have the chance to buy that magnificent animal," the stationmaster replied. "The gent who sold the carriage to me rode off on the horse."

Roger blinked in surprise. "What man?"

"Gordon something-or-other."

Roger was stunned. "You *bought* it from him?"

"Didn't I just say so?"

Apparently, Roger was lacking several details that Eva had purposely omitted from her brief note. "Then how did Eva get here?"

The owner stared at Roger as if he were dense. "On the

stagecoach with her husband, of course. She bought the buggy and got shot at. Then they piled into the stagecoach with the other four passengers and sped off."

"Shot at?" Roger crowed in disbelief. He braced his arm against the rough-hewn wall for support. *"Husband?"* His head spun like a windmill while he tried to grasp the startling information.

"Yep, surprised the hell out of me, too," the owner confided. "A woman like her married to a half-breed bounty hunter? Ask me, that's a big mistake. Someone came gunning for him already and she got caught in the line of fire."

"Good God!" Roger howled.

Roger couldn't believe what he was hearing. Eva was the most independent-minded and spirited woman he knew. And he knew very well who her new husband was. He couldn't imagine why she would marry Raven. She had sworn off men and then poof! Had she lost her mind?

A wary thought occurred to Roger and he frowned in concern. Had that brutish scoundrel coerced her, in exchange for agreeing to take her mysterious assignment?

Obviously, the case had something to do with Gordon Carter…which must be why Eva asked him and Sadie to check in on Lydia. Just what had happened between Lydia and Gordon that put Eva on the warpath? He didn't like the speculations swirling around in his head.

Maybe he should contact the Rocky Mountain Detective Agency to check in to this situation, Roger mused. Considering Eva's great wealth, she might become a hostage held for ransom by her mismatched husband.

Roger tried to make sense of the puzzling events. If Eva had been allowed to send a note to retrieve the buggy, and she had been in plain sight of other passengers and the stationmaster, she could have called out for help. Then again, who would dare to clash with the legendary bounty hunter, even to rescue a hostage? Had Raven threatened to kill the other passengers if Eva didn't pretend to be his willing bride?

His head spun with several more scenarios, none of which seemed to fit. Roger hurried off to hitch his horse to the carriage. He recalled what an angry, determined state Eva had been in the last time he'd seen her. She was not one to wait for someone else to resolve her problems. She always took the initiative. So why marry Raven? What purpose did it serve?

Eva and that gunslinger? Together? The very idea was beyond preposterous, Roger thought as he reined the abandoned buggy toward Denver and raced home lickety-split.

Eva plopped down on a boulder beside the springs then cursed Raven up one side and down the other. When she exhausted her repertoire of epithets, she huffed out her breath. She told herself that she should focus on Blackowl's eye-opening lesson and learn to defend herself and remain on constant alert, *not* dwell on her riptide feelings for Raven.

She vowed she'd learn to handle a pistol and knife expertly like Raven and his cousin. By damn, she would *not* be ill-prepared again—ever.

The sound of crackling twigs put her senses on alert—that in itself was the first line of defense, she realized. She bounded to her feet but kept her head down as she zigzagged in and out of the trees and underbrush. From the corner of her eye, she caught sight of a mule. She began screaming her head off, hoping that whoever was stalking her would think twice about attacking while she was running straight toward the cabin.

Behind her, she heard the swish of bushes disturbed by

sudden movement and a human snarl that indicated she had indeed foiled her assassin's plans. But when she spared a glance over her shoulder, still yelling at the top of her lungs, all she saw was a flash of dark clothing and hat as a man dived headlong into the underbrush.

As she raced across the open meadow, Raven and Blackowl appeared in front of her. They provided cover while she dashed between them. She didn't stop running until she burst through the cabin door and clamped hold of Hoodoo as if he were her salvation.

"Easy, little gal," he cooed as he patted her quaking shoulders consolingly. "You're fine. I gotcha. Nobody will get past those two skilled gunfighters. Best two shootists in the state. Bar none. Now sit down and I'll fix you some of that elixir tea."

Eva nodded and panted for breath after her mad dash. "Oblivion sounds appealing right now."

"Good, then trot upstairs and lie down," Hoodoo insisted. "I'll bring the brew to you when it's heated."

In the distance, she heard gunshots and hoped that Raven and Blackowl had found whoever was stalking her and had brought him down so he couldn't strike again.

"Here, little gal, drink this," Hoodoo said a few minutes later. "I doubled the strength so you can sleep. It's just what you need to calm down."

Eva gulped the lukewarm brew eagerly. She vowed that when she awakened she was going to pester Blackowl until he agreed to teach her to handle a pistol and knife proficiently.

As for Raven, he could still go to hell for thinking the absolute worst about her.

Raven swore a blue streak as he watched the burro and its elusive rider dart in and out of the trees then move swiftly up the rocky trail. Since Raven and Blackowl were on foot, they couldn't overtake the wily bastard. And sure enough, the sniper was difficult to describe because he was wearing a wide-brimmed hat that shaded his face, an oversize jacket and trousers that concealed his size and stature. Plus, the garments were the common style worn by hundreds of miners in the area.

"I'm not positively certain that was the same man I saw before," Blackowl murmured as he watched the unidentified rider disappear into another clump of trees. "I definitely didn't see the mule."

Raven reloaded his rifle. "Maybe Eva is right. Maybe there are two men out there."

"You're too modest. More than two men want you dead for killing their outlaw family members," Blackowl said. "Face it, you are no more popular in what was once Cheyenne hunting ground than I am."

"At least Eva doesn't hate you," Raven grumbled as he glanced toward the cabin.

Blackowl stared intently at him. "Do you care?"

Yes, damn it, he did. But he refused to admit it. Blackowl would commence harping at him about his destiny with a Cheyenne maiden again.

Never mind that there wasn't one within seven hundred miles. There was only that dark-eyed firebrand who'd had the wits scared out of her while she was still fuming over his careless remarks.

Yet, the fact remained that Eva had no concrete evidence to convince him thoroughly that she was the sister of the wronged female whom Gordon Carter had betrayed. She *could be* the wife or partner Gordon double-crossed. It wouldn't be the first time something like this happened, Raven reminded himself. He'd dealt with all sorts of entangled circumstances in his line of work. Plus, outlaws lied to him constantly.

"Go check on Eva, will you?" Raven requested as he headed to the springs. "I doubt she plans to speak to me so soon after I offended her." Whether she had a right to be offended or not, he couldn't say for sure. "I'll bathe and shave after I check the area for the bushwhacker's tracks."

"These snipers are good," Blackowl said grudgingly.

Raven nodded. "Half the time I'm not sure which one is after whom. Maybe they are working in tandem to confuse us."

Blackowl stared into the distance. "One or the other of them will make a careless mistake eventually."

"Not unless Eva makes one first. Like she just did." Raven scowled as he strode off.

Eva awakened the next day and lay in bed for several minutes, rehashing her argument with Raven and then mulling over the incident at the springs that nearly resulted in her death or capture. She had been overly sensitive and angry that Raven didn't believe her story, but after giving the matter further consideration, she understood why he was reluctant to trust her.

All he had was her word for it. He'd likely heard dozens of claims of innocence from outlaws looking to save their necks. Plus, not every woman would take off cross-country to track down a man she claimed had stolen money from the family coffers. By being the exception to the rule, she inadvertently provoked skepticism from the jaded bounty hunter.

Sighing heavily, Eva propped herself up on her elbows. She should apologize to Raven, she supposed. She was as mistrusting of men as he was of her. Plus, she had stormed off in anger and she could have placed him and Blackowl in danger because of her recklessness.

When she descended the steps, she saw Hoodoo ensconced in his chair, stitching together a leather garment.

"Feeling better?" he asked, glancing up momentarily.

"Much better, thank you. The past few days have been unusual and difficult."

"I would imagine so. You're out of your element. Took me a while to adjust when I first arrived, too. Not the same as New Orleans, believe me."

"Where's Raven? I need to apologize to him for overreacting to his accusation that I'm after Gordon Carter because he took my share of the stolen money."

Hoodoo's gaze remained fixed on his stitching. "Are you?"

"No, but I suppose Raven hears more lies than truth in his line of work."

"Reckon he does. Can't always tell a skunk by the stripe on its back, I always say. The two-legged variety doesn't have stripes. And not that Raven is perfect, don'tcha know. He's cautious and mistrusting by habit and by nature. Hard-scrabble living makes a man that way. You don't get to make too many reckless mistakes in this wild country and live to tell about it. I got the scars to prove I barely escaped what would have been a fatal disaster, if not for Raven."

"I'd like to talk to him if he'll listen."

"He's putting the horses through rigorous training and Blackowl is helping him. I don't expect them back until supper."

"Then I'm going back to the springs to bathe first." When Hoodoo shook his frizzy head, she flung up her hand to forestall his objection. "I'll be more attentive this time. It will be good practice and training." She pointed to his double-barrel shotgun, which was propped by the door. "May I?"

He nodded reluctantly. "All right, go ahead. But have a care or Raven will skin me alive for letting you out of my sight."

She scoffed in contradiction as she picked up the weapon. "More than likely he'll thank you for getting me out of his hair. He says I'm a nuisance of the worst sort."

"Whatever the case, remain alert." A wry smile quirked his lips. "I started liking you when we met and I don't want to have to get over you too quickly, little gal."

The teasing comment touched her and she pivoted to walk back to Hoodoo. She doubled at the waist to get right in his face and look straight into those incredible blue eyes. "I like you, too," she said before she kissed him soundly on the cheek.

"Marry me. I think I just got over the hurt and betrayal caused by my two-timing fiancée."

"Name the time and place," she replied saucily as she rose to full stature. "I'll be there with bells on."

As she walked away, she heard Hoodoo snickering in amusement. She knew it wasn't a sincere proposal. He was using their newfound friendship to build his confidence. Still, it was the best proposal she'd had since her proper introduction into high society five years earlier. At least Hoodoo liked her for the woman he was getting to know, not the heiress whose father had accidentally stumbled onto a bonanza and became rich beyond his wildest imagination.

Too bad that hard-nosed, infuriating, bullheaded man who went by the name of J. D. Raven—bounty hunter and gunfighter extraordinaire—didn't see any redeeming qualities in her. If he never saw her again, she predicted he'd be ecstatic.

"You let her do what?" Raven roared at Hoodoo. "Damn it to hell, someone tried to overtake her yesterday at the very spot where you let her go again."

"You were both in the vicinity," Hoodoo said reasonably. He glanced back and forth between Raven and Blackowl. "This is the perfect chance for her to establish her self-reliance and test her alertness to her surroundings while she's still within shouting distance. Besides, she has my never-fail shotgun."

"Your never-fail shotgun jammed once when it mattered, as I recall," Raven said meaningfully. "And we both know what I'm talking about. Your scars are a daily reminder."

Hoodoo flapped his arms dismissively. "Yes, but the scars from that ordeal don't matter anymore. I'm cured. Eva said she'd marry me anytime and anyplace when I asked her today. As for the shotgun I just cleaned it so it's in good working order."

Raven and Blackowl gaped at each other then refocused on Hoodoo's grinning face. "She got to you, too," Raven snorted. "That little snake charmer turns up the intensity of her smile and men cave in like an unstable mine shaft."

Hoodoo met Raven's stony stare and smirked. "*You* brought her here, even when you've never brought another woman to this place." He switched his attention to Blackowl. "And you took her under your wing to show her that she needed self-defense skills. Seems to me that one of you oughta be working on her shooting skills instead of raking me over live coals for giving her some space to test her self-reliance."

Raven muttered as he wheeled around to stamp off. "I'll go fetch Eva for lunch…*if* she's still there. *If* someone didn't sneak up and slit her throat while she was without a bodyguard. *If* some creature didn't pounce and drag her off for its midday meal."

He mounted the blood-red bay that didn't respond to him as easily as he did to Eva. That still amazed him. Was it her scent, her touch or the sound of her voice that made this spirited red devil at ease with her and no one else?

The horse threw its head and sidestepped at irregular intervals, despite Raven's best effort to break him of his bad habits. Dismounting, Raven tied the horse in the trees then crept toward Phantom Springs.

He stopped dead in his tracks when he saw Eva rise like a mystical siren from the pool to squeeze water from her long mane of auburn hair. She was gloriously naked. Water droplets sparkled over her shapely body like chips of diamonds dancing in the bright sunlight. Desire hit him like a physical blow and he staggered back a pace. He braced an arm against a nearby tree when his knees wobbled.

Raven wanted to look away and he scolded himself harshly for not doing it. But, in the end, he stood admiring the incredible sight of her full breasts and her trim waist above the water's surface.

Lust clobbered him again—repeatedly—and he had one hell of a time breathing normally. This was the very last thing he needed. The woman occupied too damn much of his thoughts already. This unexpected display of feminine perfection was guaranteed to torment his dreams. It was bad enough that he'd seen her naked briefly two days earlier. But this was worse. He was so mesmerized he couldn't look away.

Why did this female have to barge into his life? He wasn't prepared for this spirited, beguiling and maddening woman who wouldn't reveal her last name.

He wondered if any man could deal effectively with Eva. Not Hoodoo. He wanted to marry her, even if he was old enough to be her father. Raven knew that, despite Blackowl's derisive remarks, he was attracted to her, paleface or not.

Raven's thoughts drifted away as he stared unblinkingly at Eva. He was sorry to say that he didn't announce his presence when she came ashore, unknowingly exposing every bare inch of her shapely body to his fascinated gaze.

Hell! He hadn't even had the presence of mind to secure the perimeters, in case the mysterious assassin—or assassins—lurked about.

Scowling, he shook his head in dismay. One unhindered look at Eva obliterated his thoughts and impaired the good judgment he'd spent thirty-three years cultivating. Seeing Eva naked had suddenly become his favorite pastime.

"Eva? Are you there?" he yoo-hooed—finally.

As if he didn't know, as if he hadn't seen her in all her splendor and glory—and he would continue to see her because her alluring image was forever seared like a brand on his brain.

Chapter Ten

Startled by Raven's voice, Eva reached for the shotgun. Good girl, he praised silently. Even if she couldn't aim and fire accurately, the shotgun was extremely forgiving and would serve her well.

"Give me a moment," she called back.

Too late for that, he thought. He'd seen all there was to see. "Hoodoo is preparing lunch," he said as he panned the trees to check for intruders.

She dressed quickly. "I want to apologize to you."

When Raven stepped into view, she blinked in stunned amazement. "Good gracious, you look different."

Raven brushed his hand self-consciously over his clean-shaven face. "More like my Cheyenne cousin, I'm told. Is it better or worse?"

"Different," she murmured, pensively studying his facial features. "If you're fishing for a compliment you need to cast your line in another pond. I'm not taking the bait."

He chuckled. "So you're saying that even now I don't measure up to the men in your social circle of white society."

"Don't put words in my mouth, Raven. I can speak for

myself. The fact is that I prefer you to those pretentious dandies. But don't let that go to your head, either." She flicked her wrist dismissively to change the subject. "I can understand that my actions might seem suspicious because I'm so determined to find Gordon. Despite what you think, I don't believe he's dead, just because we found Lydia's horse and no sign of the rider. Then there is the matter of the money I want to recover."

She walked right up to him, demanding his undivided attention. "I am not in cahoots with that scheming scoundrel," she said earnestly.

"But saying you aren't, doesn't necessarily make it so," he countered.

"I didn't like or approve of Gordon the first time Lydia introduced us. I disliked him more when he began flirting with me when she was out of earshot," she confided. "To retaliate, he told Lydia that I was jealous of her and that I was interested in him. Which could not be further from the truth. I despise him for trying to turn my sister against me when we are as close as you and Blackowl."

"Whose wedding band are you wearing?" he demanded abruptly.

"It's the gold ring my father gave to my mother. *I haven't deceived you,*" she repeated emphatically. "This is who I am—the determined, protective sister who wants Gordon punished and who wants Lydia's money returned."

Raven stared at her, trying his damnedest to pay attention to what she was saying instead of looking through her clothes to visualize this voluptuous woman naked.

"I know I'm an inconvenience and nuisance to you, but I'm not giving up the search until I've traveled to those obscure mining camps to root out Gordon."

"Fine, we'll leave bright and early day after tomorrow,"

he heard himself say—and silently cursed the way he'd caved in to her wishes as if he had no backbone whatsoever.

"We will?" Her face lit with excitement. "Oh, thank you, Raven, I will pay you generously and in advance, if that's what you prefer."

She flung her arms around his neck and pulled his head down to kiss him. Visions of the naked siren in the bubbling spring leaped instantly to mind. Raven groaned in defeat as his arms contracted around her. Mercy, it felt as if he'd been waiting the whole livelong day for another taste of her. Not to mention that inhaling her tantalizing scent and rubbing his body sensuously against hers was a dream come true. He savored every arousing sensation she instilled inside him.

Like a witless fool, he closed his eyes and blocked out everything except the intense pleasure sizzling through him. It didn't help matters when Eva moaned softly then arched into him as if she were enjoying the forbidden moment as much as he was.

He felt his hands move on their own accord, learning her delicious body by touch. Hungry need gnawed at him and he tried to recall if he'd ever wanted a woman quite this much. It only took a moment to realize he hadn't. This was undoubtedly the most attractive and unique female he'd held in his arms.

When he cupped his hand around her breast, he heard her breath catch. She looked up at him as he brushed her taut nipple with his thumb and forefinger. Desire flared in her dark eyes and her lips parted on a sigh. When she didn't pull away, he lowered his head to suckle her through the fabric of her shirt. But that wasn't enough to satisfy him, not after he'd seen her silky flesh. He wanted to taste her, caress her until he'd had his fill of her.

"Raven?" she gasped as he tugged at her gently then pressed her hips against his hard arousal. "If I say I want you, promise you won't accuse me of seducing you to get my way."

"You want your way with me?" He unbuttoned her shirt to expose her full, creamy breasts to his appreciative gaze. "You can have it, Eva. I'm through fighting this maddening attraction. It takes too damn much effort."

"I know you're only interested because I'm female and I'm available out here in the middle of nowhere," she murmured as she worked the buttons on his shirt.

"Yeah, that's it." It was safer to let her believe it was nothing more than convenient lust. Hell, he preferred to believe that himself.

"Same for me." She slid her hands across his chest and kissed him until his head spun in dizzying circles.

Raven's willpower drifted across the pool and trickled downstream. He was a hopeless cause, too wrapped up in this woman to think past the luscious sight and feel of her supple body beneath his hands and lips. Too much a prisoner of his selfish desires to consider consequences. He was engulfed in the here and now and need had a fierce and mighty grip on him.

When her adventurous hand glided over the bulge in his breeches, he forgot to drag air into his deprived lungs. When she dipped her hand beneath the waistband, his knees folded up, dumping them in a reckless sprawl in the grass. He removed her shirt hastily then tossed it beside his shirt to form a makeshift pallet. Then he helped her from her breeches to feast his hungry eyes on every exquisite inch of her body.

At close range, she was even more mesmerizing than at a distance. Raven marveled at her silky perfection as he bent his head to kiss her as gently as he knew how and touch her as tenderly as he could—despite the ravenous need pounding through him.

No matter what he'd told Eva to the contrary, she *had* gotten to him—to the extreme. She was far more than an impulsive tumble in the grass. She mattered to him, much as he hated that. Because her opinions and feelings were important to him, he couldn't take from her without giving of himself, without offering her the same exotic pleasures he ached to discover with her.

To that dedicated end, Raven reined in the impatient desire pounding through him and focused his attention on caressing her until her breath sighed out in ragged spurts. He smiled in satisfaction when she whispered his name and arched eagerly toward him again. He stroked her long legs and trailed his hand over her inner thighs repeatedly. When he touched her intimately, she moved toward his hand and he angled his head to flick at her moist flesh with his tongue.

"Oh…my…" she rasped shakily.

Raven had never devoted so much time to pleasuring a woman, had never wanted to. But anything less with Eva was unacceptable to him. He wanted her warm, willing and eager for him when he came to her. Already he could feel her body quivering in response to his intimate caresses. She was hot and tight and he delighted in seducing her one kiss and caress at a time.

She clutched desperately at his shoulders and gasped for air. When she dug her nails into his skin, he didn't mind.

He reached down with his free hand to unfasten his breeches then shifted sideways to remove them. Her gaze fixated on him and her eyes widened at the sight of him. When she touched his throbbing flesh, while he held her essence in his hand, the world spun furiously around him.

"My name is Evangeline Hallowell," she murmured as she wrapped her hand around him and drew him ever closer.

"Nice to meet you, Evangeline." He bent his head to kiss her at the same moment that he settled between her legs and pressed familiarly against her.

"Mmm…" She moaned at the sheer intimacy of the moment and the unexpected pressure of his hard length gliding inside her.

When he braced his hands on either side of her shoulders and surged forward, she stared up at him, watching surprise register in those mystifying, catlike eyes. She knew the instant he realized that he was her first experiment with passion. His facial expression was usually well-guarded, but there was curiosity and amazement in his gaze when he looked down at her.

Eva smiled, pleased that she had surprised a man who had experienced nearly everything life could toss at him. When he held himself perfectly still, Eva clamped her hands on his muscled hips and arched instinctively toward him. She was unsure what she needed, but she needed something desperately and he wasn't cooperating.

She heard a low rumble in his throat, saw his uniquely colored eyes flare and decided she must be doing something right. So she moved beneath him again. Delicious pleasure undulated through her like a river of fire, compelling her to surge and retreat again, even if he seemed afraid to move for fear of hurting her.

Then he groaned and drove into her, burying himself to the hilt. Eva gasped as need intensified with each penetrating thrust. She looked down to where they were joined, aroused by the intimacy of their union, overwhelmed by the turbulent passion building inside her like a gigantic tidal wave.

Heat blazed through her and she felt herself melt help-lessly around him as they moved in frantic rhythm. She heard her own gravelly moan fill the breathless silence as scorching sensations seared through her. She stared into his ruggedly handsome face in astonishment when pleasure expanded until it radiated through every fiber of her being. She had never experienced anything so incredible…. Not until she discovered the meaning of passion in Raven's sinewy arms.

Impulsively, she reached up to cup his clean-shaven jaw in her hands and drew his sensuous lips to hers the same moment that she felt another round of intense sensations unfurl like a blossom opening to sunshine. She kissed him for all she was worth, while wild spasms rippled through her body. She cried out his name on a panted breath as time stalled out and immeasurable ecstasy pulsated through her.

Eva held on for dear life when she felt Raven shudder above her. His ragged breath stirred the strands of hair beside her cheek as he rubbed his chin against her shoulder. She smiled in satisfaction as they lay together in the after-math of overwhelming need and unbelievable passion.

"You should have told me this was your first time," he mumbled as he kissed the curve of her neck.

"Would it have mattered?" she asked as she combed her fingers through his thick black hair.

"Yes, it would have. I shouldn't have been your first time, last time or anytime in between."

"No? Who should have? Someone from the Rocky Mountain Detective Agency?" she teased as she angled her head to glance sideways at him. "You're the best time I ever had, J.D. Want to try to break your own record?"

He chuckled lightly. "Give me a minute, Miss Evange-line Hallowell, I…"

She knew at that moment her name rang a distant bell. He frowned pensively then blinked like a hibernating bear emerging from his dark cave.

"Hallowell," he repeated. Then he spoiled the most amazing moment of her life by rearing up and yowling, "Holy hell! Son of a bitch!"

He rolled away, bounded to his feet and stalked naked into the frothy spring-fed pool. "Damn it, Evangeline!"

"How long are you going to keep yelling?" she asked as she stood up and listened to him swear profusely.

"Until I get over being mad at you for withholding your last name until now!" he bellowed.

Eva walked over to join him in the warm pool. When she sank down beside him, Raven refused to look at her, just glared at the bright rays of sunlight, as if they were somehow responsible for the shocking revelation.

"Well, that explains a lot," he muttered. "But it wouldn't have hurt to be open and honest with me right up front. *Damn it!*"

"You've said that already." She snickered at his blustery show of temper.

"Not often enough, damn it to hell!" he erupted again.

She glided across the pool then returned to kneel in front of him, demanding his full attention. "I anticipated this exact reaction from you, which is why I didn't give my last name. See there? You're doing it right now. You're looking at me differently because my family has money."

"Family has money?" he repeated flippantly. "*I* have money stashed in one of the banks you own, but *you* have wealth. There's a big damn difference."

Eva swatted him lightly on the chest. "What difference did that make two minutes ago when I was just the woman sharing an amazing moment of passion with you? An hour ago I was the pain-in-the-ass female you didn't want in your cabin or in your life."

His dark brows swooped down and flattened over his glowing gold-green eyes. "If it makes you feel better I still think you're a pain in the ass. More now than before. You've given new meaning to *complicated,* damn it!"

"Why? I have asked nothing of you. Plus, I'm still paying you to help me find Gordon, who did deceive my sister and stole five thousand dollars of her money. She is beside herself with anger and embarrassment. I swore to her that I would keep the story quiet and would hunt Gordon down to retrieve her money."

"And five grand is just a drop in the bucket to the Hallowells of Denver, right? Well, excuse me, your highness, but I prefer to know who I'm dealing with and this changes everything."

She pressed the heels of her hands against his muscled chest and shoved him backward so quickly that he kerplunked in the pool. He had that coming, as far as she was concerned.

When his head reappeared above the water, she got right in his handsome face. "This changes absolutely nothing," she said in a sharp tone. "I'm a paying client and you are my first lover. Those are the facts, like them or not."

Clearly, he didn't because he was still glaring at her.

"I didn't trick you into what just happened between us and I didn't plan it, either. But I told you that I'm not making demands on you so don't panic and begin doubting my intentions and ulterior motives again."

"Don't worry, firebrand," he muttered as he wiped the water from his face. "I know I'm the last man you'd really want as a husband."

A lot he knew. He was exactly the kind of man she wanted. A man who had desired her in a heated moment of passion…until she told him who she was and he ruined everything by retreating in outrage.

"Of course, Hoodoo's proposal is still on the table so that puts me down the list," he added sarcastically.

"Feel insulted and whatever else you want to feel," she stormed. "But it isn't my fault you can't handle who I am, although you can cope with everything else life throws at you. For some reason you enjoy being annoyed at me every chance you get." She wagged her finger in his face. "But hear this, Jordan Daniel Raven, if you treat me any differently now than before I'll be tempted to shoot you. I've had my fill of men who see my money and never me. Do you hear me?"

"Who can't? You're yelling your head off. My assassin will know exactly where to find me."

Scowling, Eva wheeled around and walked ashore to grab her discarded clothes. She didn't look back while she dressed, either. Then she clutched the shotgun and strode away.

Things between Raven and her had been perfectly fine during their passionate tryst. And then…wham! She had hoped he wouldn't recognize her name, but he had heard of her family. Now things between them were worse than before.

"Lunch is on!" Hoodoo announced while he stood on the stoop.

Eva glanced sideways to see Blackowl sitting atop Raven's pinto pony. His wry smile indicated that he thought it had taken far too much time for Raven to summon her for the meal.

When his gaze drifted pointedly to the secluded pool then back to her, she muttered under her breath. Blackowl could think what he wanted. She didn't care. Men! Damn them all.

* * *

That evening, Hoodoo sent Eva outside to pen up the chickens that had the run of the lawn during the day. She fed them grain then ambled back to the cabin. She stopped short when she noticed a new set of buckskin clothes and moccasins laid out on the table. She frowned curiously when Hoodoo walked through the front door, a step behind her.

"For you, little gal," he replied to her unspoken question. "If you're headed to the rowdy mining camps then you gotta dress as a boy. It's safer for you. Besides, it'll take the pressure off your bodyguards. Too many men up there have been too long without a woman and some of them are short on morals and scruples."

"So I've been told, repeatedly," she murmured as she brushed her hand over the garments. "Thank you, Hoodoo. I've never had such a wonderful gift."

"No? Raven said you have all a woman could possibly want already since you practically own Denver."

She hugged the clothes to her chest and smiled appreciatively at him. "This is what I want most of all because you made the garments for me yourself. This gift is special and I shall treasure it always."

A pleased expression settled on his scarred features. "Go try 'em on so I can see if they need alterations."

Grabbing the moccasins, designed exactly like Blackowl's and Raven's, Eva bounded upstairs to put on her mannish clothes. "They fit perfectly," she called down to Hoodoo. "There is no end to your exceptional talents…. Now when did you say we're getting married?"

Hoodoo chuckled. "You're damn…er, darn good for my pride, little gal. So, what about the moccasins? Comfortable?"

"They fit like gloves. I'm never taking them off!"

His chuckle floated up to her as she all but skipped down the steps to show off her new attire.

"Do I look like a boy?" she asked as she pivoted for his inspection.

"No," Blackowl said bluntly, as he came through the door. "Too many curves in telling places." He pointed to her belt. "Take that off and let the doehide hang loosely over your hips." He waved his hand impatiently. "And do something about your chest. It's a dead giveaway that there is a woman beneath."

"I thrive on your flattery," she said sarcastically before she reversed direction to bind her breasts with the fabric from her petticoats.

"And wear this, too," Blackowl called out.

A wide-brimmed hat sailed through the air then bounced off the wall. Eva scooped it up and tugged it down on her forehead. When she went downstairs to see if she met Blackowl's approval, Raven came in from working with the horses. He dodged her gaze, as he'd been doing since she told him her name during their tryst by the springs.

"Much better," Blackowl declared. "But you'll have to smudge dirt on your face to disguise your sissy-colored skin."

She started to take offense, but she noted the mischievous grin that twitched his lips.

"Blackowl has agreed to teach you to handle weapons tomorrow and he'll give you a few hand-to-hand combat pointers," Raven said as he stared at the air over her head. "I'll work the horses so they'll be as ready as possible for our journey."

"I'll look forward to it," Eva enthused.

"You shouldn't. You might get roughed up again," Blackowl replied. "I'm not going to go easy on you because you're a woman, Paleface."

"Wouldn't expect you to. I'll try to keep the crying and whining to a minimum." She glanced at Raven, who was doing a spectacular job of pretending she was invisible, then she returned her attention to Hoodoo.

"Thank you so much for the thoughtful gift," Eva said again, then walked over to hug the stuffing out of Hoodoo.

"Here." He pulled a new voodoo doll from his pocket and presented it to her. "I gave it my best Cajun curse."

She chuckled as she appraised the miniature effigy of Gordon Carter with pins sticking through his torso. "Wherever he is, I'm sure he's feeling the effects of your curse."

"I'm camping out with the horses tonight and I'll keep watch for our sniper," Raven announced as he grabbed his bedroll from the corner. "Blackowl, you can sleep in the cabin."

When he walked away, Eva wanted to call out to him, but she held her tongue. She'd like to shake him until his teeth rattled, but she doubted it would change his attitude toward her. What she preferred was to revisit that realm of incredible pleasure that Raven had revealed to her.

Murmuring a quiet good-night, Eva went upstairs to bed, knowing she would have no opportunity to share Raven's passion unless she initiated it. Plus, she was leaving on her crusade to find Gordon soon and privacy would be at a premium.

She frowned thoughtfully when Hoodoo's comment about taking the pressure off her hired bodyguards, by wearing men's clothes, came to mind. It troubled her that she had placed Raven and Blackowl at risk to serve her cause. At first, it was just about hiring a guide and gunfighter to locate Gordon. Now it was personal because she knew and liked both men and didn't want to see either of them hurt.

Setting aside her new garments, she slid into bed and wished Raven would join her. But she knew that wouldn't happen. He didn't even want to be in the same cabin with her.

The next evening, after an intense day of working with the horses, Raven ambled onto the covered porch. He stared into the sunset, wrestling with a dozen emotions, none of which he wanted to feel in the first place. Guilt over taking Eva's innocence needled him constantly. Discovering she was an heiress frustrated him to no end. The possibility of Eva getting hurt during her crusade to find Carter tormented him. Not to mention that forbidden desire was eating him alive.

Overall, it had been a tortuous day.

"There's a storm brewing in the mountains," Blackowl announced as he stepped outside after supper to join Raven.

"I know." It rivaled the storm brewing inside Raven. "The sniper will have more trouble finding his footing in the mud and keeping his balance on slippery boulders, while trying to bushwhack us. It will make the trip to Purgatory Gulch sloppy but safer for us."

Raven could feel his cousin's intense gaze on him.

"Thanks for spending the day teaching Eva to shoot and to defend herself while I worked with the horses," Raven said to fill the stilted silence.

"She's a quick learner…. Why have you been ignoring her?" Blackowl asked.

Because guilt, frustration and sexual torment had a fierce, unrelenting hold on him. Of course, he wasn't particularly surprised that his cousin noticed how distracted he'd been and how he'd distanced himself from everyone, especially Eva. Very little got past Blackowl.

"Because she is Evangeline Hallowell, that's why. Her

family owns half of Denver. Her father was one of the first to strike it rich in Colorado and he invested in several lucrative businesses. Practically everything he touched turned into a gold mine."

"So she's good for the money," Blackowl remarked, a smile in his voice. "I should have asked for triple the going rate for survival training and travel guide."

"This isn't funny," Raven muttered sourly.

"It is from where I'm standing. Watching you wrestle with the newfound knowledge and seeing how you're reacting to it is even more amusing."

Raven rounded on him. "Don't you get it? She owns the bank where I stockpile my bounties. She owns my favorite restaurant. And hell, she even owns the London House where I stay when I'm turning over my prisoners to the city marshal."

"Then thank her kindly for providing good accommodations when you're in town," Blackowl teased. "Maybe you should have done that instead of what you were doing at Phantom Springs when you were *supposed* to call Eva to the cabin for lunch yesterday."

Raven glanced away from his cousin's all-too-knowing grin. "I should leave her to you for the trip and remain at the cabin with Hoodoo."

"You should but you won't," Blackowl predicted. "She won't back off until she finds her fugitive and you won't let her endanger her life more than necessary."

Raven huffed out a breath. "She's making me crazy, Blackowl."

"Crazy looks good on you…temporarily, at least. But that doesn't change your destiny," he said as he ambled into the darkness. "I'll be bathing at the springs. Don't disturb me."

Raven watched his cousin vanish into the distance then

pivoted to study Eva and Hoodoo through the window. They were washing and drying dishes, noticeably comfortable in each other's presence.

The older man had cut himself off from the world and from women years ago. However, he'd acquired a new lease on life after meeting Eva. She had a special knack of rebuilding Hoodoo's self-confidence in his appearance and restoring his faith in women. For that, Raven was grateful.

Unfortunately, she was tying Raven in a dozen different knots. She dominated his thoughts and affected his male body fiercely. Pretending indifference in her presence was damn near impossible.

"What the hell am I going to do about her?" Raven asked, glancing skyward.

The reply was a distant rumble of thunder. "So much for the white man's divine guidance," he mumbled as he walked off to shelter the new saddle horses in the shed behind the cabin.

Eva's tantalizing image was there to greet him in the darkness. The thought of her stirred forbidden memories of the wild passion they had shared. His traitorous body hardened with hungry need so quickly that he groaned uncomfortably.

One tryst with Eva was enough, given who she was, given the vast difference in their backgrounds. Hell, once with Evangeline Hallowell was one time too many, he reminded himself. He could name dozens of reasons why they were mismatched, but he couldn't talk himself out of wanting her again, even if she was Denver's version of royalty.

They had absolutely nothing in common except a reckless rendezvous at Phantom Springs, he told himself sensibly. If he knew what was good for him, he wouldn't allow mindless desire to get the better of him again.

Chapter Eleven

From the window, Lydia Hallowell watched Roger Philbert halt the buggy by the front door. He bounded up the marble steps, but she opened the door before he could knock. He blinked in surprise when he noticed she was dressed in the unconventional style of breeches and shirt that her older sister preferred. Without delay, Lydia motioned him inside.

"Thank you for returning the buggy, Roger," she murmured as she led him to the study to ensure privacy.

She pivoted to stare at him, her chin elevated in a mannerism that characterized Evangeline. Roger shook his head and smiled in amazement.

"It is startling how much you and Eva look alike, even more so than my twin sister and me."

"I've heard that a lot lately," she replied then asked him flat out, "How much do you know about what's going on?"

"Enough to be insanely curious after Eva sent a note asking me to fetch your abandoned buggy," he said. "Would you mind telling me why Gordon had possession of it?"

She grimaced, wrung her hands then muttered an unladylike oath under her breath. "If I confide what happened you have to swear on your honor that you won't tell another living soul. Not even Sadie."

Roger scoffed. "You know she'll drive us both crazy if we exclude her."

Lydia expelled her breath then scraped her fingers through her curly auburn hair. "All right. Tell Sadie only what's necessary."

She wilted into the chair behind the desk and gestured for Roger to take a seat. "Gordon only pretended to like me so he could attach himself to my money. Like an idiot, I believed he cared for me and that he was sincere when he wanted to elope in my carriage," she explained. "He asked me to bring along some money to cover the extended honeymoon. Then he dumped me by the roadside and left me to make my way home in shame and humiliation."

"I'm sorry," Roger commiserated. "Sadie and I have had to dodge those kinds of land mines ourselves."

She bobbed her head and tried to blink back the tears. It took a moment to regain her composure. "I've resolved to become as strong and independent as Eva. I also plan to avoid men until I become a better judge of your despicable gender."

Roger grinned and threw up his hands suppliantly. "Just don't forget I'm one of the good guys. Plus I'm a longtime friend." He shifted awkwardly in his chair. "As your friend, I must inform you that your sister married the gunslinger she hired to track down Gordon. That's what this is about, right?"

"What!" Lydia literally came out of her chair in shock.

Roger nodded his blond head. "That's the report I received from the stationmaster where I picked up your buggy. He bought it from Gordon, who rode off on Hodge. Eva bought the carriage back. I don't have any other details."

"*Married? Eva?*" Lydia plunked into her chair, astonished. She looked to Roger for answers. "Why did she do that?"

Roger shrugged. "I don't know but I suppose Eva has her reasons. At least I hope she isn't a pawn in the bounty hunter's perverted game."

Lydia nodded pensively. "I sincerely hope so, too. Eva usually knows what she's doing. Unlike me."

Roger surged from his chair. "You'll do fine, Lydia. If you need anything Sadie and I will be happy to assist you."

"Thank you," she murmured, distracted. "Married to a bounty hunter? What is she thinking?"

"Hell if I know," Roger mumbled as he let himself out.

Lydia was up and pacing from wall to wall in nothing flat. Lydia suspected her sister had made some sort of bargain with the devil as a sacrifice on her behalf. Her shoulders slumped with a heavy burden of guilt. As usual, Eva was fighting Lydia's battles for her.

"But no longer," she said to the room at large. "I'm going to fend for myself and take the pressure off Eva."

Although Lydia vowed to reform, she was at a loss as to how to help her sister. She didn't even know where to find her. Lydia prayed Eva would contact her immediately so she could dash off to assist her—for once in her life.

Raven had chosen to spend a second night on his bedroll, in case the sniper sneaked up to the cabin. He had just dozed off on his pallet beside the horse pen when the crackle of twigs and dry leaves brought him to instant alert. Pistol in hand, Raven watched the shadowed silhouette materialize from the inky depths of the night.

It was Eva, he realized, tormented by a riptide of emotion. He wished it was the sniper because he knew how to fight that kind of threat. But he had no defense against

Eva. He wanted to shout her back to the cabin, but he didn't voice a single protest when she removed the six-shooter from his hand and set it an arm's length away.

Mesmerized, he watched her sink to her knees to remove her robe. There was nothing beneath it.

Raven groaned softly when she grasped his hand and brought it to her lips. "I want to know you the way you know me. Man to woman. No names, no expectations. Just this one last time."

Then she kissed him tenderly and his hand contracted around her breast. She sighed into his mouth and reached out to trail her fingers over the expanse of his chest. For him, it was a kiss of helpless surrender. When she urged him to his back, he did as she asked. He, who was known for his ironclad self-discipline and unfaltering willpower, gave in to temptation without a fight.

"I want to know what you like," she murmured. "I want to please you. I want to be exceptionally good at it."

Her moist breath skimmed over his male nipples then drifted over his belly. Raven felt raw lust pulsating through his body. He was too aware of her alluring scent, too consumed by her tender touch to do anything except respond. He lay there shamelessly, allowing her to caress him at will, offering no objection when she glided her hand beneath the quilt to find him throbbing and aching for her.

"Evangeline, I—" His brain broke down and flames leaped through his bloodstream when she stroked his rigid flesh from base to tip with her thumb and forefinger.

His heart ceased beating momentarily when she dipped her head to take him into her mouth. The feel of her lips brushing his sensitive flesh drove him mad with desire. The feel of her silky hair skimming over his abdomen sent hot chills down his spine. Desperate for control, he reached down to still her roving hand, but she placed it over hers then nipped playfully at his knuckles with her teeth.

"I thought you hated men," he rasped shakily.

"Not as much since I found out they're good for something besides target practice," she teased as she worked her erotic magic on his body. "But it turns out that I'm very particular about which man I choose to sleep with."

"Not much sleeping going on here… Ah…you're killing me," he groaned as her hand brushed over his aching length repeatedly, tormentingly.

"Don't die yet," she teased. "I have a dozen more things I want to do with you."

Raven was fairly certain this would be his last day on earth. Pleasure this hot and intense demanded extreme sacrifice, he was sure of it. He had never allowed a woman unlimited access to his body. But if Eva wanted to touch him then he wouldn't stop her. She made him enjoy defeat. She made him abandon self-control and like every erotic moment of it. She made him groan in unholy torment and beg for more.

When she stroked him and suckled him, he whispered her name like a chant. She glided over him, offering him a taste of his own desire for her in their kiss. His flesh boiled into steam and bone melted like molten lava when she settled over him—so close yet maddeningly far away.

"Come here," he said huskily. "I need you…now."

"You don't need me enough. Not yet," she whispered back.

And then she reached down to touch him again and again. He swore he was going to black out when searing pleasure coursed through him like a river of fire. When she shifted to sink down exactly upon him, Raven arched instinctively toward her, aching to bury himself in her moist warmth. Suddenly he was inside her and she was riding him, setting a hypnotic pace that swept him up like a cyclone spinning his mind and body completely out of control.

Raven clasped his hands on her hips, guiding her up and down in frantic rhythm. Intense sensations burgeoned until they burst over him like a comet blazing a path across the night sky, hurtling toward fiery self-destruction.

He'd thought the first time with Eva was incredible. The second was unbelievable. He'd never felt so much pleasure and emotion converge on him at once. The effects on him were breathtaking and mind-numbing—and he wanted more.

He watched her arch her back as her head tilted, sending a cascade of auburn curls tumbling around her shoulders. He felt the quakes of ecstasy claim her body, felt them vibrate through him until they shared the climactic pleasure as one living, breathing essence. The intimate caress of her body radiating through him sent him pitching over the edge of self-control, free-falling through space into unparalleled rapture.

Raven couldn't draw breath. He could only feel to such intense extremes that he swore death was imminent. He shuddered wildly and reached up to pull Eva down on top of him. He wrapped her tightly in his arms, so completely overwhelmed that he feared he'd squeeze her in two. But he needed to be as close to her as he could get when the infinite emotion consumed him.

It was out of character for him to be so devastated by passion or by the woman in his arms. He'd never let anyone under his skin and he'd developed a hard shell around his heart. Nevertheless, Eva felt like a vital part of him and he didn't want to delve too deeply into *why* she did, for fear he couldn't deal with what all these intense emotions implied.

She stirred above him a few moments later, kissed him lightly on the lips then eased away to don her robe. "I'll never forget what it was like to be with you," she murmured.

Like a fleeting fantasy come and gone, she melted into the swaying shadows. Emptiness and restlessness, the likes he hadn't experienced since he was a child, overcame him.

A moment later lightning flickered over the mountain crests then vanished, plunging the world into darkness. Raven planned to lie awake and contemplate why Eva had risked letting Blackowl, who had camped out on the cabin floor, know where she had gone in the middle of the night.

He supposed the newness of passion had made the spirited Evangeline Hallowell impetuous and daring. A wry smile pursed his lips as he stared up at the clouds that played cat-and-mouse with the moon and stars. He decided there were worse things in the world than being the experimental object of a woman's passion. Just as long as he didn't read anything into their midnight tryst, he cautioned himself.

"When all is said and done, you'll still return to your world and I'll be stuck in mine," he whispered to the enthralling vision floating above him.

Enjoy her, came that reckless voice deep inside him. She was a rare treat for a man who lived a hardscrabble life, stuck between two opposing civilizations and cultures. If she didn't complain about their passionate trysts, why should he?

Raven told himself to get some shut-eye so he'd be alert during their upcoming journey. However, the memories of incredible passion followed him into his dreams and he woke up more than once in a cold sweat, wishing for a few more forbidden hours with Eva in his arms.

Gordon Carter packed his gear on his horse and trotted up the trail to Purgatory Gulch. He had decided to try his hand at gambling in the mining district. For sure, he hadn't had any luck picking off Eva as he'd hoped.

Meanwhile, he would kill some time while waiting for the next phase of his scheme for the Hallowells to unfold.

Without a backward glance, Gordon made his way through the fog that cloaked the mountain trail. He smiled wickedly to himself, wondering how the Hallowells would react to the next part of his plan. They would be furious and outraged, no doubt. And that would please Gordon immensely.

The next morning Blackowl glanced over at Raven while he strapped his saddlebags on his pony. "Tired, cousin? Have trouble sleeping last night?"

Raven stared bleary-eyed at the soupy fog that had greeted him at dawn. "None whatsoever. You?"

Blackowl grinned scampishly. "Yes, in fact. Someone stepped over me during the night. I hope that someone didn't wear you out completely, cousin."

Raven refused to rise to the bait. He kept his expression carefully blank. "You're going to be a nuisance on this trip, aren't you? Maybe you should stay here with Hoodoo."

"And miss the entertainment? No, I'm definitely coming."

"I packed some food to send along with you," Hoodoo called out as he limped downhill. "Don't want that little gal to get hungry." He glanced this way and that. "Where is she? Bathing at the spring?"

A sickening feeling coiled in the pit of Raven's belly. "I thought she was sleeping late this morning." He glanced questioningly at Blackowl.

"I heard her go outside during the night but she didn't return. I thought she was with you."

"Damn it to hell!" Raven exploded. "Surely she didn't strike off by herself." He glanced every which way but the blood-red bay gelding was gone. "How could she know what route to follow?"

Hoodoo winced. "That must be why she asked me so many questions about the wagon trail that led to the mining camp. I thought she was just passing time while we washed dishes and cleaned up after supper last night."

Raven swore a blue streak. When that didn't ease the anger roiling inside him, he swore another blue streak.

"Why would she leave without us?" Raven muttered as he swung into the saddle, anxious to overtake that crazed female. "Just because she had a crash course in self-defense does she think she's indestructible?"

"Maybe she didn't want to see you two hurt while serving her cause," Hoodoo speculated. Then a thought suddenly occurred to him and his blue eyes popped. "Oh, hell. I tried to impress upon her that she needed to wear men's clothing and learn to take care of herself so it would make her two bodyguards' job safer and easier. She must've felt guilty about placing you in harm's way and decided to accept the challenge by herself."

Raven had the uneasy feeling Hoodoo was right on the mark. Eva had come to Raven at midnight to say farewell before riding off in the darkness, relying on the information about the trail that Hoodoo had unknowingly offered her. Now she'd been gone for hours, following the narrow path leading to the mining camps at higher elevations.

If she located Carter and confronted him alone, he'd strangle her—if Carter didn't kill her first.

"Let's ride," Raven insisted, all sorts of unpleasant scenarios dancing in his head.

Blackowl hurriedly tied the rest of his gear in place. Although it took only a few moments, it felt like an hour to Raven. They raced off like discharged cannonballs.

Raven pushed the pinto to his limits before slowing the laboring steed to a walk so he could catch his breath.

"Everything will be fine," Blackowl consoled Raven a quarter of an hour later.

"Will it?" Raven said grimly. "That's the very last thing my mother said to me when the soldiers descended on us at Sand Creek. We know how that turned out, don't we?"

Blackowl shut his mouth. Raven had the feeling Blackowl's mother had made the same reassuring remark before she urged him to flee before the bloodthirsty soldiers shot her, too.

Eva patted the bay's muscled neck as she followed the trail through the soupy fog that enveloped the rugged peaks. She couldn't see very far ahead—or behind her. However, she figured that was to her advantage if Gordon was lurking in the hills, hoping to shoot her out of the saddle.

A faint smile quirked her lips. She wondered how Raven had reacted to finding her gone this morning. Her ears were burning so she presumed he had bellowed a few salty curses to her name. But honestly, this was for the best, she reassured herself. Raven could continue training his new horse until it equaled Buck's dependable skills. Plus, Blackowl had said she had passed her self-defense tests with flying colors—or something to that effect.

When she eventually encountered Gordon, she would have the element of surprise on her side because he wouldn't recognize her in her buckskin garb. He wouldn't likely know which horse she was riding since he had sneaked up on her when she was afoot at Phantom Springs. Every advantage would make apprehending that worthless shyster easier for her.

Eva checked the watch she had tucked in her pocket.

According to Hoodoo, she should reach Purgatory Gulch in less than an hour. Anticipation bubbled inside her. Gordon Carter was not going to get away with extorting money from Lydia and mortifying her to the extreme. Plus, he was going to pay dearly for Hodge's unnecessary death.

The sudden rumble of thunder scattered Eva's vindictive thoughts. She glanced up at the low-hanging clouds that engulfed the mountain. For the past few days, it seemed a building storm had hovered in the distance, gathering strength. Apparently, it was on the move. She glanced around, trying to decide where to take refuge in case of a cloudburst.

To her vast relief, the storm passed over her with no more than a gush of cold wind before it unleashed its fury. She could see pounding rain sweeping down the path she had followed to higher elevations.

"Talk about a stroke of luck," Eva said to the bay as she patted his powerful neck. "If we had left the cabin an hour later we would have been in the middle of the downpour."

She predicted that Raven, Blackowl and Hoodoo would be forced to duck into the cabin and stay put until the fierce storm moved southeast. She wouldn't be there to be ignored by Raven, she mused as she urged her horse into a trot. Raven wouldn't have to continue pretending she was invisible, as he'd done the previous day.

A wry smile pursed her lips, recalling that she had made her presence felt the previous night when she told him goodbye. The erotic memory of their midnight tryst triggered intense sensations that she doubted she'd experience again in her life. She had cast aside all inhibitions to be with Raven one last time before she struck off to find Gordon.

"Last night was worth it," she murmured.

The bay pricked his ears then accelerated his pace as he rounded the bend, headed straight for Purgatory Gulch.

"Of all the rotten timing," Raven growled when pelting rain pummeled him and transformed the rutted wagon trail into a stream of water.

He shot out his wet arm, directing Blackowl's attention to the overhanging ledge of rock that could provide shelter. Together they reined their horses beneath the cliff—and not a minute too soon. The sky opened up and thunder boomed overhead, indicating the storm had worsened.

"The Cheyenne gods are displeased. It is the curse of your white woman, I'm sure," Blackowl teased as he dismounted.

"She isn't mine," Raven answered, begging to differ. "I wonder how she's weathering this storm."

"With defiance and impatience," Blackowl speculated. "Do you think she will do something rash if she finds this Carter person before we catch up with her?"

"You tell me," Raven mumbled as he watched the storm pound down the trail. "You trained her to handle a gun and knife. And you already know how fiercely determined she is."

Blackowl scowled. "I think we have reason for concern."

"My sentiments exactly." Raven stared uphill, hoping Eva hadn't washed away.

She had suffered enough danger and near brushes with disaster already. Even though he was annoyed as hell with her for striking off alone, he was still worried about her.

"We'll find her," Blackowl murmured encouragingly.

"I just hope it isn't at the bottom of a ravine after this flash flood tails off."

Chapter Twelve

Eva stared owlishly at the steep, rocky mountainside as she approached the bustling community known as Purgatory Gulch. What might have been a panoramic landscape was littered with mechanized machines constructed to retrieve gold and other precious metals from the bowels of the earth.

She watched in amazement as a three-story-tall hoisting wheel churned up dirt and carried it to the surface to dump it in a pile. Narrow catwalks of planks and beams provided a passage for company miners. They carted the dirt in wheelbarrows to mammoth-size screened drums that constantly rotated, sifting out gold flakes and nuggets. Discarded beams and ladders cluttered the once scenic hillside when work sites shifted to another promising location.

In the distance individual prospectors panned for placer gold along the streams and tributaries on their ten-foot-square claims. Armed with picks, shovels and pans, they used their wooden cradles to filter gold from the water.

Tents of all shapes and sizes were staked haphazardly on the rocky slopes where other prospectors had marked off their forty-square-foot claims for dry digging. The tent camps formed an outpost community around the stores and shops of the town.

Eva continued on her way along the ever-widening path that eventually became the hub of Purgatory Gulch. The town had only one street that snaked along the side of the mountain. One half mile of log and rock cabins, shanties, frame-and-canvas buildings and large tents lined the street.

Drunken men of diverse nationalities milled about. The ragtag, unshaven and unkempt crowd looked as if the closest they had come to bathing was when it rained and soaked them to the bone. Laughter, salty curses and off-color songs filled the air.

Eva ducked her head to protect her identity as she rode into town. She noticed that only one two-story clapboard building graced the community. Unfortunately, it was called Greta's Place and four scantily dressed harlots lounged on the upper balcony. They called to the men below, inviting them to exchange their pouches of gold for sexual favors.

She should have known that the only other women in town were soiled doves, Eva mused. But then, Raven and his friends had warned her that this was no place for what they referred to as "protected women," who had never associated with the rougher elements in the underbelly of society. Eva was not accustomed to living on this side of life but she vowed to adapt.

There were more saloons and gaming halls in town than respectable hotels. In fact, there was only one hotel and Eva wanted nothing to do with sleeping in what looked to be pigsty accommodations. She'd sleep on the ground before she bedded down in that filthy, hastily constructed establishment.

Eva pictured her father living in the same sort of squalor while he fended off claim jumpers and existed like an animal in the wilds to find his fortune in gold. It was little wonder that her father had been determined to provide better accommodations for miners who came to Denver.

"Hellhole" did not begin to describe this place, she mused as her gaze swept over the community a second time.

It was the perfect locale for a mangy rat like Gordon Carter to hole up, she decided.

Dismounting, Eva surveyed the saloon in front of her. The bar counter was nothing more than a wide plank braced on two wooden barrels. It sat outside a rectangular tent in which haggard-looking men sipped their brew. She could see monte cards and backgammon boards spread out on makeshift tables.

"What'll you have, sonny boy?" The brawny bartender's thick Irish accent got her attention and she pivoted to face him.

His greasy brown hair framed his doughy face. He had fists like hams and legs like tree stumps. Eva presumed this brawny, muscle-bound man quelled his own disturbances at his bar. He certainly looked tough enough to handle a brawl.

He grinned, exposing a wide gap where his two front teeth should have been. "Does a peach-fuzz-face brat like you drink anything besides mother's milk?"

Eva refused to react to the rude question. Now she understood why Raven had taught himself to maintain a deadpan expression and tamp down emotion when dealing with the annoying ruffians in the world. He had obviously endured dozens of insults because of his mixed breeding and his profession. Out of necessity he'd become a master of self-control. Eva vowed to become more proficient, too, if for no other reason than to protect her identity in this hellhole.

"I'm looking for my uncle," she said in a deep voice that was heavy with a southern drawl. "I hoped you might've seen him. His name's Gordon Carter. Six foot tall, green eyes, thick brown hair. He wears a goatee and mustache."

The bartender smirked. "Hell, brat, I don't give out nothing for free, not even advice, directions or information. Everything has a price in this gulch. You got money?"

Eva had more sense than to flash her bankroll to the likes of this shifty-eyed scalawag. She predicted she would have her money stolen, her throat slit and her body dumped off the side of a cliff in nothing flat.

"No, sir, that's why I was looking for my uncle," she replied. "He carries the pouch of gold dust."

The bartender flicked his wrist dismissively. "Then be on your way, sonny boy. I got no time for the likes of you."

A half hour later Eva was becoming discouraged. Everyone she approached to ask for information was no more helpful than the Irish saloonkeeper. In addition, her stomach was growling something fierce and she had to take time out of her search to find food. However, she was not about to enter the dingy-colored round tent that claimed to be a café. The smells the place emitted guaranteed indigestible meals. Eva decided to purchase a few items from the dry goods store that was housed in a hastily constructed log cabin.

She entered the store to see floor-to-ceiling shelves stocked with flour, sugar, molasses, coffee and a variety of canned food. She grabbed cans of beans, pickles and peaches then discreetly retrieved a banknote from her stash of money.

"Is that all you need, kid?" The thick-chested store owner bit down on his cheroot as he sacked the items.

"No, I need to find my uncle," she said then gave a quick description.

The owner shrugged his broad shoulders then handed her the sack. "There's men coming and going from here constantly, son. Your best bet is to scour the streets and saloons. If your uncle is prospecting for gold in these parts he's bound to show up here eventually."

Eva nodded her thanks then exited the store. With her sack tucked under her arm, she grabbed the bay's reins and hiked to the far side of town. She hoped to find an out-of-the-way spot for an improvised picnic—away from the drunks who had sprawled out to sleep off their hangovers.

She stopped short when she spotted Gordon Carter swaggering down the opposite side of the street, dressed in the same fashion as the local miners—heavy boots, wool breeches and a flannel shirt. She noticed that he absently rubbed his belly and chest and she smiled, wondering if he might be suffering the effects of Hoodoo's voodoo curse. Eva hoped that was the case.

Gordon paused outside the bordello where all four harlots leaned over the railing, exposing their cleavage. She was surprised their wares didn't spill from the diving neck-lines of their lingerie.

When Gordon flashed that charming smile that had captured Lydia's attention and sent her tumbling headlong into heartbreak, Eva gnashed her teeth and cursed him soundly. She had the impulsive urge to retrieve the handgun Blackowl had given her and blow Gordon to smithereens.

This is not the time or place, said the sensible voice that barely overrode the voice of revenge.

Still, outrage boiled through her as she watched him enter the brothel—much to the delight of the soiled doves who had propositioned him.

What she felt was rage for *Lydia's* sake, she realized. The emotion was even more intense than what she had experienced personally when Felix used her and discarded her in favor of a more manageable bride. No matter what,

Gordon was going to pay for breaking Lydia's naive heart and ruining her faith in men. Eva would make certain of it!

Inwardly fuming, Eva watched Gordon saunter inside. At least she knew where he was. That was a small consolation. She continued on her way and found a place to sink down cross-legged beneath a tree. She dined on her canned food while her horse grazed beside her.

All the while, she asked herself how she was going to take Gordon into custody and transport him back to civilization without him escaping. As Raven had told her, there were no law enforcement officers in these rowdy mining camps. There were several shabby cafés, entirely too many saloons, a print shop, an apothecary store, a post office, a bakery and a freight company. Unfortunately, there wasn't a city marshal's office in sight.

"Maybe I should have allowed Raven and Blackowl to come with me," she mumbled between bites.

Then she reminded herself that Raven and Blackowl faced enough hardship and dangers in their professions without hiring on with her. No, this was her personal campaign for justice and she would have to devise a clever way to apprehend Gordon and haul him to jail.

Eva finished her meal and washed it down with a cool drink from the nearby stream. From her vantage point on the hillside, she surveyed the community again, visualizing her father living this hand-to-mouth existence before he found the bonanza that changed his life forever.

Her gaze sharpened when she saw Gordon exit the brothel to retrieve a roan pony. She wondered where he had confiscated the different mounts he had used and speculated on what had happened to the men who originally owned the livestock.

Anticipation surged inside her when she saw Gordon

pack a few items in his saddlebags. She presumed he was leaving town. Even better that he was headed toward her. If he was on his way to Satan's Bluff—the second mining camp located in Devil's Triangle—she could launch a surprise attack.

Eva scrambled to her feet to pull her horse into the underbrush on the hillside so she could keep lookout on the road. Her mind raced, trying to determine when to overtake Gordon and how to restrain him. Other than giving him the good shooting he deserved, she amended.

Her spiteful thoughts trailed off when shouts erupted from one of the canvas saloons in the middle of town. To Eva's dismay, two men were herded toward her end of town. She gasped in surprise when she recognized Frank Albers and Irving Jarmon, the two gamblers she had met on the stagecoach. The drunken mob cursed them foully and threatened to lynch them for cheating at cards.

"They're in this together!" One of the outraged miners bellowed. "I saw 'em passing cards. I say we hang 'em high!"

Eva muttered a curse to Gordon's name when he nudged his horse into a faster clip so he wouldn't be overtaken by the approaching mob. Typical Gordon, she thought in annoyance. He never had the slightest concern for anyone but himself.

As much as Eva wanted to follow Gordon, the grim expressions on Frank Albers's and Irving Jarmon's faces stopped her in her tracks. They had the look of two men who knew they had spent their last day on earth. She suspected they were guilty of sleight-of-hand tricks at the card table, but the vigilante justice directed at them seemed too harsh to fit their crime.

Frustrated to no end, Eva cast one last longing glance at Gordon's departing back, assuming he was headed to

Satan's Bluff. She sincerely hoped he stayed long enough in the community for her to catch up with him after she tried her best to rescue Frank and Irving from certain death.

Her stomach dropped to the soles of her moccasins when two members of the drunken mob tossed hangman's nooses over the branch of the lone pine tree that stood beside the creek. Judging by the scars on the branch, she presumed this wasn't the first time the tree had served a vigilante court and bloodthirsty mob of executioners.

Frantically she tried to conjure up an effective way to stop this atrocity. It didn't matter that she'd only spent one morning huddled in a stagecoach with Frank and Irving and that she knew very little about them. She just couldn't live with herself if she didn't make an effort to save them.

If the drunken mob was holding a necktie party with Gordon Carter as its honored guest, she would be all in favor.

Think! Eva urged herself when Frank and Irving commenced kicking, screaming and loudly proclaiming their innocence. Several men hoisted them onto the backs of two sorrel horses. They bound the gamblers' wrists behind them, secured the nooses dangling from the tree limb and taunted their victims unmercifully. If she didn't do something—and quickly—Irving and Frank would breathe their last breaths and she would be forced to watch it happen.

Raven scowled when rain came down in sheets. The downpour turned the trail into a swift-moving current of water and tried what was left of his patience—which wasn't much. Concern over Eva's welfare and whereabouts was driving him crazy.

Finally, thirty minutes after the thunderstorm swept down the mountain, the rainwater drained off the path so he could tell where the footing had become treacherous.

He and Blackowl got underway, dodging the eroded trenches where dirt and gravel had washed away.

"This is no time to be breaking in a new mount," Raven grumbled as he veered around the washed-out ditches.

"Your Indian pony seems surefooted to me," Blackowl observed. "You're just dissatisfied because the horse can't sprout wings and fly."

"Considering the superstitious nonsense about how I'm only half human and half Indian ghost spirit you would think two cousins from the Cheyenne Bird Clan should have the ability to fly."

Blackowl chuckled. "I have heard the same sort of rumors whispered about me at rendezvous. I usually—"

Raven flung up his hand, cutting off his cousin in mid-sentence. His attention fixated on the articles of clothing that were strewn over tree limbs and bushes that jutted from the steep downhill slope beside the road. His heart stopped beating for several vital seconds and he struggled to draw breath as he surveyed the area, looking for a body—Eva's in particular.

"Not her belongings," Blackowl declared as he studied the garments scattered on the hillside. "Not her horse, either."

Raven leaned out to look down from Blackowl's vantage point. Sure enough, a brown pony lay on its side. Its legs were sprawled at unnatural angles and it showed no signs of life.

"That looks like the horse I saw your would-be assassin riding when he set off the rockslide by Seven Falls," Blackowl murmured. "I guess this means he lost his footing during the storm and won't come gunning for you again."

Raven couldn't control his mounting concern for Eva. It was coloring his every thought. "Or maybe the bastard disposed of Eva, stole her horse and made another attempt to convince us that he's dead."

"Or maybe it is true that there *were* two assassins and that one disposed of the other," Blackowl suggested.

"There is also the possibility that the sneaky bastard overtook Eva and disposed of his own belongings to throw us off track. She could be a captive that will become bait to lure us into a deathtrap."

Blackowl grimaced as he started up the winding trail. "That is possible, I suppose. I hope you're wrong, Raven."

Raven sincerely hoped he was wrong, too. But Eva had encountered so many near brushes with fatal danger already that it was making him loco. *If* she was still alive, *if* he caught up with her before disaster struck, he was going to shake the stuffing out of her for scaring a dozen years off his life.

Eva mentally scrambled to devise a workable solution to rescue the hapless gamblers. The self-appointed judge of the mob—the burly Irish saloonkeeper—stepped forward to ask Frank Albers and Irving Jarmon if they had any last words before they died.

Suddenly inspiration struck Eva like a lightning bolt and she smiled triumphantly.

Bounding into the saddle, Eva forced her horse to circle around the clump of trees and underbrush where she was hiding. Giving whoops and shouts of excitement—that alarmed the bay and left him sidestepping and tossing his head—Eva waved her arm in expansive gestures. All heads turned toward her in synchronized rhythm as her horse bounded down the steep slope.

"Eureka! We've struck it rich!" she yelled in her exaggerated Southern drawl. "Me and my uncle hit a bonanza!"

The attention-grabbing comment distracted the kangaroo court from its execution.

"Say, that's the kid who came in my store this morning, looking for his uncle."

Eva nodded vigorously as she waved to the dry goods storekeeper who had sold her canned food earlier.

"Same for me," the burly Irish saloon owner added. "He was looking for his uncle then, too."

"I found him!" Eva shouted excitedly. "We stumbled on a rich vein on the north side of this slope." That was the exact opposite direction she planned to ride in attempt to overtake Gordon. "The vein is in a deep crevice about fifty feet above ledge. You have to see it to believe it!"

Gold fever struck the mob. With the lynching forgotten, they swarmed toward her, causing the bay gelding to prance skittishly. Eva reined the horse through the surging crowd that scrabbled up the rocky terrain and disappeared around the side of the mountain in search of the imaginary bonanza.

"Thank you, son," Frank murmured as Eva leaned out to remove the noose from his neck then untied his hands from behind his back. "We thought we were as good as dead.... *Eva?*"

His voice became a startled croak and he stared frog-eyed at her. "It is you, isn't it? What the blazes are you doing—?"

"Eva Raven?" Irving hooted as he studied her face beneath the shadowed brim of her hat. He glanced this way and that. "Is your husband here, too?"

"No, he is completing an unfinished assignment." She untied Irving's hands. "I'm tracking the bushwhacker who took potshots at me during the stagecoach journey."

Frank and Irving massaged their raw-skinned necks as they focused their bewildered stares on Eva.

"So that's why you're in disguise," Frank ventured. "To protect yourself in this rowdy camp. Good thinking."

"I identified the bushwhacker who left town immedi-

ately before you two were marched out here." She glanced
at them in blatant disapproval. "Maybe it isn't a good idea
to gang up on hapless miners. They don't take kindly to
being cheated at cards."

The gamblers had enough decency to look ashamed and
contrite. "Folks in these parts seem prone to taking drastic
measures in a hurry," Frank mumbled.

"They will probably take the same attitude in punish-
ing a kid who claimed to have discovered a gold strike that
doesn't exist." Eva cast a wary glance toward the stone-
covered hillside. "I better head to Satan's Bluff before the
mob descends on me."

Irving snickered in amusement. "That was a clever distraction and we are eternally indebted to you. If not for you,
we'd be swinging from the short end of a rope right now."

When Eva reined toward the second settlement at higher
elevations, Frank called out to her. "I'm not sure you should
go there alone. Maybe you should wait for Raven to catch up."

Eva didn't mention that Raven wasn't coming. Instead,
she waved farewell and didn't look back. She had done her
good deed for the day by sparing the gamblers, but it had cost
her valuable time and she had bypassed the perfect opportunity to pounce on Gordon when he least expected it. Now
she couldn't overtake him until he stopped in the next town.

She rode away, cautioning herself not to become overanxious and make a careless mistake. If she lost the
element of surprise—and disguise—that slimy worm
might slip from her grasp.

That is not going to happen, Eva promised herself. Before
the day was out, Gordon would be her captive... She hoped.

Raven rode into Purgatory Gulch later that afternoon.
His stomach growled and his temper roiled. He scanned the

street impatiently, looking for the blood-red bay and its dare-devil rider. He saw neither. What he did notice was the same speculative glances he usually received when he entered a community—even one as wild and rowdy as this one.

Today he drew even more attention because Blackowl rode beside him. They were given a wide berth and grudging consideration. Legend had it that he and Blackowl were deadly accurate with rifles, knives and six-shooters and challenging them to a showdown was just plain suicide.

Raven halted in front of a makeshift saloon, unaware that he had encountered the same rude Irishman that Eva had contacted when she first arrived in town.

"I'm looking for someone," Raven said without preamble.

"Ain't we all," the Irishman answered wryly then lit his cheroot. "I've seen you in town before. Raven, isn't it? We don't want no trouble." He inclined his greasy head toward Blackowl. "I've seen you before, too. Owl-Something-Or-Other, right?"

"Blackowl." He bared his teeth menacingly. "I collect Irish scalps."

The Irishman bit down on his cigar but didn't respond.

Raven retrieved the three bench warrants Marshal Doyle had given him in Denver then waved them in the Irishman's doughy face. "These men robbed a couple of miners in this area. Do you know where I can find them?"

The Irishman snorted in disgust. "Yeah, two of them are rotting in hell and you won't collect any bounty on them. We hanged them last week when they shot one of my fellow countrymen in the leg while trying to rob him. One got away."

Raven nodded grimly. "This mining camp is gaining the reputation as a 'hangtown.' You don't get to be judge, jury and executioner."

"Isn't that what you are?" the Irishman asked insolently. "I've heard there are hundreds of graves marked with an *X*, thanks to you."

Raven rolled his eyes. Every time that tale was told, the numbers were exaggerated. "There aren't hundreds," he contradicted. "Only the ones who prefer death to rotting in jail don't make it back to Denver alive."

The Irishman's expression indicated that he didn't believe Raven. The legend was usually more interesting than the truth, he supposed.

"In my book, the policy of hanging criminals immediately curtails the number of robberies and murders. I'm all for expedient frontier justice. If not for that cunning little brat we would've had ourselves another double lynching this morning."

Raven snapped to attention. "What brat?"

The Irishman blew smoke rings in the air. "The one dressed in buckskin and moccasins. "He claimed he was looking for his uncle Gordon. I shooed him away from my saloon but he turned up later when we were all set to hang two cheating gamblers. The kid started yelling about how he and his uncle had found a rich vein of gold on the north side of the mountain."

Raven glanced discreetly at Blackowl, who was also having trouble keeping a straight face. Leave it to Eva to be resourceful and inventive. Hell, that's how Raven had come to have a pretend wife who had him chasing her all over creation.

"Everybody got excited about the possibility of a new mother lode in the area and we raced off, following the kid's directions." The Irishman bit down on his cigar and his face puckered in a scowl. "We wasted two hours combing the hillside. We finally gave up and walked back to town. By that time, the two men we planned to hang for cheating at cards were long gone. So were the two horses we hoisted them onto so we could leave them swinging from a rope."

"You think one of the men might have been the kid's uncle?" Blackowl asked.

The Irishman nodded his greasy head and Raven noticed the sunlight glinting off the specks in his hair. "I'd bet my right arm that the kid's uncle was one of those hooligans who fleeced miners at the card table," the Irishman was saying when Raven got around to listening. "If you happen onto that sneaky brat, remember that he's an accomplice to horse thieving. He can hang alongside his uncle and his cohort."

"I'll see that justice is served," Raven said as he pivoted around to mount his horse.

Together Raven and Blackowl rode toward the outskirts of town, continuing to draw speculative stares. Two men darted from a saloon, bounded onto their mules and rode off in the opposite direction in a flaming rush.

"What do you suppose those two are guilty of?" Blackowl asked as he watched the men's hasty departure.

Raven shrugged nonchalantly. "Doesn't matter. I don't have warrants for their arrest." He halted when he saw the lone pine tree where two nooses swayed in the breeze. "I wonder if Gordon Carter was one of the doomed gamblers."

Blackowl frowned thoughtfully. "If Eva did manage to take advantage of having him tied up and sitting on a horse, prepared to have his neck stretched, what would she do with him?"

"She claimed she planned to shoot, stab, poison and hang him," Raven recalled as he stared at the nooses. "Why would she pass up the golden opportunity to watch him die?"

An uneasy sensation trickled down Raven's spine as he

glanced over his shoulder toward town. "What if there really are two men who are trying to ambush us and they decided to join forces?"

"Then why come here?" Blackowl questioned.

"I have no clue. This case has me baffled. The bush-whacker—or bushwhackers—struck with guerilla tactics then disappeared when the storm began building."

"Maybe they decided to clear out since they were unsuccessful in killing you," Blackowl speculated. "They did manage to lurk around long enough to keep you on defensive alert for several days."

Raven figured Blackowl might be right on that count. More than once a fugitive he was tracking took potshots at him then cleared out. But Raven still wasn't certain what had become of Eva after she diverted the mob and freed the two men who had cheated death by dodging the noose. His worst fear was that the men had managed to turn the tables on that daring spitfire. She might be their captive by now.

If Gordon Carter was still alive and had taken Eva hostage he had several lucrative options. He could use her to control Raven or hold her for ransom. Gordon knew exactly how much she was worth to her younger sister, Lydia.

"If Eva did manage to capture the man she is chasing she might have headed for Satan's Bluff," Blackowl said, breaking into Raven's troubled thoughts. "The freight trail that connects the mining camps to Canyon Springs and Mineral Wells is traveled more frequently. For certain, she didn't reverse direction. Otherwise we would have encountered her already."

Raven nudged his paint pony past the hanging tree and set a swift pace. He glanced skyward, noting that another bank of threatening clouds had gathered northwest of the mountain peaks. This was not a good time for a rainy spell, not when Eva was who knew where, trying to apprehend Gordon single-handedly.

"Life was easier when Eva was underfoot," he muttered. "At least I could keep up with what that little daredevil was doing. Now I don't know what has happened to her."

"And that disturbs you greatly," Blackowl commented. "Be careful, cousin, your weakness is showing and that is not a good sign."

"It's only because I feel responsible for her," Raven defended himself.

"If you say so," Blackowl said, and smirked.

Raven glared at his cousin's wry grin and continued somberly. "The other possibility is that neither man, who was about to be hanged, was Gordon Carter. Perhaps *my* bushwhacker overtook Eva. He might be holding her captive. Maybe he intends to contact us so he can lure us in for the kill. In which case, Eva becomes an eyewitness who must be silenced permanently because she knows too much."

The comment wiped the teasing smile from Blackowl's bronzed features. "I will personally kill any man who harms one hair on Eva's head."

Raven arched a dark brow.

Blackowl grunted. "She is the only paleface I like besides Hoodoo."

Raven hated to admit that he'd grown overly fond of Eva himself. Which probably explained why apprehension was tying his thoughts and his emotions into knots. He wanted to strangle Eva for riding off alone to encounter any number of unexpected catastrophes. But he didn't want another man to lay a hand on her. That was his exclusive right.

Once again, he chose not to delve too deeply into why he felt so protective and possessive of her. He was afraid he wouldn't like what he discovered about his ill-fated feelings for Eva. If he knew what was good for him, he would continue to consider that hellion a royal pain in the ass.

Chapter Thirteen

Eva ducked into a grove of trees when she heard the clip-clop of horses approaching from behind her. To her dismay, Frank and Irving rode into view.

"What are you two doing here?" she asked, exasperated, as she sidestepped down to the path.

"Can't go back to Purgatory Gulch, now can we?" Frank said. "Those spiteful miners are looking to hang us."

"Besides, we figure we owe our lives to you so we're going to serve as your bodyguards until your husband catches up with you," Irving added.

"I don't need bodyguards." She had dismissed the two she had so she wouldn't have to fret about placing them in danger.

"Suit yourself, but we're still going to be your traveling companions, Eva—"

She flung up her hand to shush him. "The name is Evan Hall," she informed them. She figured the shortened version of *Evan*geline *Hall*owell would suit her charade perfectly. "No sense having a woman's name when I'm disguised as a boy."

"Makes sense," Frank agreed, smiling conspiratorially.

"Wouldn't want to accidentally reveal your identity by calling you by the wrong name."

Irving nodded pensively. "A woman in these parts has to be particularly careful."

"I intend to be."

Eva nudged the bay into a trot. She was anxious to locate Gordon. If everything went according to plan, she could have him in shackles and tossed over the back of a horse like a feed sack by sunset. The prospect inspired her. For the first time in almost a week, she had positively identified Gordon. She suspected he was also her would-be assassin who had taken more shots at her than she cared to count.

Who else could it possibly have been? she asked herself. When Gordon realized she was following him, he must have tracked her all the way to Raven's cabin. Otherwise, he would have come up the wagon trail between Canyon Springs and Satan's Bluff since it was more familiar to travelers.

Once she had Gordon in custody she would demand all the details, she mused. By nightfall, she would reach Satan's Bluff and overtake Gordon.

She glanced over her shoulder at her companions. On second thought, she might need to enlist Irving and Frank's assistance at some point in the capture. But when she had Gordon bound up like a mummy he wouldn't be any trouble.

Anticipation spiked inside her once again. She could accomplish her mission and transport Gordon to Canyon Springs tomorrow. She could turn him over to the sheriff for safekeeping and have him stand trial somewhere besides Denver to curtail unwanted publicity. Then she could take the train home to inform Lydia that justice had been served.

Eva knew she would never see Raven again, unless it

was a chance sighting from a distance, while he was in town turning over his prisoners to Marshal Doyle.

The thought caused waves of emptiness and longing to swamp her. For a woman who had sworn off men three years earlier, she had recently changed her tune. Well, she would have to change it back, she told herself resolutely. Mooning over Raven was a waste of emotion.

The sooner she accepted the fact that he didn't want or need her to make him happy the better off she would be. Still, she was going to miss him terribly. She'd miss ruffling Raven's feathers, miss their playful banter, the mental challenges and the incredible passion.

He was still her pick as a husband. Eva smiled ruefully, knowing that if Raven ever decided to take a wife she wouldn't even be on his list of prospective brides.

She glanced skyward, noting that another storm was building on the horizon. She had the uneasy feeling that she wouldn't be able to dodge this one. Hopefully, she would have Gordon bound and gagged by the time the storm descended on Satan's Bluff.

Determined of purpose, she quickened her pace to lead the way up the steep mountain trail.

Two hours later Eva watched the storm clouds form an ominous line from northeast to southwest. Above the lofty summits lightning flashed and thunder rumbled. If she planned to apprehend Gordon before the storm descended, she needed to locate him quickly.

She studied the wide, well-traveled road that angled down the slope toward Mineral Wells and Canyon Springs. To the right was the narrow trail that she presumed led uphill to Hell's Corner—the third raucous boomtown in the mining district.

Ducking her head to conceal her identity, Eva rode into the community that was home to hundreds of individual prospectors.

Satan's Bluff was a rough-and-tumble town that sat on an elevated cliff overlooking a craggy canyon. Two meandering streams divided the canyon. They were lined with tents and wooden lean-tos. Like its sister city, only one street ran through the middle of town. Log cabins, false-front buildings and oversize tents lined the street. Banjo music filled the air and it seemed that most of the miners had called it quits for the day, in anticipation of the storm. They had congregated to take their leisure in the saloons, gaming halls and cafés.

Eva glanced from one hitching post to the next in search of the brown horse Gordon had been riding when he high-tailed it out of Purgatory Gulch. She spotted the horse in front of a tent that served as a gaming hall. She scanned the area, wondering if the soiled doves had also set up shop in this community. No doubt, Gordon would become an eager client after he drank his fill in one of the nameless saloons.

She panned the street again. Sure enough, three shanties—connected by a boardwalk and sporting red-globe lanterns—sat on the edge of town. The small red-light district was butted up against a steep, rock-strewn hill.

"Now what, *Evan?*" Frank asked, grinning conspiratorially. "If you don't mind, I think I'll wet my whistle and try my hand at monte. Will you be okay for a while?"

"I'll be fine," she insisted, anxious to be rid of the gamblers.

This was her personal crusade, after all.

"The first order of business should be to trade or *lose* the horses you rode in on," she reminded them. "Eventually someone from Purgatory Gulch will show up here and remember you're the ones who were sitting on those borrowed sorrel horses and were about to swing from ropes."

Both men tugged nervously at the collars of their shirts. "Point taken," they mumbled in unison.

"And it wouldn't hurt to dress like the locals," she advised. "I'll be too busy to save your necks this evening."

Frank stared somberly at her. "Be careful, you hear?"

"I will," she assured them before she rode over to the dry goods store to purchase canned food for her supper.

Eva also purchased a chain and leather straps to serve as manacles for her prisoner. Once she captured Gordon, she would find an out-of-the-way place to stash him for the night. First thing in the morning, she would head down the mountain to Canyon Springs.

It was almost dark when Eva stationed herself outside the gaming hall where Gordon was entertaining himself—on the money he had extorted from Lydia, no doubt. She conjured up and discarded several ideas to entrap him. Shooting him out of his chair held the most appeal but she figured she would be swinging from whatever passed as the hangman's tree in Satan's Bluff by midnight.

When a haggard-looking man, whom she guessed to be in his late fifties, hobbled past she reached out to tap him on the shoulder. "Sir, I need a favor."

The stoop-shouldered man with leathery features glanced over at her. He arched a curious brow as he leaned on his makeshift cane that was carved from a tree branch. Eva had noted earlier that most miners were younger than forty. No doubt, the grueling physical labor required to chisel gold from rock was a strain for older men. Most of them became freighters, café owners or shop managers.

"What is it, boy?" the man said in a wheezy voice.

Unlike the burly Irish saloonkeeper who had demanded

payment for information, this man didn't thrust out his gnarled hand, palm up. Eva felt exceptionally generous so she shook his hand and passed him a large banknote.

His eyes widened in surprise. "You don't have to—"

"I want to," she interrupted. "I need you to deliver a message to the man who is sitting at the corner table." She craned her neck around the tent flap to single out Gordon. "Tell him that one of the ladies of the evening saw him ride into town and she wishes to make his acquaintance."

The crusty old prospector looked at Gordon then squinted speculatively at her, causing deep grooves to wrinkle his forehead. "Are you sure you want me to do that? If you're out for some sort of revenge, which I expect you are, you might be wading into deep water."

"I have two assistants." Sort of, she amended silently.

If things went sour, she could prevail on Frank and Irving to assist her. However, nothing would please her more than to apprehend Gordon by herself—and she would never let him hear the end of it.

"All right then," the miner said finally, and nodded his shaggy head. "I'll direct the gent to the shanties on the edge of town."

When the prospector hobbled off, Eva tugged on the bay's reins and led him toward the poorly constructed shanties. With her pistol tucked in the waistband of the doeskin breeches, she flattened herself against the outer wall and lingered in the shadows to await Gordon's arrival.

Two minutes later she saw Gordon exit the gaming hall and stare at the three red-globe lanterns that hung outside the shanties. He rubbed his hand absently over his chest and belly then slicked back his hair. Eva grinned wickedly, certain the voodoo magic was at work, thanks to Hoodoo's curse.

As Gordon approached, she tried to recall every word

of instruction and precaution Blackowl had tried to pound in her head during her crash-course training. She waited, her senses on high alert, her heart thumping in her chest, her hand folded around the butt of her pistol.

The reckoning, she mused as she watched Gordon's swaggering approach. This bastard was long overdue.

Raven rode hell-for-leather, pausing only to let his horse catch its breath when absolutely necessary. The paint pony's stamina didn't match Buck's and the thought made Raven lament losing such a good horse.

The sense of urgency driving him to reach Satan's Bluff was born of his concern and the uncertainty about whom Eva had confronted at the would-be hanging. Her good deed might have backfired in her face, especially if the men realized she was posing as a boy. Either that or Eva had located Gordon and who knew what kind of trouble she faced.

To make matters worse, the line of storms building in the northwest looked ominous. Lightning flickered in the distance. The unsettled weather was as disruptive as the unsettling emotions Eva had touched off inside him since she exploded into his life with the force of a cannonball.

Raven breathed a gusty sigh of relief when he spotted the glowing lanterns on the bluff. This place was aptly named, he mused as he pulled back on the reins, allowing the winded skewbald pony to slow to a walk. The golden lantern light reminded him of coals burning against the backdrop of mammoth slabs of rock that jutted helter-skelter from the mountains. He likened it to the flaming embers in the white man's image of hell. Black clouds billowed up like angry fists and lightning bolts struck down the tormented souls congregated on the devil's playground.

"Getting a mite philosophical, aren't you?" Raven scoffed at himself.

"Come again?" Blackowl stared quizzically at him as he eased his horse up beside him.

Raven angled his head toward the mining camp perched on the windswept bluff. "If there is a devil, I swear he's in attendance here tonight."

Blackowl nodded. "Evil spirits seem to be swirling about. Makes me twitchy. I have a bad feeling about tonight."

"So do I." Raven urged his pony into a trot. "I want Eva under wing before hell breaks loose."

Eva waited nervously as Gordon strutted up to the door of one of the brothels and raised his hand to knock. She pounced from the shadows and rammed the barrel of the pistol into the back of his neck.

"Don't move," she growled menacingly as she dug the pistol barrel a little deeper into his flesh. "Hands up where I can see them, Gordon."

He slowly raised his arms, as she demanded. "Eva? Is that you?"

"None other. Too bad your aim was off the mark when you tried to bushwhack me repeatedly. But at this close range, I doubt I'll miss. One careless move, Gordon, and you'll be lying in a pool of your own blood."

When he tried to shift sideways, she kicked him in the back of the knees as Blackowl taught her. Gordon grunted uncomfortably then stiffened when she shifted the pistol barrel to the base of his skull.

"Lydia sends her warmest regards, of course." Eva took grand satisfaction in taunting the devious bastard. "She also knows you lied to her when you tried to turn her against me."

"I was just annoyed at you because you rejected my affectionate attention," Gordon had the nerve to say. "You were the one who interested me. Lydia was my second choice."

"Don't insult my intelligence," she snapped as she forced him to walk backward with her.

She berated herself for not having the forethought to grab the leather strips from her satchel so she could shackle Gordon immediately. She had to back him toward her horse—and hope he didn't attempt to make a break for it. Keeping that in mind, Eva paid close attention to his every move.

"It really is you that I care about," Gordon purred.

"Shooting at me is a strange way of showing it," she scoffed. "You have no affection for anyone but yourself. I've dealt with conniving suitors like you countless times before. You are just a more obnoxious version of the others."

When he tried to shift sideways abruptly to catch her off guard Eva was ready and waiting. She whacked him upside the head to discourage him from trying to escape.

"Ouch! Damn you, bitch!" he snarled as she forced him to take another reluctant step backward while she remained as close as his own shadow.

"Ah, so now your true feelings for me come pouring out," she said, and smirked.

"That's right," he muttered bitterly. "The truth is that you're a royal pain in the ass."

"So I've been told," she said, undaunted. "I knew you resented me because I cautioned Lydia against placing too much trust in your premeditated charm and empty words of affection for her."

Keeping the pistol firmly imbedded in the back of his skull, Eva eased up beside the bay gelding. Lightning flashed overhead, making it easier to see what she was doing while she dug into her satchel with her free hand to retrieve the leather strips.

She heard the clatter of approaching horses but she didn't look back to see who had arrived at such a swift pace. Her first order of business was to bind Gordon's hands. Then she would summon Irving and Frank to help her toss Gordon over the back of his own horse and tie him in place.

When Gordon moved suddenly, trying to duck beneath the bay gelding's belly and escape, Eva grabbed a handful of his hair and jerked him upright. *"Stand still!"* she snapped harshly.

"Eva?"

She made the crucial mistake of glancing over her shoulder when Raven's deep baritone voice erupted unexpectedly behind her. Gordon took full advantage of her distraction. He elbowed her in the side of the head, momentarily stunning her. Then he wrenched the pistol from her hand.

She recovered her senses quickly enough to attempt to kick him where he could be hurt the worst, just as Blackowl had taught her. Unfortunately, Gordon jackknifed his body and she kicked nothing but air.

Wild fury blazed through her when Gordon spun around to hook his arm around her neck and yank her roughly against him. He had deftly turned the tables on her and now *she* was the one who had a pistol barrel digging into her temple. The fact that she had been so close to apprehending him single-handedly infuriated her to no end!

Thunder boomed overhead as Eva stared into Raven's face. He looked like murderous fury, which is exactly how she felt.

"Let her go, James," Raven snarled viciously.

Eva blinked, bemused. "This is Gordon Carter. He's the man who extorted money from my sister."

"Hello, Raven. Blackowl," Gordon said, grinning triumphantly. "Long time no see."

"Not long enough, James," Raven said scathingly.

"James who?" Eva demanded, baffled and confused.

Raven had assumed that his would-be assassin was one of Widow Flanders's hirelings or one of Buster Flanders's vindictive kinfolk. He never dreamed that his hated stepbrother had taken a new identity to extort money from unsuspecting young women. But here the bastard was, clamping Eva against him like a protective shield and holding a gun to her head.

Outraged frustration poured over Raven as he stared down at James. Eva was at his mercy and James was gloating the way he always did after he had successfully played a cruel prank on Raven when they were teenagers.

"Learning that you and Gordon Carter are one and the same explains a lot," Raven growled. "No doubt, you saw your chance to take potshots at both of us. Of course, you were always a lousy shot."

"You would have thought that my stint in the army, fighting Indians, would have sharpened my aim. But I still managed to kill my share of your heathen kinfolk," James said maliciously. "Of course, I pretended every one of those savages I slaughtered was you and your full-blood cousin."

"How ironic," Raven countered acrimoniously. "Every worthless criminal I've planted facing west and X-ed out reminded me of you."

James flashed a goading smile. "Now here we are, with me holding the upper hand." He inclined his head toward Eva. "I figured this spiteful termagant would come charging after me. Or, at the very least, send someone to track me. I made it easy for her to pick up my trail by leaving the buggy behind. Imagine my delight when I had the unexpected bonus of getting my half-breed stepbrother and his redskin cousin in the bargain. We can finally settle the score between us."

"Who were the men you disposed of so you could switch clothes, horses and mules constantly?" Eva wanted to know. "I plan to settle the score for *them* as well as *Lydia*."

James scoffed haughtily. "You're in no position to settle anything. Besides, the hapless miners I shoved off cliffs won't be missed…. Hold still, damn it!"

Raven tensed when Eva kicked James/Gordon in the shin. He gave her a hard shake to bring her under control but she was in a fit of temper and fought him until he hit her in the head with the pistol barrel. It took every ounce of self-restraint Raven could muster to squelch the wild urge to launch himself off his horse and pounce on James, consequences be damned. But at the same time, he didn't dare place Eva's life at an even greater risk, for fear he'd have to watch James shoot her.

This time James was too damn close to miss.

"What do you want, James?" he sneered hatefully.

"To walk away from here unscathed, for starters." James shifted his forearm upward to place it solidly against Eva's windpipe, making her gasp to catch her breath. "And of course, I already mailed off a note to Lydia from the stage station. I demanded a ransom for the return of her pesky sister. Whether or not I was able to overtake Eva along the way didn't really matter," he added with a careless shrug. "Lydia won't know the difference. She should receive my ransom demands tonight or tomorrow at the latest."

"Bastard," Eva wheezed with what little breath James granted her.

When James grinned smugly, Raven gnashed his teeth.

Again, he had to resist the intense urge to leap off his horse and go for his stepbrother's throat.

Even as a teenager, Raven had detested that haughty expression James wore so well. His stepbrother's animosity had always been as vicious as it was obvious. Raven had left his father's home in Pueblo, hoping he would never have to see James Archer again.

No such luck. The son of a bitch had reappeared and had disrupted Eva's life. He had caused as much turmoil for Eva as he had for Raven.

"I'll be your hostage," Raven volunteered. "Let Eva go."

James barked a caustic laugh. "How noble of you. You must have become sentimentally attached to this feisty hellion. Don't know why though. She has too much spunk and spirit to bother with, believe me. I got fed up with her several times while charming her sister into doing my bidding. But she's worth a hell of a lot of money to me. Half-breed bounty hunters, on the other hand, are worth nothing to anyone," he added cuttingly.

The insult rolled over Raven like water down a duck's back. He didn't give a damn what James thought of him. Besides, there were too many other emotions bombarding him at the moment. He felt powerless and frustrated—and maddeningly guilty because he had unintentionally diverted Eva's attention while she had the drop on this ruthless bastard. *He* was the reason that she was a defenseless captive.

When Raven instinctively eased his horse forward, James jerked Eva back a step. "Stay where you are. I mean it, Raven," he snapped sharply. "That goes for you, too, Blackowl. If you don't think I'll shoot this troublesome daredevil you are mistaken. A wounded captive is less trouble to control than a healthy one."

Teeth clenched, while dozens of vile curses danced on the tip of his tongue, Raven watched his stepbrother lash Eva's wrists together—one-handed. He didn't make the mistake of removing the pistol from the side of Eva's head for even a second, much to Raven's dismay.

"I told Lydia to drop off the money at the stage station where I left her buggy," James informed him as he wrapped another leather strap around Eva's neck like a dog collar.

Cold fury coursed through Raven's veins when James twisted the strap, demonstrating how easily he could choke her if she offered the slightest resistance.

"If you want to see this smart-mouth vixen alive then *you* will fetch the ransom money for me and leave it on the ridge by Seven Falls. You have three days to make the trip. After that…" He shrugged negligently. "I can't promise Eva will still be alive and kicking if you don't meet my terms. She's a lot of trouble, after all, and I'm short on patience."

Raven cursed James to hell and back while his stepbrother tossed Eva over the bay's back. Before Raven could go for his pistol to take a shot that was risky at best, James bounded up behind her then jerked her up in front of him like a shield once again.

The bay gelding shifted beneath the additional weight of the second rider, but he quieted when he turned his head to sniff Eva's leg. This was one time Raven wished the contrary bay would buck and send James flying through the air. Raven was pretty sure he could draw his pistol and fire two shots into the bastard before he hit the ground.

"If you can distract him for a moment I'll try to wing him," Blackowl said in Cheyenne.

"Speak English!" James ordered brusquely. "And no funny business or she's dead. You understand, Raven? No matter what else happens here tonight, *she dies,* if for no other reason than *you* want her to survive."

A sense of impending doom descended on Raven as raindrops splattered around him. Even though the bay gelding tossed his head when James jerked roughly on the reins, the horse backed behind the shanty so James could blend into the inky shadows.

"Three days," James called out in the darkness. "That's all the time you get."

"Tell Lydia that I said she is not to give this son of a bitch one red cent—awk!"

Raven cringed when Eva's voice fizzled out. No doubt, James had twisted her leather collar, making it difficult for her to breathe or speak.

"I hated that bastard the first time I met him," Raven muttered to Blackowl.

"So did I," Blackowl muttered back. "Now what do you want to do?"

"Besides skin him alive, you mean?"

"That goes without saying," Blackowl snorted. "Unfortunately, that will have to wait."

Never in his adult life had Raven felt so helpless or vulnerable. He wanted to race after James, who skulked along the back side of the bordellos and shops in town, making himself an impossible target of gunfire. Ordinarily Raven's policy was to give chase, despite the voiced threats. He was usually able to strike fear in the hearts of his fugitives, even when they held a hostage.

However, this was different. This was personal. His adversary was James Archer, who was using Eva as his shield of defense.

Raven and James shared a mutual hatred that dated back fifteen years. If James suspected that Raven had developed a personal interest in Eva then he would delight in using it against him. It was next to impossible for Raven to be objective when every troubled thought and turbulent emotion centered on ensuring Eva's safety.

Plus, she was daring and defiant enough to take dangerous risks, he reminded himself. That scared the living daylights out of him.

He sat atop his horse, pounded by rain. He was uncertain what to do next, and he had never had trouble acting under pressure—until now. Raven was shocked to realize that he was *terrified*. He'd almost forgotten what that felt like. But he remembered now.

Chapter Fourteen

"I can follow the bastard at a distance to see where he stashes Eva," Blackowl volunteered as he stared into the rain and the darkness. "You can fetch the ransom money from the stage station and bring it to your cabin."

Raven shook himself from his tormented trance. He couldn't leave Eva behind. Already he was haunted by the fear that he had seen her alive for the very last time.

He forced himself to draw in a fortifying breath, then another. "You go fetch the ransom from Lydia," Raven requested. "James is my stepbrother. I'll track the spiteful son of a bitch myself."

"Raven? Is that you?"

He dragged his gaze away from the shadowed silhouettes in the mist then half twisted in the saddle to see Frank Albers and Irving Jarmon trotting toward him.

"Glad you're here," Frank said, out of breath. "I guess you finally caught up with your wife. We owed her a favor so we kept an eye on her as best we could until you got here."

Raven divided his attention between his fleeing stepbrother and the two gamblers he'd met on the stagecoach. "What favor are you talking about?"

"We nearly got ourselves hanged this afternoon," Irving explained. "Eva came to our rescue. When she said she was following the man who took potshots at her, we came along."

"*You* were the two men about to be hanged?" Blackowl asked.

Remembering his manners, Raven gestured toward his cousin. "Frank Albers and Irving Jarmon, this is Blackowl."

The men nodded in greeting then Frank glanced this way and that. "Where's Eva?"

"Kidnapped," Raven growled sourly. "Why weren't you helping her apprehend the bushwhacker after she saved your necks?"

"We offered," Irving defended quickly. "She said she'd give a shout if she needed our help."

Raven squeezed his eyes shut and cursed the image that rose in his mind's eye. Eva was entirely too independent. Hell, she even lit out from the cabin without waiting for him and Blackowl. *Why?*

"What can we do to help?" Frank asked earnestly.

"I'm not sure you can because I have no guarantee that two cheating gamblers who barely missed a lynching are trustworthy enough to fetch the ransom money that Eva's abductor demands," Raven grumbled.

Frank squared his thin-bladed shoulders and met Raven's hard stare. "I may be a lot of things, Raven, but I honor a debt when someone spares my life. If you want me to deliver ransom money to save Eva then I'll do it."

"And I'll help him," Irving chimed in. "We *owe* her and that makes all the difference."

Raven cast a quick glance toward the far end of town as raindrops continued to soak his clothing, leaving him cold, inside and out. "All right. We can use the assistance. Blackowl will explain the details of the demands and give you directions to my cabin." He glanced at his cousin. "You can catch up with me later. I'll make sure you have a trail to follow."

Raven turned to bear down on the gamblers like the dark angel of doom. "If you try to double-cross me for the ransom money I will personally hunt you down," he snarled.

"And I'll be right beside him," Blackowl vowed fiercely.

"There will be no place you can hide that I won't find you." Same went for James Archer, but Raven hadn't had the chance to issue that deadly promise. "Do I make myself clear?"

Irving and Frank both gulped hard then nodded their heads vigorously.

Assured that the two men knew he was dead serious, Raven reined his paint pony through the middle of town. He didn't slow his pace, just dodged the drunken pedestrians who stumbled around in the rain. Raven wasn't sure where James planned to stash his captive, but he intended to be nearby, waiting for his stepbrother to make a careless mistake.

Swearing profusely, Raven focused on the fleeing twosome illuminated by a flash of lightning. Guilt and regret pummeled him as he trailed them at a discreet distance. If he hadn't called out to Eva at that critical moment, she wouldn't be embroiled in this disaster. Unfortunately, he had been so relieved to find her that he had reacted without thinking.

Then his worst nightmare unfolded when he realized his stepbrother was using the name of Gordon Carter to extort money from unsuspecting women.

"Damn it to hell," he muttered as he watched the twosome gallop uphill toward Hell's Corner. The prospect of seeing Eva perish at James Archer's spiteful hands drove Raven as close to loco as he ever wanted to come.

* * *

Lydia silently fumed as she paced the floorboards. She reread the ransom note delivered a quarter of an hour earlier that evening. "Curse you to hell and back, Gordon!"

Dear God, she thought apprehensively. Eva was in fatal danger because of Lydia's foolish romantic impulsiveness. It was bad enough that she had fallen victim to Gordon's scheme. He had humiliated her to the extreme. But to place Eva's life in jeopardy in order to avenge Lydia's embarrassment? That was unacceptable. Lydia couldn't bear the thought of losing her sister as a sacrifice for restoring her pride and honor.

Whirling around, Lydia darted toward the back door then jogged to the stables to fetch a mount. She hesitated, uncertain which horse to ride since that low-down lying extortionist she thought she loved had stolen Hodge. Finally, Lydia decided to take the spirited black gelding that was Eva's favorite mount.

Wearing the same male attire Eva favored, Lydia rode bareback to the Philberts' estate. Despite the late hour, she hammered loudly on the door. Roger appeared a few moments later with Sadie a step behind him.

"Are you all right?" he asked in concern as he surveyed what had become her everyday attire.

"No," she muttered angrily.

"Come in, Lydia." Sadie swerved around her brother to grab her arm and guide her to the parlor. "What's wrong now?"

"Only everything!" she wailed. "I've killed my sister!"

"What!" the Philbert twins howled in horror.

Lydia thrust the ransom note at Roger. "I might as well have killed her. Eva struck off to avenge my humiliation of falling prey to that shyster who stole my money and left me stranded in the middle of nowhere." The embarrassing tale poured out of her in fits and starts—in between inconsolable sobs. "Now Gordon has somehow managed to take Eva hostage. I have no idea where they are or what happened to that bounty hunter she married. He might even be in on this scheme for all I know!"

Panic and fear gushed through her, causing the room to spin wildly around her. Lydia staggered shakily then clutched Roger's arm for support. "I've lost them all. First Mama then Papa and now Eva," she whimpered desolately.

Before she wilted into a heap on the floor Roger scooped her up in his arms and carried her to the sofa. By the time he laid her down, she was bleeding so many tears that the twins were a blurred image swimming before her eyes.

"Everything is going to be fine," Sadie tried to reassure her as she patted her arm.

"No, it won't," Lydia said between shuddering gulps. "I've lost everyone I care deeply about."

"We'll find Eva." Roger handed her a glass of brandy. "Drink this. It will make you feel better."

"Nothing will make me feel better," she muttered but she took a sip nonetheless—and nearly choked on the strong liquor. Then she took another drink that went down easier the second time so she helped herself to another.

"According to this missive, you are to deliver thirty thousand dollars to the same stage station where I picked up your abandoned buggy," Roger said.

Lydia knew he was trying to distract her from bawling her head off all over again. It worked to some extent, but she was so frightened and concerned about Eva's safety that she was still shaking uncontrollably. She reminded herself that Eva wouldn't fall apart like this and neither should she. But her sister was the one who usually took charge. She *had* to pull herself together, for Eva's sake!

"First thing in the morning Roger will go to your bank and withdraw the money, won't you, Roger?" Sadie insisted.

"Certainly." He smiled encouragingly as he clasped Lydia's hand tightly in his. "Then I will ride out to the stage station to drop off the pouch of money at the designated location."

Lydia wiped the tears from her cheeks then levered herself up on a wobbly elbow. "I'm coming with you."

"Whatever you wish," Roger agreed. "But for now, you should get some sleep. You can stay with us tonight."

"No!" Lydia bolted upright. "I have to be at home, in case I receive more instructions. In case…" She flicked her wrist to dismiss the grim thought that descended on her. She might receive the dreadful news that Eva had not survived this calamity. A calamity that Lydia had caused.

The thought put her in tears again, despite her attempt to become as strong as Eva had always been in a crisis.

"Fine, then we will stay with you tonight." Roger hoisted Lydia to her feet. He turned back to his sister. "Sadie, can you pack an overnight bag while I fetch the buggy?"

When Sadie dashed off, Roger led Lydia outside. She was too distraught to object to being led around like a child and carted home. Eva wouldn't have stood for it because she was the strongest, most determined female Lydia had ever met. And by damned, Lydia would follow her example to do her sister proud. No more dramatics. No more useless tears. She was already the spitting image of her older sister and she would learn to match her determination and fortitude, too.

Lydia inhaled a restorative breath and squared her shoulders while she waited for Roger to hitch up the buggy.

During the short ride home Lydia marshaled her self-confidence and courage. If she had the opportunity to confront Gordon, she would deal severely with that conniving bastard. She would repay him for every humiliation she had suffered and for every ounce of concern for Eva's welfare.

She felt ten times better when she visualized taking a shotgun in hand and blasting that scoundrel full of buckshot. As Eva was fond of saying, most men had no particular use other than for target practice. Which reminded her that she should save a couple of bullets for that incompetent bounty hunter who had married Eva. Apparently, he wasn't man enough to protect her from harm—or he was using her for his own devious purposes.

Eva cursed herself up one side and down the other as Gordon—or rather James, she silently corrected—carted her uphill during the rainstorm. If she hadn't become distracted by the unexpected sound of Raven's voice, none of this would have happened.

Why had he shown up in Satan's Bluff? she wondered. Because he had three bench warrants in his saddlebag and he decided to track down the men for bounty? Or was it because he was worried about her?

Well, it didn't matter now, she supposed. She wouldn't see him again so she couldn't ask what motivated him. Despite her objections, he was most likely on his way to retrieve the ransom money James Archer demanded.

The thought of her conniving captor made her furious all over again. Her future—or lack thereof—was grim. So why should she be an accommodating hostage? She wouldn't be rewarded for good behavior, so why should she submit to this heartless scoundrel?

When she squirmed restlessly on the saddle, James gave

the leather choke necklace a painful twist. Cursing him soundly, Eva struggled to draw breath. She retaliated by up-raising her bound hands to clobber James in the face.

"You vicious little hellion," he growled as he held his bleeding nose. "I ought to—"

Sizzling lightning flared in the darkness and struck a tree on the west side of the trail, interrupting his threat. Deafening thunder exploded overhead. Eva took it as a sign to attempt escape. She knew how the bay gelding would react to the sound effects of the storm if she didn't pat his neck reassuringly. Therefore, she made no effort to calm him, just waited for him to bolt sideways in alarm.

The instant the wild-eyed horse reared up Eva flung herself from the saddle, catching James off guard. She bit back a wail of pain when she landed on her shoulder, but she rolled away from the flailing hooves before her horse unintentionally trampled her.

James swore furiously as he struggled to keep his seat on the bucking horse. When he swung his arm wildly, slapping the horse on the head, she cursed his cruelty and remem-bered how he had beaten Hodge. Eva silently cheered when the bay gelding ducked his head between his front legs and kicked up his back hooves again. The sight of James soaring through the air to splatter into the mud was gratifying.

Taking advantage of James's graceless sprawl, Eva bounded to her feet and raced off in the direction they had come.

"Come back here, damn you!" James roared as he scraped himself off the ground to give chase.

When he snarled so close behind her, she wheeled abruptly to strike him with her bound hands again. She heard the crunch of bone and knew she had broken his nose with the hard blow.

He howled in outrage, cursed her foully and covered his nose with his hand.

Eva darted sideways when he tried to backhand her. The glancing blow tossed her off balance momentarily but she uprighted herself. When he grabbed her forearm, she wheeled around to kick him squarely in the crotch.

James gasped in pained fury as he hit his knees. He stopped chasing her all right. She had granted herself a head start. But he resorted to firing wildly with the six-shooter. Frantic, Eva ducked then glanced around to determine where her horse had gotten off to. Even when a flash of lightning illuminated the rain-drenched trail, she didn't see her horse.

Curse it, Raven was right, she realized. He claimed a horse wasn't completely trained until it came when you whistled. If the horse could answer her call she could leave James far behind—and run right over the heartless bastard on her way by.

Her spiteful thoughts scattered when another shot rang out. Eva flattened herself on the ground—a moment too late. The bullet grazed her shoulder, the same one she had injured when she leaped off her horse. Despite the burning pain, Eva surged to her feet and raced downhill as fast as her legs would carry her.

"I'll shoot to kill!" James raged over the sound of pelting rain. "Don't think I won't!"

Eva didn't slow her swift pace. Although James wasn't a particularly good marksman, she wasn't taking any chances. But she did make the careless mistake of glancing over her shoulder to see where he was while she was running at full speed.

She didn't see the oversize rock on the trail until she stumbled over it. She tried to hurl herself backward to prevent pitching over the crumbling edge of the road. Despite her vow to keep silent so she wouldn't give away her location to James, a wild shriek flew from her lips when she tumbled down the steep slope.

Desperate, she tried to retreat but her forward momentum left her pinwheeling over boulders and under-brush. Hands still tied, she rolled over the sharp rocks and tried to protect her head from a brain-scrambling blow.

Lightning flashed again and thundered rolled. Eva slammed into an unyielding boulder then moaned when blinding pain exploded in her skull. Her last thought before she blacked out was that James wouldn't be able to find her in the darkness, not without risking a painful fall himself.

Raven felt his heart slam into his ribs—and stick there—when he heard gunshots in the distance. When Eva's wild shriek echoed in the darkness, his heart stopped beating altogether.

Frantic, he nudged his horse and trotted up the sloppy trail, wishing he could call out to Eva but refusing to alert James to his whereabouts. If James commenced shooting wildly at him, he might hit Eva—if he hadn't already.

When lightning flickered overhead, Raven spotted his stepbrother hobbling up the trail on foot. Eva was nowhere in sight. Conflicting emotion rippled through Raven. He longed to chase down James to avenge Eva, who had risked life and limb to avenge her sister. Not to mention that Raven wanted to skin the son of a bitch alive for taking Eva hostage.

Yet, Raven didn't dare leave the area until he knew what had happened to Eva. She could be anywhere in the wild tumble of boulders, trees and underbrush. She could find herself at the mercy of vicious predators and she might be seriously injured already.

Raven didn't know what had happened to her and the uncertainty was killing him, bit by excruciating bit. All he knew was that she had to be somewhere between where he sat on his horse and where James had disappeared around the bend of the trail. Where the blood-red bay had gotten off to was anybody's guess…

The image of the horse Eva called Hodge popped instantly to mind and he wondered if James had forced Eva and her mount off the road and left them tumbling down the jagged slopes. James had disposed of a few miners and their horses in the same heartless manner already. The thought of Eva lying in a broken heap beside her horse tormented him beyond measure.

"Eva!" he bellowed at the top of his lungs.

He waited anxiously but there was nothing but the sound of whipping wind and rain. Feeling helpless and frustrated, Raven dismounted to lead his horse to the nearest tree for shelter. Unless Eva called out to him there was little to do but wait until daylight.

Then he suddenly remembered the bottle of whiskey he had tucked in his saddlebag. Hurriedly he grabbed the bottle and dug out one of his shirts. Groping in the darkness, he found a tree branch that would serve as a makeshift torch. He wrapped his shirt around the top of the branch then doused it with whiskey. Careful to keep the match dry, he lit the improvised torch and watched it flare to life.

Fortunately, the storm let up gradually as it swept southeast. Pounding rain became intermittent sprinkles. Raven scanned the terrain. One side of the trail sloped upward and Raven noticed the tree that had been struck by lightning. He was greatly relieved when he saw the bay gelding, its reins dangling, munching on weeds. The other side of the trail tumbled into a labyrinth of deep crevices, boulders and scrub bushes.

Instinct sent him striding across the path to sidestep down the rocks, hoping he could locate Eva before his torch burned itself out. He called her name repeatedly but received nothing for his efforts.

"Raven? Is that you?" Blackowl shouted in Cheyenne.

His shoulders slump in relief. Two sets of eyes were better than one. "Down here!"

"Where is that sidewinder James Archer?" Blackowl asked as he appeared above Raven on the edge of the path. "Dead, I hope."

"No such luck. He ran off," Raven muttered.

"Why'd you let him get away?" Blackowl asked, baffled.

"Because Eva is out here somewhere and I can't find her," he breathed as Blackowl veered around the obstacles to join him. "I saw the flash of gunshots in the darkness then I heard her scream, but I couldn't see what happened." He handed the torch to his cousin. "Light the way while I search."

"Paleface!" Blackowl shouted. "Where are you?"

With meticulous precision, Raven and Blackowl reconnoitered the area. After thirty frustrating minutes, they heard a faint moan below them on the hillside. Raven scrambled toward the sound, calling Eva's name every step of the way. He stopped short when the torchlight glowed down on the deep crevice that had practically swallowed her up.

"Eva? Can you tell how badly you're hurt?"

"No," she mumbled dazedly. "I hurt all over and I'm not sure which pain is serious." There was a slight pause then she said, "What are you doing here?"

He sent her a withering glance. Did she really think he would abandon her to his stepbrother? "I don't negotiate with kidnappers. I don't follow their commands, either. Besides, I was worried about you."

"Oh, well that's nice to know."

Eva smiled, despite the pounding ache in her head and the throb of pain in places she wasn't aware she had. Raven had come after her, bless him. She had figured she was as good as dead after her hapless fall down the mountain at night.

When she took inventory of her scrapes and aches, she realized her hands were bloody from checking the gunshot wound on her shoulder and her arm was stinging something fierce. It hurt to breathe and she figured that couldn't be good. Overall, she felt battered, bruised and exhausted. Nonetheless, she was so relieved to see Raven that she wanted to fling her arms around his neck and hug him for rescuing her from certain death.

As he came toward her, it dawned on her that he wasn't alone. She saw Blackowl holding a torch over his head. When he saw her wave at him, he scurried downhill.

Raven sank down on his haunches to reach out to her, but Eva winced when she tried to grab his offered hand. She heard him swear foully when the torchlight spotlighted her, revealing the bloodstains that trickled across her throat.

"The son of a bitch shot you!" Raven growled in outrage.

"That's because I broke his nose and kicked him in the crotch, as Blackowl instructed," she panted. "When I made a run for it in the darkness he fired blindly. I don't think the wound is deep. It just burns like hell blazing and so does my arm."

"I don't care if all you sustained was a scratch," Raven muttered bitterly. "James will pay dearly, count on it."

When Blackowl joined him on the ridge to offer a helping hand, Raven crawled into the crevice. Eva whimpered slightly when he hooked his arm around her waist to drag her up beside him.

"You scared me half to death," he murmured against the side of her neck.

"What? Over a piddling little fall down the mountain? That's child's play compared to what you and Blackowl endure on a regular basis."

She saw him crack a faint smile, saw those hypnotic green-gold eyes glow in the torch light. "You can drop that tough-as-nails act, sweetheart. I know you're hurting. It's okay. I won't think any less of you if you want to bawl your head off…"

His voice trailed off as he brushed his hand over her hip. "Blackowl, hold the light directly over my head."

"What's wrong?" Blackowl asked worriedly as he leaned out as far as he could to illuminate the V-shaped crevice Eva had fallen into. Then he barked a laugh. "Like father like daughter, I see."

Bemused, Eva watched Raven rub his fingers together then she saw the golden flakes sparkling in the light. "Gold?" she chirped, incredulous.

"Yep," Raven replied. "The rich just keep getting richer. The rain exposed the vein of ore and it stuck to your doehide clothing."

"I suppose you've heard the tale about how my father's stubborn mule suddenly set his feet and caused him to tumble downhill. He unknowingly unearthed a bonanza while he was trying to scrabble uphill," she said as he lifted her carefully.

"I hadn't heard the tale," Blackowl said, and snorted. "Typical paleface. Wandering around Cheyenne haunts and taking what doesn't belong to him."

Eva gasped in pain when Raven handed her off to

Blackowl. Her ribs throbbed painfully and she struggled to breathe. She tried valiantly not to cry, but tears slid down her muddy cheeks nonetheless.

"Did you find my horse?" she panted raggedly. "James didn't kill him, too, did he?"

"Not to worry, the bay gelding is grazing on the west side of the trail," Raven reported.

"And James? Did you apprehend him?" she asked eagerly.

"No, I came looking for you first and he ran off on foot."

Eva should have been pleased to learn she was his first concern. And she was, but having that slippery bastard race off with no more than a broken nose and a wet set of clothes offended her strong sense of fair play. She had yet to accomplish her mission. Now she would have to contend with injuries that would slow her down.

"He can't be too far ahead of us," she mumbled as she held her throbbing rib cage. "We can still—"

"*No.*" Raven's tone of voice brooked no argument. "First things first. We will treat your wounds and make camp here for the night."

She expelled a sigh that indicated her displeasure.

Raven curled his hand beneath her skinned chin and uplifted her gaze to his. "James won't go free, I promise you, Evangeline. He will answer to me for abusing you."

"No, he will answer to me for humiliating my sister."

"You two can argue later," Blackowl said dismissively. "First we tend your injuries and mark your claim."

"Ouch!" Eva hissed in agony when Raven lifted her into his arms again then strode to the opposite side of the road. "You don't happen to have some of that Indian tea with you, do you?"

"Something better," Blackowl answered for Raven as he hurried over to dig into his saddlebags.

He returned a moment later to place strange-tasting seedpods between her lips. "Chew vigorously," he instructed.

Eva did as he asked then sipped from the canteen Raven held up to her. The foul-tasting pods prompted her to take another large gulp of water.

"I need to look at your shoulder," Raven said before he turned to Blackowl, who had spread a pallet beneath the shelter of a tree. "Give me a few moments to see how many injuries we need to treat, will you?"

He nodded agreeably. "I'll mark the claim site."

When he left, using a small torch he'd made for himself, Raven eased the shirt from Eva's shoulder. "You're damn lucky James is a lousy shot." He dabbed poultice on the wound. "Where else do you hurt?"

"My arm," she replied. "And my ribs, though I doubt there is much you can do about that."

"The peyote will help you relax." He bent down to press his lips to hers. "I'm glad you're still alive."

Eva smiled drowsily, amazed at how much she enjoyed the taste of him and relieved that the Indian remedy took effect immediately. "Even if I'm a pain in the ass?"

"Even if," he whispered back to her before he kissed her gently.

And that's the last thing she remembered before the world turned pitch-black and swallowed her up in silence.

Chapter Fifteen

The next morning Blackowl frowned disconcertedly as he watched Raven give Eva another strong dose of peyote. "Why are you knocking her out completely again?"

"If I don't she'll insist on chasing down James and she is in no condition to do anything except recuperate." Raven carefully repositioned her broken arm against her abdomen. Then he wrapped her in the bedroll so he could strap her to the travois he had made at first light to transport her.

Blackowl smiled wryly. "I don't want to be you when she comes to her senses and realizes we are heading in the opposite direction than she anticipates."

Raven wasn't sure he wanted to be him, either, when the ranting and raving commenced. But he had been through everything else with this headstrong hellion. Why not endure a temper tantrum of gigantic proportion?

"I think we'll let James come to us." Raven scooped Eva's limp form into his arms and carried her to the travois he had hooked up for the bay gelding to drag behind him. He let the horse sniff Eva on the way past before he strapped her into the Indian-style carrier.

Blackowl smiled perceptively. "So you think James will try to intercept the gamblers and steal the ransom they are supposed to deliver."

Raven nodded as he swung into the saddle. "James was so overly confident that he sent Lydia Hallowell a ransom note *before* he knew whether he would be able to capture Eva. He'll try to take the money before Frank and Irving discover she is free. By now I imagine James has confiscated another horse in Hell's Corner and has ridden down the trail from Hell to Purgatory."

"Maybe the spirits will prevail and he will take a fall that breaks his neck," Blackowl said cheerily as he handed off the bay's reins to Raven.

Raven would like nothing more than to have his cruel stepbrother meet with disaster. James certainly had it coming, considering the long list of crimes he'd committed. Taking shots at Eva on several occasions and then leaving her to die intensified Raven's thirst for vengeance. He knew Eva would pitch a fit, but she had to wait in line to have her revenge on James until *after* Raven finished with the bastard.

Glancing back to ensure the downhill jaunt didn't cause Eva more discomfort than necessary, he headed to Satan's Bluff. He planned to take the timesaving Indian trail that led to his cabin so Hoodoo could care for Eva. Raven smiled, knowing the older man would relish the duty since he'd become overly fond of Eva.

When they reached the mountain meadow that led to the Indian trail Raven handed off the bay's reins to Blackowl. "I'm going to stop in Satan's Bluff long enough to file Eva's claim. I'll catch up with you as soon as possible."

Raven urged the paint pony into a swift pace while Blackowl veered across the mountain meadow. He considered trying to overtake James and let his cousin tend to Eva. However, she was so banged up and bruised that he couldn't bring himself to leave her for too long.

None of this would have happened if he hadn't shouted her name while she held James at gunpoint, he reminded himself sourly. Now she was battered and exhausted and James still was running loose. Raven owed Eva for her pain and trouble and he would be there to care for her.

Eva moaned groggily then opened her eyes to stare at the ceiling above her. It looked vaguely familiar but the strong sedative Raven had given her left cobwebs in her mind and she had trouble formulating thought. When she tried to roll onto her side, every muscle screamed in pain.

"Dear God…" she groaned as she raised her arm to rub her throbbing head. *Thunk.* "Ouch…" Bleary-eyed, she stared at the splint on her left arm that she had unintentionally clanked against her skull.

Obviously, she had broken her arm during her fall. She wasn't surprised because she remembered that it had hurt like hell. When she noticed the bandage on her shoulder, the events of her harrowing escape from James returned in full force.

She glanced around the room and realized she was in Raven's bed in his cabin. Eva frowned, befuddled. How had she gotten here so quickly and without remembering the journey? And where was James Archer? Surely Raven and Blackowl had captured him by now.

"Hoodoo!" she croaked, surprised that her voice sounded as if it had rusted from overexposure to the rain and wind.

"You're finally awake? Well it's about time," he called from downstairs. "I'll bring up leftovers from lunch."

Eva blinked, disoriented. Lunch? What time was it? She

couldn't determine the time of the day because the curtains upstairs were closed. Thanks to the sedative, she barely knew where she was, but she did admit she felt famished.

A few minutes later Hoodoo hobbled up the steps with a plate of food. Eva smiled in eager anticipation when the appetizing aroma wafted across the loft to greet her.

"I've missed you and your cooking, Hoodoo," she rasped as she pushed herself up against the pillows. She glanced down to note she was wearing her nightgown, but she didn't recall how and when she'd come to have it on. Raven was responsible, she presumed.

Hoodoo smiled as he sank down on the side of the bed. "You've had a rough few days, I hear," he said as he spoon-fed her stew.

Her taste buds went into full-scale riot at first bite and she eagerly waited for him to offer her another gulp.

"I can tell you for sure that the three of us were beside ourselves when we realized you had ridden off alone to capture James." Hoodoo's disfigured face puckered disapprovingly. "If I had known it was James who had been hounding you and Raven, I would have taken after him with my shotgun. I've heard too many infuriating stories about that scoundrel. After what he did to you, I want to carve him into wolf bait. But I know Raven and Blackowl will deal severely with him."

Eva swallowed her food then frowned. "They haven't captured him yet?"

Hoodoo shook his frizzy brown head. "No, they figure he'll try to intercept the two men you saved from a hanging. They are headed to the cabin with the ransom money."

Eva angled the spoon away from her mouth then sat upright in bed. "The meal is incredible, as always, but I need to dress," she said hastily. "Could you grant me a moment of privacy? I need to be on hand when James is captured."

"No!" Hoodoo protested. "Raven gave me strict orders to make sure you received plenty of bed rest. He'll have my head if you go haring off again."

"I'll have his head for sedating me to such extremes that I didn't know where the blazes I was," she grumbled as she flung back the quilt to note her legs were a mass of scrapes and bruises.

"*See there?* You got no business riding off," Hoodoo lectured.

"Then at least let me bathe at Phantom Springs." She requested. "You claim the water has healing powers that work wonders."

Hoodoo smiled agreeably. "That's exactly what you need."

Eva walked over gingerly to retrieve her satchel and grab a clean shirt and breeches. When Hoodoo went downstairs, she pulled on her clothes.

"How long have I been sedated?" she called down to him.

"Two days."

"Two?" Eva howled in dismay. "Frank and Irving will be transporting the ransom money and James might be lying in wait already."

"That's the way Raven and Blackowl have it figured," Hoodoo replied.

She pulled on her boots then crammed her belongings in her satchels. "How long ago did Blackowl and Raven leave?" she asked as descended the stairs.

"Four hours," Hoodoo reported. "They presumed James would arrive early to search out the best location for an ambush between here and the stage station. They hoped to overtake him before someone gets hurt."

"If James is the one who gets hurt I couldn't be more pleased," she muttered as she glanced at the splint on her left arm. "He definitely has it coming."

Eve walked outside feeling guilty that she had tricked Hoodoo into thinking that she was settling for a bath when she intended to saddle the blood-red bay and ride off to make sure James didn't escape again. She hoped Hoodoo would forgive her…eventually…

Raven frowned, bemused, as he stared through the field glasses to survey the entourage on horseback. "I could swear that's Eva down there with the gamblers and an un-identified man. But how is that possible? She's sedated and lying in bed at the cabin."

Blackowl took the spyglass and frowned, too. "Same hair color, same style of shirt and breeches. How—?"

"Must be her sister," Raven interrupted then smiled. "Not only do they look amazingly alike, but Lydia is ob-viously as determined to be involved in this manhunt as Eva… See anything of James?"

Blackowl scanned the tree-choked foothills and wild tumble of rocks. "No, not yet. If he's here, he's doing a damn fine job of concealing himself." He glanced sideways at Raven. "Are you sure you want to use these travelers as bait to trap James?"

"Not particularly but we have no choice since we can't locate James. We're running out of time and I don't want to give away our location to him."

Raven was glad Eva wasn't here to scold him for using her sister to lure in James. But who would have thought Lydia would have insisted on delivering the ransom money in person? Damn, those Hallowell sisters were a stubborn lot, he mused.

"Oh, hell," Blackowl grumbled a moment later.

Raven jerked up his head and looked around. Blackowl thrust the spyglass at him then hitched his thumb to the west.

"Damnation," Raven grumbled when he saw Hoodoo and Eva racing down the trail, with Hoodoo following a short distance behind and waving his arms in agitated gestures. "Well, so much for my explicit instructions that Eva was to remain bedfast until we returned to the cabin. Obviously, she sneaked away from Hoodoo and he came charging after her since she was determined to make tracks so she could be a part of James's capture."

"Maybe James will decide to back off before his luck runs out," Blackowl remarked.

"Doubt it. Money is an obsessive motivation for my stepbrother. Always has been. After all, he sold my father's possessions and kept the money for himself. He doesn't care whose money it is—he wants it all."

"James has to know you will come looking for him," Blackowl murmured as he panned the area painstakingly.

"I predict his typical arrogance will prevail. Nothing would please him more than to outsmart me by intercepting the brigade and making off with the ransom money." Raven backed from the underbrush. "Keep close watch for James while I flag down Eva. I don't want her to stumble into our trap."

Raven strode quickly to his horse then mounted up. He cut cross-country to overtake the twosome, hoping James hadn't spotted the latecomers. Focused on Eva, who was sitting astride the muscled bay, Raven ignored the first rule of survival. He didn't pay attention to his surroundings.

A gunshot rang out nearby and echoed around the canyon. Burning pain seared his forehead and the coppery scent of blood flooded his senses. He blinked, stunned, when trickles of blood clouded his vision and obliterated his thoughts.

Raven sagged over his horse, oblivious to everything except the fierce pain that made him swear his head had exploded.

Eva jerked upright when she heard the report of a rifle echoing around her. She couldn't see where the shot originated or where it landed, but a sense of urgency overwhelmed her. She nudged the bay, forcing him into a gallop. She wanted to be on hand to see James apprehended. By damned, she was entitled. This was *her* private manhunt to avenge her sister and she was ready to rake Raven over live coals for excluding her.

She blinked in surprise when she stared downhill to see Irving, Frank, Roger and Lydia scrambling from their horses to take cover in the underbrush. Why Lydia had become personally involved in this ransom exchange Eva couldn't fathom. Not only was Lydia on hand, but she was dressed in breeches. Was this the same sister she'd left in Denver less than two weeks ago?

Riding at a fast clip, Eva charged toward the entourage that had disappeared into the protection of the trees.

"Eva, no!" Hoodoo shouted. "This could be a trap!"

No sooner were the words out of his mouth than a shot zinged past her shoulder. She flattened herself on the bay gelding and thundered toward the place she had last seen her sister. Somewhere to her left she heard more gunshots ring out. She presumed Blackowl and Raven were returning fire. Even Frank, Irving and Roger were shooting at an unseen target in the bushes.

A flash of color caught her attention and she glanced sideways. She did a double take when she spotted Raven racing toward the entourage on his paint pony. The shooting stopped abruptly when he waved his arm to draw attention.

Eva realized almost immediately that the rider sitting astride the paint pony was dressed in Raven's customary black shirt and hat but he didn't move with the same muscular grace.

"Hold your fire, everybody! It's Raven," Frank Albers shouted at his companions.

When Lydia and the three men appeared from the underbrush, Eva waved her broken arm over her head. "Lydia! Get down! It's a trap! That isn't Raven!"

It was a race to see who reached the foursome first. If James managed to pounce on Lydia, *she* could become the new hostage and he would confiscate the ransom.

Eva vowed, there and then, that her sister would not endure the agony she had suffered at James's hands. The showdown would come, here and now, she promised herself resolutely.

Like two medieval knights jousting on horseback, Eva and James plunged straight toward each other. He divided his attention between Lydia's location and Eva's daring attempt to intercept him. Eva took full advantage of his distraction. She used her splinted arm like a club to knock James off balance when their paths intersected.

He yelped as he somersaulted off the back of Raven's paint horse. He hit the ground with a thud and a groan. His hat went flying, exposing his true identity to the onlookers.

Eva skidded her horse to a halt. Before she dismounted, Lydia shot across the meadow with a thick tree branch in hand.

"You bastard!" Lydia shrieked as she upraised her arm and thwacked her former fiancé on the shoulder. "How dare you try to ransom my sister after what you already did to me!"

She tried to club him on the head, but he raised both

arms to shield himself so she thunked him good and hard on the shin instead.

When James howled and tried to roll away from the multiple body blows directed at him, the three men rushed forward to hold him at gunpoint. Eva watched in supreme satisfaction as Lydia vented all her pent-up outrage on the man who had caused her so much heartache and humiliation.

"You missed a spot." Eva called her sister's attention to James's kneecaps and listened to him yowl when Lydia thumped both knees—good and hard.

"Your turn." Lydia thrust the club at Eva so she could give him a good thrashing.

James yelped when Eva hammered his elbows for good measure.

She returned the makeshift club to Lydia. "Have another go at it. Smash his fingers while you're at it. I want this scoundrel to remember us each time he sees his welts and bruises. After what he did to—" She slammed her mouth shut then decided Lydia had a right to know the fate of her prized horse. "He killed Hodge and beat him brutally."

"What!" Lydia cried in outrage.

Then she proceeded to beat the hell out of James and no one intervened. The men stood and watched her wallop him repeatedly until he begged for mercy—and found none forthcoming.

"Where's Raven?" Eva asked suddenly.

She glanced around, expecting his arrival. She had been focused completely on protecting Lydia from James's possible attack. Then she'd become sidetracked watching her sister have her revenge.

She had forgotten about Raven.

How could she have forgotten him? He had saved her life more times than she could count. Not to mention that she had committed the unforgivable by allowing herself to fall in love with a man who had little use or need for her in his life.

And there it was. The truth she had tried so hard to deny to herself. *She loved Raven.* But she didn't know where he was or what happened to him.

Unholy terror pulsated through her as she lurched around to retrieve her horse. She suddenly remembered the first gunshot that had sent her thundering downhill to protect Lydia. Dear God, had Raven been shot? Is that why James had been able to confiscate his horse and clothing?

Despite the awkward splint, she pulled herself into the saddle then grabbed the reins to the paint pony. She rode off in the direction from which James had come, hoping beyond hope that she hadn't delayed too long to find Raven alive.

Her heart dropped to her stomach when she spotted Hoodoo and Blackowl hunkered down beside their horses. All she could see was Raven's moccasined feet sprawled on the ground. Everything inside her rebelled at the prospect of Raven being seriously injured—or worse. He was practically invincible, prepared for *everything*—or so he had told her the first night they met. If something happened to him because of her…

Her thoughts trailed off and she burst into tears. She reined the bay gelding to a halt then vaulted from the saddle. She raced forward to see that Raven was bare-chested and bareheaded. His face was as white as salt and blood streamed from his head wound and dribbled over his cheeks like a river of red.

"Raven! Oh, God, J.D.!" she shouted as she elbowed the two men out of her way to crouch beside him. "I'm so sorry!" she wailed. "This is exactly what I tried to guard against when I went after James alone."

Her wild-eyed gaze bounced back and forth between

Blackowl and Hoodoo's grim expressions. "Is he going to be all right?"

Hoodoo shrugged noncommittally. "Dunno, little gal. Head wounds can look worse than they are, but he hasn't regained consciousness. He should have by now… And thanks so much for sneaking off," he added disapprovingly.

"I'm sorry, Hoodoo. I wanted to be there, badly."

Eva scooted sideways so she could cradle Raven's head in her lap. She motioned for Blackowl to hand her the cloth he was using to compress the wound. She frowned in confusion when she felt the large knot on the back of Raven's head.

"James must have clubbed him, too," she guessed accurately as she turned his head sideways to show the men the bloody knot on his skull.

"I'll fetch the poultice to treat the gunshot wound," Blackowl said as he climbed to his feet. "We'll make him as comfortable as possible so we can take him back to the cabin."

"No, he's coming home with me so he can have the best medical care money can buy," she insisted.

Eva felt so horribly guilty about Raven's condition she cried again. Raven had placed her safety above his need to track down James because she had fallen down the mountain. Yet, she had rushed to her sister's rescue.

She had placed Lydia's welfare above Raven's. It tormented her to no end that she'd failed him when *he* needed *her* for the very first time. To compensate she'd turn her bedroom into an infirmary. While he recuperated, she'd give him round-the-clock care and cater to his every need.

"Where are those foul-tasting peyote buttons you crammed down my throat?" she demanded of Blackowl.

"They're in my pouch, but Raven won't want—"

"Raven is not in charge of his convalescence, I am," she

said sharply. "He sedated me when I was injured and needed to be transported. Obviously he approves of that policy."

When Blackowl opened his mouth to object, Eva glared him into submission. He sighed audibly then grabbed the peyote.

"Is this him? Is this your husband who couldn't protect you from that sneaky shyster?" Lydia demanded huffily as she walked up behind Eva.

She glanced over her shoulder, noting again that she and her sister were identically dressed. "Yes, this is Raven and he protected me just fine," she defended. "I wouldn't be alive now, if not for him and Blackowl and Hoodoo."

She hitched her thumb toward the two men and noted that Lydia stared overly long at Hoodoo's disfigured face before she surveyed Blackowl's bronzed features and powerful physique. "Lydia, this is Hoodoo Lemoyne and Raven's Cheyenne cousin, Blackowl."

While Lydia and Blackowl sized each other up, Eva crammed the peyote buttons into Raven's mouth to dissolve and take effect. When she removed the compress from his head wound, she realized it was deep enough to require stitches.

"Blackowl?" she murmured, gesturing to the clean wound.

He came down on one knee to inspect the injury, then nodded in agreement. "I can stitch him up. There's a pouch in my saddlebag—"

"I'll fetch it for you," Lydia volunteered quickly. "What else can I do to help?"

Eva stared at Lydia, who usually fell to pieces in a crisis. "Who *are* you and what have you done with my sister?"

Lydia returned shortly with needle and thread in hand then tapped herself proudly on the chest. "This is the new improved me," she announced. "I have decided to be exactly like you and to assert myself. And most importantly I'm not taking another man at his word so long as I live."

"Some are trustworthy," Eva insisted.

"Name one," Lydia challenged.

"Here are three," Eva replied. "Then there is Roger Philbert, who has been a loyal friend to both of us."

"Fine, there are four. The rest I'm not sure about." Lydia handed the needle and thread to Blackowl then looked back at Eva. "I still don't understand why you married the bounty hunter. *Hiring* him should have been sufficient."

Eva decided to save the long involved explanation for later. The first order of business was to tend to Raven, then bind up James for transport to jail. While Hoodoo and Blackowl treated Raven's wounds, Eva drew her sister aside.

"It is your choice what to do about James," she murmured.

"James?" Lydia stared blankly at her. *"James who?"*

Chapter Sixteen

"James Archer—alias Gordon Carter, and who knows what other names he goes by—is Raven's vicious stepbrother," Eva reported. "But if you prefer to have James incarcerated at Pueblo or Canyon Springs to avoid rumor or gossip pertaining to you then that's exactly what we'll do, Lydia."

Lydia pulled a face then glanced back to where Frank, Roger and Irving had tied James to a tree. "Those are my only choices? I want to shoot him."

"So do I, but there are entirely too many eyewitnesses who would have to testify against us," Eva said dryly. "The tale would be all over Denver."

Lydia waved her hand dismissively. "I don't care about gossip anymore. I'm not wasting my time with meaningless soirees or trying to live my life according to someone else's expectations. I'm planning to broaden my horizons to include more challenge and adventure in the wilderness."

Eva smirked. "The last time I took you on an excursion in the mountains you claimed city life suited you better."

She elevated her chin. "I've changed my mind. I've decided to live on the edge like you."

Eva held up her broken arm. "Then beware of nasty falls."

Lydia flung her arms around Eva's neck suddenly and hugged her close. "I was so dreadfully worried about you. I've felt horribly guilty because every bruise and pain you've suffered is my fault. If I had seen Gordon for what he was, none of this would have happened!"

Eva nuzzled her sister affectionately, knowing exactly how she felt. Eva had been hounded by guilt because Raven, Blackowl and Hoodoo had risked danger and devoted so much time and effort on her behalf.

"Everything is fine now. I'm taking Raven home with me so he can recuperate." Eva pulled away to stare intently at her sister. "Are you serious about wanting to undertake an adventure?"

Lydia bobbed her headed eagerly.

Eva grinned. "I fell downhill and landed on an overlooked vein of gold ore. Although Hoodoo told me that Raven registered the claim in my name, I want to transfer it to Hoodoo, Blackowl and Raven. If not for them, I would have perished in a gold mine that no one knew was there."

"You want me to work the claim?"

"Yes, if you'll allow Blackowl and Hoodoo to accompany you to determine its potential. It might fizzle out in a few pans of dirt or become a productive site." She leaned close to her sister to continue. "As for Hoodoo, he was mauled by a bear and has become self-conscious about his appearance. But he's a dear, considerate and helpful man so be kind to him."

"You can count on me," Lydia said determinedly. Then her expression became quite serious. "I want to know what is going on with you and the bounty hunter."

Eva shifted uneasily. "I had to resort to drastic measures

to enlist his help because he turned down the case. I pretended to be his wife to force him to let me travel with him on the stagecoach. He was more or less stuck with me."

Lydia grinned wickedly. "That should teach him not to tangle with a Hallowell."

"But then I fell in love with him," Eva burst out.

Lydia's smile turned upside down. "How can this possibly work?" She looked back at Blackowl, who was completing his task. "That would be as ill-fated as a match between me and that brawny Cheyenne warrior I just met."

"Probably," Eva agreed. "But at least this time I'm wise enough to realize that what Raven feels for me is professional duty and responsibility."

Lydia reached out to give her hand a sympathetic squeeze. "I'm sorry, Eva. But now you have your eyes wide open and you can foresee the pitfalls. Unlike your crushing disappointment with Felix Winslow and my mortification with Gordon Carter, who isn't even a real person, for God's sake!"

"Raven is ready for transport," Hoodoo called to her.

Eva wheeled away to check on Raven then she pivoted back to her sister. "Decide what you want to do with your ex-fiancé. We can have him jailed in Canyon Springs in a matter of hours."

"We'll take him to Denver," Lydia decided. "By the time word of his kidnapping attempt and his ransom demands spread around town, my short-term association with him will be old news." She shrugged lackadaisically. "Besides, he is a closed chapter in my life and I am anxious to begin my grand adventure."

Eva walked off, making a mental note to outfit her sister with the doehide clothing that would conceal her gender. However, with Hoodoo and Blackowl as her companions she would be safe and protected. All Eva had to do was persuade them to accompany Lydia to Satan's Bluff and transport the necessary equipment to the site to mine the gold ore.

Eva smiled impishly, wondering what the negotiations would cost her. Blackowl would invariably claim he didn't want to spend more time with "palefaces" than absolutely necessary.

Raven awoke to the feel of miniature carpenters hammering at his skull. He felt so sluggish and lethargic that he couldn't muster the energy to open his eyes. He lay there, trying to recollect the last thing he remembered.

After a long, confused moment, he recalled riding frantically toward Eva and Hoodoo before they prematurely sprung the trap for James. Damn, what had happened to Eva? Had she become James's hostage again?

Scowling at his inability to recall the details, he massaged his throbbing head and inspected the bandage covering the wound. The back of his skull hurt like a son of a bitch. He touched the knot carefully then grimaced when he unintentionally triggered another sharp pain.

Several minutes passed before Raven decided to open his eyes to see how his headache responded to sunlight. Sure enough, his skull throbbed and blinding light stabbed at him. Shielding the top portion of his face with his hand, he surveyed his surroundings through cloudy vision. He was shocked to find himself lying on a frilly blue canopy bed in a palatial room fit for royalty.

"Where the hell am I?" he chirped.

Clearly, he had died and gone to heaven. No one had bothered to inform him of his change of address. He was floating in a lazy haze, lounging on a mattress as soft as a cloud.

When the door swung open, Raven stared blankly at Eva. "Oh, damn, you're dead, too. I failed you again."

She smiled at him as she all but floated into the room with a tray of food in hand. Her dark eyes sparkled impishly as she sank down beside him. "Dead? No, you aren't that lucky, Jo-Dan. You are under my care."

"So this is hell, not heaven," he mumbled but he was smiling because she looked so damn appealing in her trim-fitting green gown. Despite the new splint on her broken arm and the telltale scrapes and bruises—souvenirs of her wild adventure in the wilderness—she looked positively radiant.

She leaned sideways to set the tray on his belly. "Hell is what you make of it," she replied. "Be optimistic and enjoy your accommodations while you recuperate."

He looked around the spacious room again. "Where are we?"

"In my room in Denver," she reported.

"Your room!" he hooted as he shoved himself into a sitting position. *"In Denver?"*

Eva reached out to place her hand on his bare chest then pressed him back down, which was probably for the best because the abrupt movement made him light-headed.

"I'm a long way from my cabin, which is where I should be," he grumbled, taking inventory of the elaborately decorated furnishings that made him feel completely out of place.

She grinned mischievously. "Not so far away when you consider your caregiver crammed peyote down your throat to knock you out for a day or two. As you did with me, might I remind you. But I had our family doctor give you a strong dose of laudanum to keep you sedated when you arrived here."

He muttered under his breath and rubbed his jaw, noting that he had a thick growth of whiskers. "That's a fine way to treat a man who was trying to save you from another shooting. What became of James, by the way?"

Eva offered him a spoonful of tasty soup. "When he tried to swipe the ransom money I whacked him with my splint and knocked him off his horse."

Raven grinned. "A shame I missed that."

"It was quite gratifying," she admitted. "But it did my heart good to watch Lydia grab a makeshift club and pound James into the ground."

"Sorry I missed that part, too."

"Now Marshal Doyle has James locked up *tight*. He is chained to the bars, at my insistence," she continued. "Our lawyer has charged him with kidnapping, attempted murder and extortion, to name only a few of his crimes. The story circulating around Denver is that I exposed him as the shyster he was and he retaliated against me. Lydia's involvement with him is a mere footnote in the tale."

"How is your sister holding up?" he asked between bites.

"Amazingly well." She offered him a drink of milk. "I was able to retrieve the stolen money James had stashed in his saddlebags and return it to Lydia. She was greatly relieved, but now she's too preoccupied with the new gold mine to care about her ordeal with James."

Raven's brows shot up his forehead and then he winced when he felt the twinge in his scalp. "She's in Satan's Bluff?"

Eva nodded her auburn head. "Hoodoo and Blackowl gladly agreed to accompany her, equipped with the necessities to determine what kind of yield to expect from the mine."

Raven stared skeptically at her. "*Gladly agreed?* How did you swing that, hellion?"

Eva fed him another spoonful of soup. "I offered a generous fee for their trouble. Then I informed them that

Lydia was instructed to transfer ownership of the claim to them and to you."

Raven gaped at her and nearly choked on his soup.

She dug a letter from her pocket and waved it in front of his face. "I think Lydia has developed a *tendre* for your cousin, though she claimed she had also sworn off men forever. Her letter if full of 'Blackowl said this' and 'Blackowl did that.'" She snickered. "Also, Hoodoo asked her to marry him twice. The fact that Lydia and I look alike has its drawbacks. Apparently, either of us will do. Since I'm out of sight I'm also out of Hoodoo's mind."

"Ah, well, you did tell me more than once that *you* had sworn off men for the rest of your life," he reminded her.

Her smile faded as she brushed her hand over the tousled black hair that drooped over his forehead. "We have a slight problem, Raven."

"Do we? Only a slight problem? Like breaking an arm? Getting shot in the head?" he quizzed her.

She glanced away, refusing to meet his inquisitive gaze. "Word has spread through town that we are married. Not that I care because it is a fine deterrent for adventurers who are eager to attach themselves to my fortune."

He nodded pensively. "Yes, now Felix Winslows and Gordon Carters of the world will look elsewhere for an un-suspecting pigeon."

"To regain your freedom you will have to get a pretend divorce to nullify our fake marriage," she explained. "Divorce is nasty business, whether real or pretended, but it is my fault that your name has been linked to mine and the news has set gossips' tongues to wagging. I'm sorry I dragged you into this."

The prospect of having no attachment whatsoever to Eva left him feeling empty and dissatisfied. It shouldn't have because he knew it was best for Eva to remain in her world while he returned to his own.

"I'll take care of the situation as soon as I'm back on my feet," he assured her.

She turned away to fluff his pillow so he couldn't gauge her reaction to his comment. He really wanted to know if she was relieved or slightly disappointed. However, he wasn't about to ask, for fear he might do something stupid—like admit his aversion to letting her go and never seeing her again.

"The doctor will arrive shortly to check on you," she informed him. "Perhaps he will dispense with the laudanum since you are coherent. How's your headache by now?"

"Still there."

Contentment stole over him when Eva leaned down to press her lips gently to his. It seemed like weeks since he'd kissed her, since he'd inhaled that unique fragrance he associated with her, since he felt her lush body brushing against his.

"I'll leave you to rest," she whispered against his lips. "I'm dreadfully sorry you were injured because of my crusade. That's why I struck off alone for Purgatory Gulch. I didn't want to place you in danger. Even so, James got off a lucky shot then he took your clothes and horse. He tried to masquerade as you so he could swipe the ransom money from my sister, but I knew it wasn't you and I alerted everyone.

"Now here you are, flat on your back. With a headache from hell, I suspect. Forgive me?" she murmured softly.

"If you'll forgive me for failing you when James took you captive and you ended up with a gunshot wound and broken arm."

"I didn't hold you responsible."

He grasped her good arm then curled his hand around the back of her neck to draw her lush mouth back to his. "*I* did."

He kissed her hungrily, deeply, and wondered how many kisses he could accumulate before the doctor gave him a clean bill of health and shooed him out of this incredibly comfortable bed in what looked like a fairy-tale palace.

"Ahem…" The physician, a black leather bag in hand, cleared his throat to make his presence known. Then he rapped his knuckles on the doorjamb. "May I come in to check on our local hero?"

"By all means, Dr. Fields," Eva insisted as she withdrew.

Raven frowned, puzzled. "Local hero?"

"Quite the story in the newspaper," the gray-haired physician remarked as he eased down on the edge of the bed to replace the dressing and bandage. "It all sounded quite exciting and perilous, but you sacrificed your own safety to save Eva from disaster. Very admirable, Mr. Raven."

Raven said nothing, just wondered how many ways Eva had spun the facts to make him appear the hero for the week.

"Whoever sewed up the gash on your head did a fine job," Dr. Fields praised.

"It was his cousin," Eva reported.

Raven grimaced when the physician slid his hand behind his head to inspect the tender knot.

"If you're dealing with blurred vision I'm not surprised," Dr. Fields said.

Raven was amazed James hadn't opted for a bullet in the back. If James hadn't wanted to avoid getting blood on his black shirt, when he exchanged it with his own, Raven predicted he would be looking down from that great Cheyenne hunting ground in the sky right now. Instead, James had knocked him senseless and bypassed a lethal gunshot that might have drawn unwanted attention.

"You can get out of bed this evening." Dr. Fields remarked as he came to his feet. "Limited activity, of course. You have a concussion, Mr. Raven, so you should stay in bed as much as possible."

Raven murmured his thanks to the doctor and watched Eva escort the gray-haired man into the hall. Although he planned to remain awake, his eyelids dropped to half-mast. He decided it would be a good idea to catch another nap so he could gain enough strength to walk out of Eva's life before he lost the willpower to get up and go.

That evening, Eva went in to check on Raven before she bedded down in her sister's room. She smiled ruefully, re-membering that Raven had insisted on moving about after supper. They had taken a slow tour of the upstairs before dizziness forced him to lie down again. He seemed ill at ease and uncomfortable with the plush accommodations her father had designed for her mother—who had died before the mansion was completed.

Eva slipped quietly into the room to see Raven sprawled in her bed. He had announced that he had business to attend the next day and that he would be leaving Denver shortly thereafter. The thought tormented her to no end. She knew she had no lasting hold on him, but she had hoped he wouldn't be in a flaming rush to leave town. Other cases awaited him, of course, and he was eager to tend to business.

To him, she was a completed assignment and money in his pocket. To her, he was the beloved man she never expected to find after she'd lost faith in men.

Knowing this would be her last night with him, Eva quietly approached the bed to snuff the lantern. The impulse to lie down beside him one last time before he walked out of her life overwhelmed her. Shedding her nightgown, she eased between the sheets and felt instantly content.

Then she realized he wasn't asleep. His hand glided over her bare hip then moved up to cup her breast. Desire sizzled through her as he levered himself up on his elbow.

"I was wrong," he whispered. "This is heaven, after all."

And then Raven kissed her so tenderly that her heart turned over in her chest. She would never forget how he made her feel when he touched her, how desperately she wanted him. For all the lonely tomorrows to come, tonight would have to be a vivid memory that lasted a lifetime.

Eva wanted him to remember her for all times, as well. She couldn't speak the words trapped in her heart because she had promised not to tie him down or make selfish demands. But she could weave her love around him like a silken cocoon. He would know that he meant something unique and special to her, she promised herself. And perhaps someday he would return from his forays and stop by to see her for a few days. It was better than never seeing him at all, she consoled herself.

She wrapped her arms around his neck, careful not to clank her cumbersome splint against the knot on his head. But she needed to be as close to him as she could possibly get. She ached to memorize the exquisite feel of his masculine body pressed familiarly to hers, to savor his scent and his gentle touch, and experience the intimate emotions and sensations that he alone called from her.

She kissed him until she was forced to come up for a breath of air. "I don't think this is the limited activity Dr. Fields prescribed," she teased.

"But it's exactly what I need," he murmured as he spread a row of warm kisses along the column of her neck. "With you here, I'm feeling no pain."

And it was true, Raven realized. Hungry need over-shadowed everything else. He had awakened when Eva cuddled up beside him and he longed to share her passion before he did what was best for both of them—leave town the next morning.

When she expelled a wobbly sigh and arched into his caresses, Raven dipped his head to flick his tongue against her pebbled nipple. Then he suckled her gently, adoring the soft sounds of pleasure he provoked from her. With dedicated tenderness, he worked his way down her satiny body one kiss and caress at a time until she was writhing impatiently.

Although his need for her played hell with his self-control, Raven refused to rush through their last night together. It had always been like this with Eva, he recalled. She caused him to break every hard-and-fast rule he'd made about avoiding emotional involvements. She distracted him to the extreme and she aroused him until he was lost in a mindless fog that demanded sensual satisfaction.

"Raven, I—"

He shifted position to kiss her thoroughly and felt the urgent need in her embrace. Right or wrong, she wanted him and that pleased him to no end. He vowed to invent new ways to pleasure and excite her as never before.

He inched down her lush body again, memorizing every texture and contour by touch and by heart. When he glided his fingertips across her moist flesh, she quivered and he smiled in satisfaction. So much woman, he mused. So much indomitable spirit. So much incredible passion. She knew no equal, and for a time she belonged only to him and he belonged only to her.

He dipped his head to flick at her with his tongue and tease her with light caresses. When he slid his finger inside her damp heat, he swore he was burning alive. He wanted nothing more than to be inside her, to become a part of that wild flame that burned down the night and erased all rational thought from his mind.

"Come here, damn you," she panted. "I want you now."

When her hand folded around him and she stroked him, urging him closer, he couldn't deny what she wanted, what he wanted so much that he shook with need. He braced himself on his hands and looked down into her enchanting face illuminated by the moonlight that sprayed through the bay window.

As he eased her thighs apart with his knees she curled upward to kiss him as if there were no tomorrow and he was her last breath. The searing impact of emotion that coursed through him sent his senses reeling. When he sank into her welcoming warmth, he became a living, breathing part of her and she became a vital part of him.

They moved in perfect rhythm, drifting in a world of rapturous sensations that defied description. Wild tremors consumed them as they soared to previously unattained heights of ecstasy then plummeted into a reckless free fall of mind-boggling rapture.

Eva gasped when intense pleasure bombarded her repeatedly. She held on to Raven for dear life, struggling to draw breath. When he shuddered above her then clutched her tightly in his arms she savored the sweet intimacy of the moment, committed the feelings and sensations to living memory.

The words she longed to say ached to fly free but she bit them back, for fear they would spoil the moment and make Raven uncomfortable—just as he had retreated emotionally and physically after they first made love and he discovered who she was.

Every kiss and caress she offered him in the aftermath

of unrivaled passion was a silent I-love-you. If Raven couldn't translate her affection for him then it wasn't because she hadn't tried to communicate with every beat of her heart and the soundless whisper of her soul.

"Stay the night, Evangeline," he murmured as he eased down beside her. "I don't want to let you go just yet."

She kissed his cheek then nuzzled her head against the crook of his arm. "Since you asked so nicely, Jordan Daniel."

She smiled as he draped his arm over her hip and sighed deeply. If she had a lifetime to spend cuddled up beside him it still wouldn't be enough, she decided. But it would be a start because she had never been anywhere in her life that felt as much like the place she belonged than when she was with Raven, like this.

The next morning Eva came awake and stretched leisurely in her bed. Her eyes flew open when she realized she was alone. A gigantic sense of disappointment flooded through her as she glanced around her room. Raven's saddlebags weren't on the marble-top dresser where she had placed them. The money she had paid him to take this case sat on the nightstand and Raven was nowhere to be seen.

Emptiness swallowed her alive. She had known this day was rapidly approaching. She had tried to prepare herself mentally, but losing Raven still tormented her. There should be a rule written down somewhere that the man you love had to love you back to the same intense degree. If that were so, Raven would never leave her again.

Rising, Eva freshened up then dressed in her breeches and shirt. She went downstairs to have breakfast in the empty dining room. Lydia usually livened up Eva's days but she was still away from home. Eva wasn't quite sure what to do with herself. She had never had trouble filling her days with activity. But when Raven left without a word, she was at loose ends and she couldn't muster the enthusiasm to do much of anything but mope about and feel sorry for herself.

Her deflated thoughts trailed off when she heard the front door open and close unexpectedly.

"Eva? Are you here?" Lydia called out.

Eva was on her feet in a single bound to seek out her sister. They nearly collided when she rounded the corner to dash into the foyer. "What are you doing back in Denver already? Is that a good or bad sign? And how did you get here so quickly?"

"It's a very good sign and Blackowl and I made part of the trip by train," Lydia reported.

Blackowl on a train? That surprised Eva.

"All three of us have been digging at least twenty ounces a day from the pit," she added excitedly.

Eva smiled in satisfaction when she calculated the earnings at five hundred dollars a day per person.

"Your accidental discovery is going to make the three men enough money to live comfortably," Lydia predicted as she veered into the dining room to help herself to what was left of Eva's breakfast.

Eva scrutinized her sister, whose delighted expression faded into a melancholy smile. "Now what's wrong? Did you meet with trouble in that raucous mining town?"

"No," Lydia replied as she munched on the toast. "No one knew I was a woman since I was wearing your cap and buckskin clothing. I was just wondering how soon after I swore off men for the rest of my life that I might change my mind."

Eva did a double take. "You are seriously considering Hoodoo's proposals?" she chirped.

Lydia flicked her wrist then grinned wryly. "You and I both know that Hoodoo proposes for practice. He's building his self-confidence. But you're right. He is a dear, delightful man and he would make a fine husband."

Eva was pleased to note her sister's perceptiveness. She had grown up quickly the past two weeks.

"I was…um…thinking of Blackowl," Lydia said confidentially before sipping coffee.

Eva sank down in a chair across from her sister. "Don't set yourself up for another heartache, Lydia. Blackowl says he's not particularly fond of palefaces. Has he taken advantage—?"

"No," Lydia interrupted. "Nothing much has happened."

"Nothing much?" Eva repeated, staring intently at Lydia. "How much, *exactly,* is nothing much?"

Lydia waved her hand dismissively. "Don't fret. I can take care of myself. I'm nineteen, after all."

Right. She owned the world. "I'm going to have a heart-to-heart talk with Blackowl," Eva muttered.

"No, you aren't. I have allowed you to run interference and overprotect me since we lost Papa. It's high time I began taking care of myself." Lydia smiled proudly. "Venturing into that mining camp and digging for gold has allowed me to fend for myself, even if Blackowl and Hoodoo were nearby to intervene if I had serious problems. I intend to be just like you, Eva."

Eva stared contemplatively at her sister. It was time to let go, she realized. Lydia was coming of age and she was spreading her independent wings. Eva sincerely hoped Blackowl didn't take advantage of Lydia's infatuation for him. She made a mental note to pull him aside and establish the ground rules, despite Lydia's refusal to let Eva speak on her behalf.

When Lydia bounded up the steps to freshen up, Eva stared out the window, still feeling lost and alone. Perhaps she would join the threesome to dig for gold in the mountains. She desperately needed something to occupy her time before thoughts of Raven drove her completely crazy.

Curse it, he had been gone but a few hours and she missed him already.

A tear slid down her cheek and she brushed it away. "Goodbye, J.D.," she whispered to the ruggedly handsome image floating above her. "I do love you, even if that's the last thing you want to hear from me."

Chapter Seventeen

Raven noticed the waitress who took his breakfast order at the café was studying him speculatively. Obviously, there wasn't anyone in town who hadn't heard that he and Evangeline Hallowell were husband and wife. He remembered what Eva had said about being treated differently when folks found out who she was. Now he knew what she meant.

True, people were still leery of him, but they looked at him differently now that he had supposedly married Eva. He wondered if folks thought he had threatened to dispose of her if she didn't agree to marry him. Probably. He doubted that a single citizen in Denver thought he was good enough for a Hallowell heiress—including himself.

"Here you are, Mr. Raven." The waitress set a steaming plate of food in front of him. "Will your wife be joining you this morning?"

"No, I have professional business to conduct," he replied. Then he added, "Tomorrow perhaps."

The owner, who was eavesdropping beside the kitchen door, smiled in anticipated pleasure. Raven suspected the place would be scrubbed within an inch of its life if Evangeline Hallowell were scheduled to grace the place.

Raven finished his meal then exited to breathe in a deep breath of fresh air. He was still suffering occasional bouts of dizziness, but he'd be damned if he spent another day in bed. Inactivity made him twitchy and he was prolonging the inevitable.

He glanced left, surprised to see Blackowl striding toward him. The fact that his cousin had ventured into Denver at all amazed him. Raven doubted Blackowl would have come if he hadn't been serving as Lydia's bodyguard.

Blackowl halted abruptly in front of Raven, seemingly oblivious to the attention they both received. "I think you should travel to the Cheyenne Reservation in Indian Territory to choose a wife," Blackowl insisted adamantly. "I'll go with you and pick one for myself."

Raven frowned, bemused, as he continued down the street to tend to his next order of business. "Did something happen while you were working the mine that inspired you to take a wife?"

Blackowl refused to look at him—which was a clear indication that something was bothering him. Raven stopped short then half turned to face his cousin directly.

"Why this sudden insistence to leave town and marry immediately?" he demanded.

"Because of Eva's sister," Blackowl blurted out. "I cannot have another paleface female disturbing me constantly."

A wry grin pursed Raven's lips as he studied his cousin's exasperated scowl. He knew what Blackowl was going through. The riptide of emotion, the ill-fated attraction that played hell with a man's disposition. Raven had been fighting the same inner battle because of Eva. He knew for a fact that combating persistent emotions could drive a man as close to crazy as he ever wanted to come.

Spinning on his heels, Raven continued down the board-walk. "If you're headed to the Cheyenne Reservation you'll have to travel without me. I have an errand to run. Then I'm headed to the marshal's office to complete paperwork on the two men who were lynched last week by a mob in Purgatory Gulch. Also, I need to give my statement about my multiple confrontations with James."

"Then *you* take that pint-size paleface back to our new mine," Blackowl demanded sullenly as he fell into step. "The mine has panned out exceptionally well. I think we will have more money than we know what to do with very soon."

Raven chuckled. "You don't sound very pleased with the prospect—"

When Raven tried to veer into the jewelry shop beside the bank, Blackowl grabbed his arm to detain him. "Do not do this, cousin," he pleaded, staring pointedly at the glittering rings behind the window. "Don't give Eva a ring and make this pretend marriage real. Be true to our clan. Let's leave town *right now*."

Raven stared grimly at his cousin. "The man who owns this shop is the same one who broke Eva's heart and used her much the same way James used Lydia. I intend to issue a threat he won't soon forget, if only to satisfy my vengeful need to speak on her behalf. Are you coming in or not?"

Blackowl glanced through the window at the scrawny little man who was puttering around the store. "I'm coming. I can work up great enthusiasm for this particular errand."

"So can I," Raven agreed.

"What's his name?" Blackowl wanted to know.

"Felix Winslow. Let's go make his acquaintance."

Assuming his most intimidating stance, Raven mentally

geared himself up to confront the skinny weasel. He shoved open the door then stalked into the shop to introduce himself.

"Miss Evangeline? The Philbert twins are here to see you," the butler announced.

"Tell them I'll be right there."

Eva glanced toward the staircase to see if Lydia was on her way down after she had bounded off to her room to freshen up a quarter of an hour earlier. But Lydia hadn't reappeared. Eva pasted on a smile and walked into the foyer to greet her longtime friends.

Roger removed his stylish hat and studied her closely. "You look a little better," he observed.

"You poor dear," Sadie cooed with sympathetic concern as she appraised Eva's bruises and broken arm. "A tumble down the side of a mountain? Gracious! It's a wonder you're still alive."

"Only on the outside," Eva mumbled, half under her breath.

Sadie cocked her blond head sideways. "Pardon?"

Eva smiled slightly. "I was lucky indeed."

"I should say so," Sadie declared. "Roger told me all about how you overtook that horrible scoundrel and knocked him right out of the saddle with your splint."

"That was rather gratifying," she had to admit.

"We stopped by to see if you might enjoy a ride around town," Roger offered. "You've been cooped up caring for your…er…husband for several days. How is he, by the way?"

Gone, and I don't expect him to return. "Much better. He went out this morning to take care of some business." She strolled over to fetch her jacket. "A morning drive sounds wonderful."

But it didn't compare to being snuggled up in Raven's

muscular arms, sharing his incredible passion. He was gone and a measly carriage ride was not going to compensate. She knew she would be miserable for a while. Filling the lonely hours to take her mind off him would require considerable effort. She simply had to adjust to life after Raven, she lectured herself sternly.

"Where are you off to?" Lydia called from the top of the staircase.

"Roger and Sadie invited me to take a ride. Want to come along?" Eva called back.

"I'd love to." Lydia hurried down the steps, dressed in a clean pair of breeches and a shirt.

"You're looking well," Roger complimented. "We can wait if you and your sister would like to change clothes."

Lydia grinned as she ambled past him. "No need. Like Eva, I couldn't care less what high society thinks of my attire."

Roger bowed slightly, amusement twitching his lips as he glanced from Eva to Lydia. "The eccentric Hallowell sisters," he teased as he opened the door. "Such a refreshing twosome. I think that's why I like you so much."

"What a lovely day for a ride," Sadie enthused when she stepped onto the porch.

Eva glanced at the cloudless sky. "Isn't it though."

It might as well have been dreary, the air heavy with the threat of rain. It felt all the same to Eva because Raven had taken the sunshine with him when he'd left.

Raven mounted his horse then trotted down the street to Marshal Doyle's office. Blackowl was right beside him, still harping about leaving for Indian Territory immediately after Raven completed his paperwork at the marshal's office.

"Now that you have your business with Felix Winslow settled and out of the way, I'll restock supplies for our journey," Blackowl volunteered as he veered toward the dry goods store. "I'll catch up with you at the jail in a few minutes."

Raven nodded, distracted. His thoughts centered on his upcoming encounter with his stepbrother. He was anxious to see James locked in jail and cuffed to the bars. However, if he had been given a choice, he would have preferred to take his turn with the bastard after the agony James had caused Eva. But Raven supposed it was fitting that Lydia was the one who had gone on the warpath and had pounded James into the ground with an improvised club to retaliate for her humiliation.

"I heard you were back in town." Marshal Doyle nodded a greeting as he lounged in his chair behind the cluttered desk. "I've heard other intriguing rumors as well."

"Have you?" Raven removed his hat to call Emmett's attention to his mending wound. "Was it that I nearly got my head blown off by a man whose shooting skills are mediocre at best?"

The marshal shrugged a bulky shoulder and grinned. "Naw, every joker gets lucky with his aim once in a while. A new part in your hair doesn't make headlines. Now, marrying an heiress? That's newsworthy. Evangeline Hallowell is said to be a free spirit and I do admit that I was highly impressed when I met her, but—"

Raven flung up his hand to silence the marshal. "I came by to have a few words with the prisoner."

Emmett shook his head very deliberately. "Not unless you unload all your hardware. You can't stab or shoot him for injuring you and your new wife. Her lawyer intends to have a field day with him in court and the newspapers thrive on these high-profile stories."

"You are no fun whatsoever, Emmett," Raven grumbled

as he laid his pistols and knife on the desk. "Oh, by the way, two of the men you sent me to arrest were hanged in Purgatory Gulch last week. The other one is still at large. Unless he was one of the nameless men James shoved over a cliff so he could steal another horse and pocket money and personal belongings."

Emmett frowned disconcertedly. "I'm going to have to do something about that vigilante justice in Devil's Triangle. The long arm of the law doesn't stretch far enough into those mountains." He glanced hopefully at Raven. "You interested in camping out there for a few months to clean up that place?"

"Nope. Although I now own a gold mine in the area, it will keep me busy enough when I have time to head back in that direction."

Emmett's jaw dropped to his chest. "You're quitting the business?"

Raven shrugged evasively as he opened the door that led to the jail cells. "Haven't decided yet," he said before he shut the door firmly, granting himself privacy to speak with James.

Cold fury mingled with amusement—of all things—when Raven got his first look at his stepbrother. His stylish clothes were filthy. Raven wondered if the Hallowell sisters had dragged James through the mud before planting him on a horse to cart him to Denver. It certainly looked like it.

Several days' growth of whiskers lined James's jaw. His usual arrogance was nowhere to be seen, but his long-held bitterness remained visible. His green eyes glowed with hatred and resentment as he glowered at Raven.

"What the hell do you want?" James sneered derisively. "To gloat about marrying that rich bitch? If it wasn't for the money, I'd say the two of you deserve each other."

"If you weren't such a lousy shot, you wouldn't be behind bars," Raven countered mockingly. "Don't blame me for your predicament, James. You had plenty of chances."

As much as he wanted to take James apart with his bare hands for nearly getting Eva killed, seeing him confined to a ten-by-ten-foot cell and surviving on prison rations was extremely gratifying. A quick death would have been too merciful, Raven realized. This way James could serve the rest of his days in the penitentiary, knowing his half-Cheyenne stepbrother, whom he despised, was free to come and go anywhere he pleased.

James stared at Raven for a long moment. "Why did she pick you when she has refused everyone else's courtship?"

Apparently, curiosity was killing James. It tormented him beyond words that Raven had supposedly married into one of the richest, most influential families in Denver.

A wicked grin pursed Raven's lips as he turned to leave. "It's my Cheyenne charm," he replied before he closed the door on the foul-smelling cells in the room behind him.

"You bastard!" The wild, shrill feminine voice bounced off the walls and came at Raven from all directions at once.

The pleasure of taunting James was instantly forgotten. Raven froze in his tracks. Widow Flanders stood in the open doorway of the marshal's office. Her gray eyes were narrowed in a murderous glare. Her dingy brown hair was in tangled disarray. Her calico gown looked as if she had slept in it for several days on end. She had both hands clamped around her departed husband's six-shooter and it was aimed at Raven.

And here *he* was unarmed. His weapons lay atop the marshal's desk and the marshal was sprawled motionlessly on the floor at the widow's feet.

"Well, hell," Raven muttered as he stared down the

spitting end of the pistol. "You better not have killed Emmett. He's a good man and I like him."

"He'll just have a knot on his head for trying to interfere. *You're* the one I want dead," the widow snarled without taking her squinty-eyed gaze off Raven.

He grimaced, knowing what a knot on the head felt like. Emmett was in for a mind-scrambling headache.

"I told Emmett I would dance on your grave. But when I offered to pay to have you gunned down I couldn't get any takers from my clan of yellow-bellied brothers-in-law."

Raven didn't bother to mention that his own stepbrother had been taking potshots at him for over two weeks—for free. That might set off the crazed hag.

"Now I hear you've married money," she hurled in a begrudging tone. "When I saw you ride over to the marshal's office I decided to take matters into my own hands. I'm not afraid of you!" Her smudged face puckered with disdain. "You murdered my Buster. How am I supposed to get by without him?"

"No more stolen money stashed away to support yourself?" he remarked insolently. "Sorry to hear that."

"Like hell you are," she seethed.

Raven cast a discreet glance toward his weapons again, estimating how much time he needed to grab a pistol to defend himself. He also wondered if Widow Flanders was a better shot than James. Of course, at this close range, she didn't need to be an expert markswoman to blow him to smithereens.

She cocked the hammer and sighted down the barrel. "I hope you told your bride 'fare thee well' when you left her bed this morning. You won't get another chance. Once you're dead and gone I *will* dance on your grave!"

* * *

Eva perked up immediately when she noticed Raven's paint pony tethered on the hitching post in front of the jail. She shouldn't have been surprised that Raven wanted to swing by the office to make sure his stepbrother was enjoying all the *dis*comforts of the foul-smelling jail.

Her thoughts trailed off and alarm sizzled through her when she noticed the door was standing wide open. A scraggly-looking woman was squared off, as if she were involved in a showdown with someone inside the office.

"Dear God!" Eva yelped when she suddenly remembered Widow Flanders had placed a death wish on Raven's head. Apparently, she had decided to do the dastardly deed herself.

Frantic, Eva snatched the reins from Roger's hand and snapped them over the horse, prompting it to clip-clop down the street at a faster pace. She aimed the carriage directly at the open door.

"Eva? Have you gone mad?" Roger growled as he tried to reclaim the reins. "If you hit the boardwalk you'll overturn the carriage… What the blazes—?"

Despite Roger's concern and Sadie and Lydia's gasps of alarm, Eva bolted to her feet and dived off the moving carriage. She expected to hear the pistol discharge any second and she had the unmistakable feeling that Raven was the spiteful widow's target. The thought of losing him terrified her and she was hell-bent on preventing his death.

"Stop!" Eva screeched, hoping to draw the woman's attention.

The widow glanced over her shoulder to see who caused the commotion. Eva remembered that she had made the same crucial mistake the day she had captured James—momentarily. Then, as now, distraction altered the course of events.

Eva launched herself at the stout woman and grabbed

her around the knees, sending her sprawling on the floor. The pistol exploded prematurely and the shot went wild. It slammed through the wall that separated the cells from the outer office. Eva remembered hearing a yelp from the other side of the door, but she was too intent on wrestling the pistol from the widow's grimy fists before she took another shot at Raven, who had dropped to the floor and rolled behind the desk.

"Get off me!" the widow screeched like a demented banshee. "Eye for an eye!"

Eva had quite enough of wrestling the smelly widow around on the dirty floor where the marshal lay like a displaced rug. She used her splint like a club to wallop Widow Flanders upside the head, stunning her momentarily. But the vicious woman bared her claws and came up fighting.

Eva managed to get in another brain-rattling blow before she felt herself being hoisted completely off the floor. She looked up to see Raven grinning in amusement while he held her aloft against his hip.

Cursing colorfully, the disheveled widow reached for the discarded pistol but Raven planted a moccasined foot on the weapon then scooted it from her grasp.

"Lady," he said, "you might have killed me, but if you had, you would have realized that dealing with my wife just wouldn't have been worth it. If I let her loose on you again, she'll tear you to pieces. Guaran-damn-teed."

The widow glared at him and Eva, but she made no move to reach for the pistol again.

"Wise choice," Raven said as he set Eva to her feet then scooped up the discarded weapon. He handed it to Eva then gathered his knife and peacemakers from the desk. "If she upsets you in the slightest, sweetheart, shoot her."

Eva smiled devilishly when the widow cast her a speculative glance. "If you're thinking I won't bat an eye at shooting someone who has evil designs on my dear husband, then you are correct, madam. You can join your outlaw husband for all I care."

"Good Lord!" Roger crowed as he, Sadie and a half-dozen onlookers crowded around the open door. "Are you going to shoot her, Eva?"

"She tried to shoot Raven. What do you think?"

Roger stared somberly at the widow. "Ma'am, I wouldn't move a muscle if I were you. I've seen Eva in action twice. She definitely means business."

The widow half collapsed and lay submissively on the floor while Raven dribbled water over Emmett's head. The injured marshal groaned then wiped the water from his face.

Groggily, Emmett climbed to his hands and knees. "What happened?"

"Widow Flanders tried to make good on her death threat," Raven explained as he assisted Emmett to his wobbly legs then steadied him. He inclined his dark head toward Eva. "That's when my wife showed up to rescue me."

Eva inwardly snickered when the bumfuzzled marshal glanced from her to Raven. Clearly, he was trying to figure out what the supposed marriage was all about.

It was about one-sided love, but Eva kept the truth to herself because she was enjoying the fact that Raven was smiling at her. *Really smiling,* as if she had pleased and amused him in some way.

Ah, he had a glorious smile and she wished she could be around to see him smile like that more often.

"Help!" A wailing voice reverberated around the jail cells.

Bemused, Eva and Raven opened the door, while the marshal and Roger pulled the widow to her feet to lock her up. To Eva's surprise, James was sitting on his cot, cradling his bleeding shoulder. He looked disheveled. Not at all the cocky rascal who had swaggered through ballrooms, boasting of a fortune he had acquired at someone else's expense.

Eva and Raven turned simultaneously to stare at the hole in the paper-thin wall.

"The widow must have shot him accidentally when I knocked her arm aside. The bullet went astray," Eva declared. She turned to glance at the widow, who was being marched into the cell beside James. "Nice shot, Mrs. Flanders."

The widow didn't seem to appreciate the irony because she hissed and growled like a disturbed cat.

"I need attention!" James demanded as he stared at the red stain spreading across his shirt. "I could bleed to death."

"I'm busy," the marshal said unsympathetically. "I'll get to you in a minute… Roger, fetch the doctor, will you?"

"Gee, your wound looks like the gunshot I received from you, James," Eva pointed out. "As I recall you didn't lift a finger to help me."

His reply was a scowl.

Following on Roger's heels, Raven curled his hand around Eva's good arm to escort her to the outer office. "I owe you my life," he murmured against her ear, sending goose bumps skittering across her skin.

"It still doesn't make us even," she insisted. "I owe—"

Her voice trailed off when she spotted Lydia and Blackowl standing together at the back of the crowd of bystanders gathered at the front door.

"What's happened now?" Lydia questioned as she tried to shoulder her way through the crowd. "Are you all right, Eva?"

"She's fine," Raven answered for her.

To her surprise, Raven closed and locked the door.
When he turned back to her, his expression was somber.
"Now, about our pretend marriage, Evangeline…"

Chapter Eighteen

Eva marshaled her composure and stiffened her spine. She knew this was her last encounter with the legendary bounty hunter she had come to love. Earlier she had wondered why Raven had looked at ease and in such good humor—considering the widow had nearly succeeded in blowing his head off. It must have been because he knew he was leaving Eva behind very soon. He was thrilled to be rid of her, once and for all.

She wanted to sit down and bawl her head off.

"How did you handle passing the word about our pending divorce?" she managed to ask without her voice cracking completely. "I want to make sure we have our stories straight before I tell it around town."

Someone pounded on the door and said, "What's going on in there?"

It sounded exactly like Lydia.

Raven didn't reply, just shifted restlessly from one foot to the other. Eva watched him curiously. She promised herself that no matter what he said, she was not going to blurt out her feelings for him or beg him to stay. That would make him uncomfortable—especially if this turned out to be his official farewell.

"Blackowl and I paid a visit to Felix Winslow this morning," he said out of the blue.

Eva blinked owlishly. She had no idea where he was going with this conversation and it kept her completely off balance. All she could think to say was, "Oh?"

"I didn't like that skinny, self-important gent," he remarked. "I told him I didn't want to see him within speaking distance of you...or else."

Eva managed a chuckle. She could visualize Felix cowering beneath Raven's ominous glares. She wished she could have been there. "Or else what?" she asked.

Raven's gold-green eyes glistened with mischief. "I left it up to his imagination. Furthermore, I didn't want to put the slightest restrictions on my methods of retaliation."

Someone pounded even harder on the door. It was Blackowl. "I have the supplies gathered, Raven. It's time to ride."

Eva swallowed hard and battled the tears that threatened to flood her eyes. He was leaving and she wouldn't see him again. "Where are you going?"

"Blackowl thinks we should travel to Indian Territory to select Cheyenne brides. He claims that is our destiny."

"I see," Eva said quietly—and wondered if he could hear her heart breaking in two.

Raven reached into his shirt pocket then held up two items of jewelry in front of her. Eva stared stupidly at the diamond ring and gold band that he placed in the palm of her hand.

"You bought these from Felix?" she squeaked, confused.

"Yes." Raven grinned wryly. "He gave me an exceptionally good price." He took the rings and placed them on her finger. "I want you to wear these instead of your mother's gold band."

Still dumbfounded, she stared at the expensive rings that sparkled in the sunlight then she peered up at him. "Why?"

"Raven! Open this door!" Blackowl roared as he rattled the hinges. "We have places to go!"

"In a minute, damn it!" Raven yelled back.

"Raven?" Eva prompted, puzzled.

He expelled his breath in a rush then he said, "I'm in love with you, Evangeline. And I think you love me, too. No one but Hoodoo and Blackowl ever cared enough to save me the way you did when you came flying through the doorway to tackle Widow Flanders before she blasted me to kingdom come. That has to mean something…doesn't it?"

His words echoed through her head and her mouth dropped open wide enough for a sparrow to roost. "You love me?" she chirped incredulously.

"Eva!" Lydia shouted. "What is going on in there?"

"Give me a minute!" Eva shouted back. "I'm busy!"

"I'm crazy about you," Raven admitted as he pulled her into his arms and held her possessively against him. "I wasn't sure I could feel anything, or *wanted* to feel anything after suffering through the heartache of losing my family in the massacre. But you touched every emotion I had buried deep inside me and made me feel alive for the first time in years. I don't want to go back to the empty existence I led before I met you."

He sketched her features with his forefinger, rerouting the tears that dribbled down her cheeks. "I've never wanted anything or anyone as much as I want you, Eva." He kissed her tenderly then said, "I've been searching for my soul for years and I've discovered it's with you. I want to wake up beside you all the days of my life."

"Oh, Raven," she whispered brokenly. "I—"

He pressed his fingertip to her trembling lips to shush her. "Since you saved me from the bloodthirsty widow I was hoping you cared enough to agree to a real marriage. Not just a convenient arrangement to hold the money-hungry adventurers at bay." He brushed his thumb over her flushed cheek then asked, "Do you, Evangeline?"

"Yes!" With a squeal of delight, she flung her arms around his neck—ever mindful of her splint and his head wound—and showered him with smacking kisses.

Raven savored her zealous response and thanked his lucky stars that he'd worked up the courage to ask her to be his wife. It hadn't been easy, what with Blackowl hounding him to ride away from temptation. His cousin was afraid he'd become too sentimentally attached to Lydia so he wanted to clear out fast…and take Raven with him.

But his heart knew where he belonged. It was here in Colorado with Eva.

"I've been miserable since the moment I woke up this morning to find you gone," she murmured against his lips. "I was afraid you were going to tell me goodbye for good."

"I discovered that is impossible."

"I don't care where you go or what you do, so long as you'll take me with you," Eva insisted. "I don't want to be without you, Raven. Not ever."

"Agreed," he said without hesitation. "I thought we might divide our time between here and my cabin. There's the gold mine to oversee and Blackowl to console because he's fascinated with Lydia and is nobly trying to keep his distance, in case she doesn't feel the same way."

Eva tipped her head back, her dark eyes twinkling with pleasure and approval. "She does."

She traced his lips then arched a curious brow. "Are you

certain you want to make this official? You know what a pain I can be. In addition, I have developed a reputation as a free-spirited misfit in Denver. Today's fiasco will only contribute to the rumors that I'm as unconventional as a woman can get."

Raven hugged her close then kissed the tip of her upturned nose. "To be honest, you aren't quite the pain in the ass that I've made you out to be, sweetheart. Besides, a man with a reputation like mine can't possibly settle for a normal kind of woman," he teased affectionately. "Despite what others might think, I'm convinced that we are a perfect match."

She beamed in pleasure. "I will be honored to marry you, Jordan Daniel Raven. I will love you the rest of my life."

He stared down into her beguiling face, knowing this spirited, vital woman had made his wildest dreams come true because she loved him. And he loved her with every part of his being, with every beat of his heart.

"I'm thinking of giving up bounty hunting in favor of training and selling horses." He pressed her ever closer, loving the feel of her lush body meshed familiarly to his. "I'm sure we would make a fine pair of manhunters, given your impressive skills in capturing James and the widow. But I've dodged enough bullets. I was hoping you might be satisfied with a less dangerous lifestyle."

"I'll adapt," she promised as she toyed with the buttons on his shirt, leaving him wishing they were anywhere besides the office, where onlookers were trying to beat down one door and the marshal and the two people who hated him most were behind the other.

"Making love with you for the rest of my life will be excitement aplenty," Eva whispered provocatively. "I'd like to begin right now—"

"Oh, excuse me," Marshal Doyle mumbled as he burst in through the door that led to the cells. He raised a questioning eyebrow then inclined his head toward the locked door.

"Crowds," Raven said as he smiled adoringly at Eva. "I'm having a devil of a time getting a moment alone with my wife."

"Then why don't the two of you go on home and lock your own doors," Emmett suggested with a knowing grin.

"I do believe we will." Raven clasped Eva's hand and opened the door to embrace the rest of his life with the woman he loved standing beside him forever…and forevermore.

* * * * *

Turn the page for a sneak preview of
AFTERSHOCK, *a new anthology*
featuring New York Times *bestselling author*
Sharon Sala.

Available October 2008.

n●cturne

Dramatic and sensual tales of paranormal romance.

Chapter 1

October
New York City

Nicole Masters was sitting cross-legged on her sofa while a cold autumn rain peppered the windows of her fourth-floor apartment. She was poking at the ice cream in her bowl and trying not to be in a mood.

Six weeks ago, a simple trip to her neighborhood pharmacy had turned into a nightmare. She'd walked into the middle of a robbery. She never even saw the man who shot her in the head and left her for dead. She'd survived, but some of her senses had not. She was dealing with short-term memory loss and a tendency to stagger. Even though she'd been told the problems were most likely temporary, she waged a daily battle with depression.

Her parents had been killed in a car wreck when she was twenty-one. And except for a few friends—and most recently her boyfriend, Dominic Tucci, who lived in the apartment right above hers—she was alone. Her doctor kept reminding her that she should be grateful to be alive, and on one level she knew he was right. But he wasn't living in her shoes.

If she'd been anywhere else but at that pharmacy when the robbery happened, she wouldn't have died twice on the

way to the hospital. Instead of being grateful that she'd
survived, she couldn't stop thinking of what she'd lost.

But that wasn't the end of her troubles. On top of everything else, something strange was happening inside her
head. She'd begun to hear odd things: sounds, not voices—
at least, she didn't think it was voices. It was more like the
distant noise of rapids—a rush of wind and water inside
her head that, when it came, blocked out everything around
her. It didn't happen often, but when it did, it was frightening, and it was driving her crazy.

The blank moments, which is what she called them,
even had a rhythm. First there came that sound, then a cold
sweat, then panic with no reason. Part of her feared it was
the beginning of an emotional breakdown. And part of her
feared it wasn't—that it was going to turn out to be a per-
manent souvenir of her resurrection.

Frustrated with herself and the situation as it stood, she
upped the sound on the TV remote. But instead of *Wheel
of Fortune,* an announcer broke in with a special bulletin.

> "This just in. Police are on the scene of a kidnapping
> that occurred only hours ago at The Dakota. Molly
> Dane, the six-year-old daughter of one of Holly-
> wood's blockbuster stars, Lyla Dane, was taken by
> force from the family apartment. At this time they
> have yet to receive a ransom demand. The house-
> keeper was seriously injured during the abduction,
> and is, at the present time, in surgery. Police are hop-
> ing to be able to talk to her once she regains con-
> sciousness. In the meantime, we are going now to a
> press conference with Lyla Dane."

Horrified, Nicole stilled as the cameras went live to
where the actress was speaking before a bank of micro-

phones. The shock and terror in Lyla Dane's voice were physically painful to watch. But even though Nicole kept upping the volume, the sound continued to fade.

Just when she was beginning to think something was wrong with her set, the broadcast suddenly switched from the Dane press conference to what appeared to be footage of the kidnapping, beginning with footage from inside the apartment.

When the front door suddenly flew back against the wall and four men rushed in, Nicole gasped. Horrified, she quickly realized that this must have been caught on a security camera inside the Dane apartment.

As Nicole continued to watch, a small Asian woman, who she guessed was the maid, rushed forward in an effort to keep them out. When one of the men hit her in the face with his gun, Nicole moaned. The violence was too reminiscent of what she'd lived through. Sick to her stomach, she fisted her hands against her belly, wishing it was over, but unable to tear her gaze away.

When the maid dropped to the carpet, the same man followed with a vicious kick to the little woman's midsection that lifted her off the floor.

"Oh, my God," Nicole said. When blood began to pool beneath the maid's head, she started to cry.

As the tape played on, the four men split up in different directions. The camera caught one running down a long marble hallway, then disappearing into a room. Moments later he reappeared, carrying a little girl, who Nicole assumed was Molly Dane. The child was wearing a pair of red pants and a white turtleneck sweater, and her hair was partially blocking her abductor's face as he carried her down the hall. She was kicking and screaming in his arms, and when he slapped her, it elicited an agonized scream that brought the other three running. Nicole watched in horror as one of them ran up and put his hand over Molly's face. Seconds later, she went limp.

One moment they were in the foyer, then they were gone.

Nicole jumped to her feet, then staggered drunkenly. The bowl of ice cream she'd absentmindedly placed in her lap shattered at her feet, splattering glass and melting ice cream everywhere.

The picture on the screen abruptly switched from the kidnapping to what Nicole assumed was a rerun of Lyla Dane's plea for her daughter's safe return, but she was numb.

Before she could think what to do next, the doorbell rang. Startled by the unexpected sound, she shakily swiped at the tears and took a step forward. She didn't feel the glass shards piercing her feet until she took the second step. At that point, sharp pains shot through her foot. She gasped, then looked down in confusion. Her legs looked as if she'd been running through mud, and she was standing in broken glass and ice cream, while a thin ribbon of blood seeped out from beneath her toes.

"Oh, no," Nicole mumbled, then stifled a second moan of pain.

The doorbell rang again. She shivered, then clutched her head in confusion.

"Just a minute!" she yelled, then tried to sidestep the rest of the debris as she hobbled to the door.

When she looked through the peephole in the door, she didn't know whether to be relieved or regretful.

It was Dominic, and as usual, she was a mess.

Nicole smiled a little self-consciously as she opened the door to let him in. "I just don't know what's happening to me. I think I'm losing my mind."

"Hey, don't talk about my woman like that."

Nicole rode the surge of delight his words brought. "So I'm still your woman?"

Dominic lowered his head.

Their lips met.

The kiss proceeded.

Slowly.

Thoroughly.

* * * * *

Be sure to look for the AFTERSHOCK
*anthology next month, as
well as other exciting paranormal stories
from Silhouette Nocturne.
Available in October wherever books are sold.*

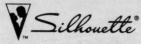

Romantic
SUSPENSE

**Sparked by Danger,
Fueled by Passion.**

The Coltons Are Back!

Marie Ferrarella
Colton's Secret Service

The Coltons: Family First

On a mission to protect a senator, Secret Service agent
Nick Sheffield tracks down a threatening message only
to discover Georgie Gradie Colton, a rodeo-riding single
mom, who insists on her innocence. Nick is instantly
taken with the feisty redhead, but vows not to let his
feelings interfere with his mission. Now he must figure
out if this woman is conning him or if he can trust her
and the passion they share....

Available September wherever books are sold.

**Look for upcoming Colton titles
from Silhouette Romantic Suspense:**

RANCHER'S REDEMPTION by Beth Cornelison, Available October
THE SHERIFF'S AMNESIAC BRIDE by Linda Conrad, Available November
SOLDIER'S SECRET CHILD by Caridad Piñeiro, Available December
BABY'S WATCH by Justine Davis, Available January 2009
A HERO OF HER OWN by Carla Cassidy, Available February 2009

REQUEST YOUR FREE BOOKS!

Harlequin® Historical
Historical Romantic Adventure!

2 FREE NOVELS PLUS 2 FREE GIFTS!

YES! Please send me 2 FREE Harlequin® Historical novels and my 2 FREE gifts (gifts are worth about $10). After receiving them, if I don't wish to receive any more books, I can return the shipping statement marked "cancel". If I don't cancel, I will receive 6 brand-new novels every month and be billed just $4.94 per book in the U.S. or $5.49 per book in Canada, plus 25¢ shipping and handling per book and applicable taxes, if any*. That's a savings of 20% off the cover price! I understand that accepting the 2 free books and gifts places me under no obligation to buy anything. I can always return a shipment and cancel at any time. Even if I never buy another book, the two free books and gifts are mine to keep forever.

246 HDN ERUM   349 HDN ERUA

Name _____ (PLEASE PRINT) _____

Address _____ Apt. # _____

City _____ State/Prov. _____ Zip/Postal Code _____

Signature (if under 18, a parent or guardian must sign)

Mail to the **Harlequin Reader Service:**
IN U.S.A.: P.O. Box 1867, Buffalo, NY 14240-1867
IN CANADA: P.O. Box 609, Fort Erie, Ontario L2A 5X3

Not valid to current subscribers of Harlequin Historical books.

Want to try two free books from another line?
Call 1-800-873-8635 or visit www.morefreebooks.com.

* Terms and prices subject to change without notice. N.Y. residents add applicable sales tax. Canadian residents will be charged applicable provincial taxes and GST. Offer not valid in Quebec. This offer is limited to one order per household. All orders subject to approval. Credit or debit balances in a customer's account(s) may be offset by any other outstanding balance owed by or to the customer. Please allow 4 to 6 weeks for delivery. Offer available while quantities last.

Your Privacy: Harlequin Books is committed to protecting your privacy. Our Privacy Policy is available online at www.eHarlequin.com or upon request from the Reader Service. From time to time we make our lists of customers available to reputable third parties who may have a product or service of interest to you. If you would prefer we not share your name and address, please check here. ☐

HH08R

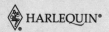

Inside ROMANCE

Stay up-to-date on all your romance reading news!

The Inside Romance newsletter is a FREE quarterly newsletter highlighting our upcoming series releases and promotions!

Click on the <u>Inside Romance</u> link on the front page of **www.eHarlequin.com** or e-mail us at insideromance@harlequin.ca to sign up to receive your FREE newsletter today!

You can also subscribe by writing us at: HARLEQUIN BOOKS Attention: Customer Service Department P.O. Box 9057, Buffalo, NY 14269-9057

Please allow 4-6 weeks for delivery of the first issue by mail.

IRNBPA208

™ *Silhouette*®

SPECIAL EDITION™

NEW YORK TIMES
BESTSELLING AUTHOR

DIANA PALMER

A brand-new Long, Tall Texans novel

HEART OF STONE

Feeling unwanted and unloved, Keely returns
to Jacobsville and to Boone Sinclair, a rancher
troubled by his own past. Boone has always
seemed reserved, but now Keely discovers a
sensuality with him that quickly turns to love. Can
they each see past their own scars to let love in?

Available September 2008
wherever you buy books.

COMING NEXT MONTH FROM
HARLEQUIN®
HISTORICAL

- **THE SHOCKING LORD STANDON**
  by **Louise Allen**
  (Regency)
  Encountering a respectable governess in scandalizing circumstances,
  Gareth Morant, Earl of Standon, demands her help. He educates
  the buttoned-up Miss Jessica Gifford in the courtesan's arts. But he
  hasn't bargained on such an ardent, clever pupil—or on his passionate
  response to her!
  *The next passionate installment of Louise Allen's Those Scandalous
  Ravenhursts miniseries!*

- **UNLACING LILLY**
  by **Gail Ranstrom**
  (Regency)
  Abducting Lillian O'Rourke from the altar is part of his plan of
  revenge. But Devlin Farrell had no idea that he would fall for his
  innocent captive. Devlin may be baseborn, but to Lilly he's the truest
  and bravest gentleman....
  A dramatic tale of love, danger and sacrifice...

- **LONE STAR REBEL**
  by **Kathryn Albright**
  (Western)
  Returning to an unstable Texas, Jack Dumont is determined not to
  engage in the disputes brewing, wanting only to reunite with his
  brother. But beholding the entrancing beauty that is Victoria Ruiz, Jack
  realizes that to gain her love, he must fight hard for her land—and for
  her....
  Rebellion, freedom and romance—all in one passionate Texan tale!

- **TEMPLAR KNIGHT, FORBIDDEN BRIDE**
  by **Lynna Banning**
  (Medieval)
  Beautiful, talented Leonor de Balenguer y Hassam is more interested in
  music than marriage, while Templar knight Reynaud is seeking his true
  identity. Traveling together, both keeping secrets, attraction flares, but
  Reynaud knows he can't offer Leonor what she deserves....
  *Travel on a thrilling, passionate journey through medieval France and
  Spain!*

HHCNM0808